THE WATCHER

NEW YORK TIMES AND USA TODAY BESTSELLING AUTHOR

MELANIE MORELAND

Dear Reader,

Thank you for selecting The Watcher to read. Be sure to sign up for my newsletter for up to date information on new releases, exclusive content and sales. You can find the form here: https://bit.ly/MMorelandNewsletter

Before you sign up, add melanie@melaniemoreland.com to your contacts to make sure the email comes right to your inbox! **Always fun - never spam!**

My books are available in paperback and audiobook! You can see all my books available and upcoming preorders at my website.

The Perfect Recipe For **LOVE**

xoxo,

Melanie

The Watcher by Melanie Moreland
Copyright © 2022 Moreland Books Inc.
Copyright #1193845
ISBN Print 978-1- 990803-10-9
All rights reserved

MORELAND
BOOKS INC.

Edited by Lisa Hollett of Silently Correcting Your Grammar
Proofreading by Sisters Get Lit.erary Services
Cover design by Feed Your Dreams Designs
Cover Photography by Wander Aguiar Photography
Cover Model Travis S
Cover content is for illustrative purposes only and any person
depicted on the cover is a model.

used without permission. The publication/use of these trademarks is not authorized, associated with, or sponsored by the trademark owners.

Readers with concerns about content or subjects depicted can check out the content advisory on my website: https://melaniemoreland.com/extras/fan-suggestions/content-advisory/

DEDICATION

Matthew
My protector.
My friend.
My husband.
I love you.

CHAPTER ONE

Damien

I sipped my whiskey, letting the rich flavor roll down my throat. Outside, the sky was dreary and overcast, matching my mood. The bar was mostly empty, the weather keeping people inside. I ran a hand through my hair, catching my reflection in the mirror behind the bar. My mouth was turned down in a frown, the creases in my forehead deep. I blew out a long breath and rolled my shoulders, relaxing my tight muscles. I was feeling off. Tense yet bored. Restless yet tired. I couldn't put my finger on it, but I wasn't myself. I had escaped my too-quiet condo to be around people. Yet I had no desire to mingle with anyone here.

It was a conundrum.

I tapped the bar, and Taylor, the bartender, topped up my glass.

"Dinner?"

"Shepherd's pie on tonight?" I asked hopefully.

"You know it. I'll put in the order. You want to move to a table?"

I glanced behind me and nodded. There was a comfortable booth available, and I could relax and eat dinner.

"Yeah."

"Mum's got sticky toffee pudding up tonight for later."

"With custard?"

He nodded with a grin.

"Make sure to save me one."

I liked this bar. Family-run, home cooking, it was like an English pub in style and décor. I had been coming here for years. The food was delicious, the whiskey selection top-notch, and the staff friendly but not intrusive. The front half was a long bar, the heavy wood dark with age. There were a few scattered tables, a pool table, and a space for darts. The back half was tables and booths. Often on a Friday or Saturday, the place was full, people eating and drinking everywhere, music playing, and someone always looking for a fellow dart player or to start a game of cards. Today, it was quiet, with only a dozen patrons scattered around the place.

I stood, reaching over for my glass, when the door to the bar burst open. A woman stumbled in, breathing hard, her eyes wild. Our gazes locked, the fear in her eyes driving me forward. I was at her side in a moment, gripping her elbow. Her hair was long, the rain causing the color to darken. It hung down her back in a damp wave of espresso. Her eyes were an unusual gray-green color, rimmed in a dark green. Long lashes framed them. They were stunning. And terrified.

Before I could speak or ask what was wrong, she flung her arms around me.

"I'm so sorry I'm late!" she exclaimed loudly.

I blinked at her words.

"I'm sorry," she whispered against my neck. "Please play along."

Then she crashed her mouth to mine.

It took me about three seconds to catch up, all the ennui and lethargy leaving my body, everything in me strumming with alertness and need. Of their own volition, my arms wrapped around her, hauling her close to my chest. She was soft and curvy, fitting against me perfectly. One hand crept up, fisting her hair, holding her close. Desire filled me as I held her, and I flicked my tongue against her mouth, slipping inside and groaning as her taste exploded on my tongue. Cinnamon and spice, sweet and tangy—all things good and rich filled my senses.

Until she pulled back, our gazes locking.

I felt my mouth curve into a wide smile. "You're forgiven."

I stepped back and closed the door, one arm still wrapped around her. I felt the shiver race through her body at the chill from outside, but it was the constant tremble of her limbs that told me how frightened she was. The fear in her gaze did something to me.

"I've got you," I murmured.

I glanced over to Taylor, who was watching us with curious eyes.

"Make it dinner for two," I called over. "My girlfriend is late but will join me. Add a glass of red to the order."

Then I headed away from the door toward the back and stopped at a booth, indicating she should sit.

For a moment, she hesitated, then slid in. I glanced behind her, noticing a solitary figure outside. Obviously male, his dark gray hood was pulled low over his head, obscuring his face. He was tall and his frame lean. I tilted my head, noting the fisted hands and tense set of his shoulders. I could feel his hate and anger from the other side of the glass. I stepped toward him, and he turned and hurried away.

"Is he still there?" she asked, the anxiety in her voice evident.

"He's gone now. Were you being followed?" I asked, sliding in across from her.

"Y-yes."

I had a lot of other questions, but I remained

silent, knowing I had to tread carefully.

Taylor slid my whiskey and a glass of wine on the table and walked away. I pushed the glass toward her. "Have a sip."

She shook her head.

"Of course, I'm sorry," I replied, shaking my head. She was scared and being followed—she wasn't going to accept a glass of wine from a stranger. I picked it up and took a drink.

"It's perfectly safe," I assured her.

Her hand trembled, and she took a long sip from the glass, letting out a sigh.

"I'll pay for my wine and leave. I'm sorry." She met my gaze, the beauty of her eyes startling me again. Set under delicate eyebrows, they were wide and lovely. Even scared, they were beautiful.

"I ordered you dinner. You can eat and relax. You'll be safe."

She frowned, her brow furrowing. "Why would you do that?" she asked.

I shrugged, leaning my arm across the back of the booth. "Because I can," I replied. "Obviously, you're in trouble and you need help. I can offer that help to you. But first, you need to warm up, relax, and eat, then you can tell me what happened."

She blinked. "Why?" she repeated.

I smiled. "Because you chose me to help you. You kissed me." I couldn't help winking at her. "Not that kissing you was a chore."

"Really," she replied, edging toward the end of the booth. "I'll be fine."

I put my hand out to stop her. "Don't go."

She looked down where my hand rested on her sleeve. "I don't want to cause you trouble."

I shook my head. "Trouble and I are old friends."

Taylor arrived with dinner, the shepherd's pie bubbling in the casserole dishes, the steam wafting in the air bringing the delicious aroma to my nose. The mixed salads and warm loaves of bread rounded out the tray. I looked at her after he left, the food sitting on the table.

"You wouldn't make me eat alone now, would you?"

She hesitated.

"Please," I said simply.

Her shoulders slumped. "Okay. Just dinner, though. Then I'll leave you in peace."

I leaned closer. "You might want to rethink that, pretty lady. Of all the men you chose to kiss, I was the right pick. I can help you."

Her eyes widened, but she said nothing.

I held out my hand. "Damien DeSalvo."

She let me wrap my fingers around hers. "Raven Bailey."

Raven. The name suited her.

"A pleasure. Now eat up. You have a story to tell, and I want to hear it."

CHAPTER TWO

Damien

The shepherd's pie was delicious. The salad crisp. My unexpected dinner companion had little appetite, though. Every time the door opened, she tensed. Each time a new voice rang out, she jumped. Finally, I slid my hand across the table, covering hers that held her fork like a weapon.

"That's for eating, not gouging someone's eye out with," I stated mildly. "And if you're still really worried, you should know that I could take whoever was threatening you out in about forty-five seconds. They wouldn't even get close."

Her worried eyes met mine, a frown between them. I smiled, wanting her to relax. "You picked the right bar to come into, Raven. Trust me on that."

"Are you some sort of assassin?" she asked, half joking.

I slid a card from my wallet and handed it to her.

She read it, mouthing the words. "Damien DeSalvo. You own a security firm?" she queried. "Really?"

"The best in the business. With my background, I'm highly trained. You're perfectly safe, so I would like you to eat this delicious meal and relax. While you're with me, nothing will happen to you."

She glanced down, and I slipped my hand under her chin. "And I'll make sure nothing happens after either."

I tapped her nose. "Eat, please. The food is incredible, and you are far too pale. A meal will help."

She let out a long exhale of air, her shoulders loosening. She picked up her fork again and began to eat. "It's good," she agreed.

"Way better than what I make." I chuckled.

"You don't cook?"

I shrugged. "I get by. Simple things. I like to grill. But I enjoy a well-made meal. My old boss used to get his frustrations out by cooking. Some of the best Italian food I've ever eaten." I winked at her. "Sometimes we'd rile him up just so he'd go upstairs and cook."

She smiled, a soft laugh escaping her mouth. She was extraordinarily pretty when she smiled. Her unusual eyes lit up, and a small dimple appeared by the left one, giving her an impish look. Her hair was beginning to dry, the dark color almost black against her creamy skin. She had pierced ears with three earrings in each ear, and I spied a hint of ink behind one of them. I felt a burning curiosity to know what it depicted and what it meant to her. All my ink had a story, and I wanted to know hers.

It shocked me how much I wanted to know everything about her.

But for now, I would settle for knowing she was fed, warm, and safe. The rest would happen.

Of that, I was certain.

"Do you have a lot of famous clients?" she asked.

I rarely spoke about Elite Security, or the clients we handled. But I noticed when I spoke, she concentrated on my words and she ate, so I made an exception and shared a few humorous stories. She laughed when I talked about the client who got so drunk, we had to take him out the service exit hidden under a trolley cart so the press didn't see him. She covered her mouth with her hand as I described the amorous couple in the back of the limo, we had to drive around the city on an extended route until they were decent enough to escort back into their hotel.

"How did you look at them with a straight face?" she asked.

I grinned. "I didn't. I charged them extra for deep cleaning the limo. Thank God leather cleans up well."

She giggled, the sound light and airy. But it worked, and she ate her dinner. We shared a sticky toffee pudding after. She had never heard of the dessert and, after a few bites, declared it her favorite.

"They make the best in the city here," I informed her.

"I need to look up the recipe."

"You like to cook?"

She nodded. "As much as I can in my tiny apartment." Then her face darkened. "I'm wondering if I have to move."

I waited until Taylor refilled our coffee cups and took away the dessert plate.

"I need you to tell me about this man. Everything you can."

She shook her head. "I don't want—"

I interrupted her. "I am involved now. I can't ignore it or you."

She worried at her lip. "He scares me. What if—"

Again, I stopped her. "I can handle myself. Trust me. But it's you I'm worried about. Now tell me. Please."

She looked down at her coffee and sighed. "Okay."

RAVEN

Damien covered my hand with his larger one, squeezing my fingers. I looked up and met his concerned gaze. When I had burst into the bar earlier, I had no plan other than to get into a place with other people. The way he had reacted to seeing me had been an unexpected surprise. He had reached my side fast and played along with my impromptu performance. Considering how terrified I had been of the man following me, I had felt completely safe in the arms of the tall stranger who appeared in front of me. He was solid and warm, his scent reminding me of the crispness of fresh air and water.

And the way he kissed me. It felt right, real, and perfect. Not as if he was a stranger I had just met, but someone I knew intimately—which was impossible, but that was how it felt.

I took a sip of coffee, studying him. He was handsome. Dark brown hair and blue eyes. Heavy brows that emphasized his stern look. A full mouth and a sharp jawline with a tightly trimmed beard. He was intense and focused. He was probably a foot taller than me, and he was solid. Broad shoulders, thick arms, and a well-defined torso. He exuded power. Even frowning, he was sexy. And when he smiled, his sexiness exploded.

But he wasn't smiling now. He was waiting, and I knew he wouldn't let me leave without knowing my story. Again, given why I had been running, I should be worried, but something about him told me I could trust him.

"I moved here last fall from up north. I got the chance of a full-time job here."

"What do you do?"

"I'm a teacher."

"What grade?"

"Kindergarten and grade one."

"So, you like kids," he observed.

"I do. I love watching them learn."

"Do they call you Miss Bailey? Ms. Bailey?"

"Ms. Raven, actually. I prefer it."

"I see." He took a sip of coffee. "So, you've been here about ten months?"

"Yes. This is my first year at the school."

"Any family up north?"

I shook my head. "My mom died a short while ago. My brother lives out west. My dad died when I was a teenager. I couldn't find a full-time job, and when this one came up, I jumped at it. There was nothing left holding me up there."

"No friends, boyfriend to stay for?"

"No," I replied shortly. I had no desire to get into that with him.

He nodded, not reacting to my terse response. "Culture shock, I imagine."

"It was. It's so busy here. So many people." I took another sip of my coffee, appreciating the fact that he wasn't rushing me.

"I was lonely," I admitted. "Most of the teachers are in relationships where I work. There's only one other single staff member. I met a couple of other teachers from a different school, and we're friendly…" I trailed off then shrugged. "I'm a bit shy, so I have trouble meeting new people."

He smiled. "I can see that about you."

He had a beautiful smile. It changed his whole countenance. It became warm, open, inviting. I wanted to bask in it. But it disappeared fast.

"I decided to try online dating. One of the other teachers I'm friendly with loves it. She's met some great people." I shook my head. "So far, that hasn't been my experience."

"So, you met this man online?"

"Yes. I filled out a profile on one of the dating sites—"

"Which one?"

"The Real Connection."

"Okay. And you met this…"

"Andy. Andy Smith. I talked to a few men, met a couple for coffee, but the ones I agreed to meet were too pushy and made it plain what they wanted. I spoke with Andy for a couple of weeks, and he asked if we could meet for coffee. He seemed really nice, and we got along well in the chats. He was funny and sweet. I agreed."

"And?"

"He seemed fine. A little shy. He wasn't as funny, but I put that down to his shyness. He told me he lived with a couple roommates, that he worked for a bank, and he was an only child. There was no spark between us, but he seemed nice."

"How much of your information did you share?"

"Not a lot. I told him I was a teacher, I was still new to the city, and I wasn't looking for a relationship, but more of a friendship. He agreed with me and asked if maybe we could go to a movie or dinner one night, just as friends. No pressure. I said that it sounded great. We talked a bit more and exchanged numbers, and he left."

He studied me briefly. "He wasn't fine, though, was he?"

A shiver went through me. "No."

"Tell me," he urged.

"He called, and we agreed to go to a movie that weekend. But I kept thinking I was seeing him places when I was out. At the store, outside the school. But when I would look again, there was no one there. One night, I got up to get a drink of water, and I looked out my window. I swore he was across the street, looking up at my apartment. Then the next moment, the person was gone. I convinced myself I was being paranoid. He didn't even know where I lived."

"He may have followed you home that first day," Damien said.

"I think so. He was weird at the movies. Too close. Too aggressive. I reminded him I wasn't interested in a romantic relationship. He said he wasn't either, he was just being nice. He said there was a guy looking at me, and he just wanted him to back off. I didn't like it, and I told him." I rubbed my forehead. "I was worried about going, but we met for supper another day and he was fine. It was just two people sharing a meal. Then we met for coffee a week later, and he was all moody and handsy again. He said a few things that put me on edge. Things he shouldn't know."

"Like?" Damien prompted.

"The grocery store I stopped at a lot. What time I usually left the school. I asked him how he knew those things, and he said I had mentioned them in our conversations, but I was certain I hadn't."

"He was following you around."

I nodded. "Then he said something about making sure people knew we were seeing each other and acting as if we were a couple. His tone and attitude were just so possessive. I didn't like that side of him, and I told him if that was how he was going to act, I didn't want to see him again. He walked out. He didn't call or text again, and I thought it was for the best. Something about his mood swings bothered me."

"Then?"

"I was out having lunch one day, and he showed up, insisting it was an accident. He was pleasant and friendly, chatted for a bit, then left. I thought nothing of it. Then suddenly, he was everywhere again. I'd see him when I was out. At the store. Walking home from work. He'd approach me sometimes, and I asked him to leave me alone. He disappeared and I was glad. Until…" I trailed off.

"Until?" he urged.

"Until two weeks ago. He showed up at my door, asking for another chance. I asked him how he knew where I lived, and he told me I had given him my address. But I knew I hadn't. I have no idea how he got into the building. I told him there wasn't a first chance. I wanted a friend, not a relationship. I was clear about that from the start. He got angry, and he told me we were meant for each other. He started pushing on the door, trying to force his way in. Thank God my neighbor came around the corner, and he backed off. I told him to leave me alone, and I slammed the door and locked it. After that, I was careful about where I went, but invariably, he would show up. I went to the police, but they said he'd done nothing wrong. That I was overreacting."

Damien cursed. "They were wrong."

"Yes. He started calling all the time. Sending texts. I changed my number, but somehow he got it again. I bought a new phone. He'd leave me notes in my mailbox. And he seemed to follow me everywhere. I added extra locks to my apartment. The super changed the lock on the front door and reminded everyone not to let in strangers. I told the school what was happening. The principal started driving me home herself, she was so upset. She wanted me to come stay with her, but I refused to put her out or involve her. I told myself he was just annoying and he'd get bored."

"Men like him never get bored with their prey."

I felt the color drain from my face at his words.

"Prey?" I whispered, fear wrapping my throat in ice.

"He's a stalker. And he's stalking you. He's not going to stop until someone makes him, Raven."

Shudders ran through me at his simple words. Deep down, I knew he was right.

"What am I going to do?"

"What happened today? What brought you to me?"

"I hadn't seen him for a few days. I thought he'd grown tired of it. I needed some things, so I went to the store. But he was there, and I ran. I just left all my groceries in the cart, and I ran. I live about two blocks from here. But he followed. Grabbed me and pulled me into the alley over there." I pointed to the side of the building. "He told me I was his. I belonged to him, and I needed to stop making him chase me. He said he was getting mad, and I wouldn't like him if he was mad. His eyes—" I swallowed and shivered again "—his eyes were crazy. I was terrified. I told him I wasn't his. I said that I had a boyfriend and I was on my way to meet him. He shook me so hard, screaming in my face, telling me *he* was my boyfriend and we were meant for each other."

"What did you do?"

"I stomped on his foot. He let go, and I ran around the corner. Saw the pub." I met his intense, worried gaze. "Found you." The tremor in my voice grew more pronounced. "I'm sorry."

He studied me, then shook his head. He reached across the table and took my cold hands in his, chafing them.

"I'm not."

CHAPTER THREE

Damien

I sensed her fear, the terror she was holding inside. She was in over her head, no one to turn to, no idea how to stop what was happening. Because she couldn't stop it—it was beyond her control.

But I could.

It angered me the way the system worked. He hadn't touched her, so therefore, nothing was done. Never mind he was mentally frightening her. It was as bad, if not worse, than laying hands on her. And I worried what would happen if he managed to get her alone and did get his hands on her. The man I had seen was tall and lean, but I had no doubt he was stronger than her. He had a good foot on her, height-wise, and his loose hoodie probably hid muscles that could easily overpower her.

But it wasn't going to happen on my watch. I couldn't explain the connection I felt to Raven— the need to protect her, to make sure she was okay, but I wasn't going to fight it. The memory of how she felt in my arms and the taste of her on my tongue was too strong. There was a reason she'd run in here, to me. I was what she needed to help her.

I wrapped my hands around her cold fingers, rubbing at the skin.

"I know you're upset and scared, Raven. I understand. But I'm right here."

She looked away, opened her mouth, then closed it.

"What?" I prompted. "What's going on in that pretty head of yours?"

"I appreciate you playing along. Having me stay and have dinner with you. Giving me a chance to calm down and relax a little…" She trailed off.

"But?"

"Now I have to go home and hope he's not waiting."

I shook my head. "I rather hope he is."

"What?" She gaped at me.

"Since I plan on walking you home, I hope he is there. I have a few things to say to him that might discourage any further interactions. I have a feeling he likes to push people smaller than himself around. If he knows someone is looking out for you, he might back off."

She frowned, chewing the inside of her cheek. "Do you really think so?"

"I hope so. But I want a good look at him. I plan on finding out as much about him as I can."

"Why?"

I squeezed her hands. "Unlike my boss, I believe in fate, Raven. You rushed into this bar where I was for a reason. That reason is no one can help you the way I can. No one can protect you like me. I was sitting there for the same reason."

"Which is?"

I tilted my head, studying her. "Waiting for you."

Color flushed her cheeks. "Oh."

She looked as surprised by my words as I was. But I was being honest. From the moment our eyes met, I felt a connection. I wanted to know everything about her. Including what in her past had hurt her and why she had left her hometown. I had seen the pain in her eyes when I asked about friends or a boyfriend. Felt the sadness in her single-word answer. *"No."*

"You aren't alone with this anymore."

She looked dazed.

"Does my directness bother you?"

She pursed her lips. "It should, given why I ran in here, but for some reason, it doesn't. I like your directness."

"Good. I will always be honest with you."

Again, that odd look crossed her face. "I like honesty."

This wasn't the time to question her. I would find out her history soon enough.

"Are you ready to go home?"

She blew out a breath and nodded.

I went to the bar and paid the bill, then walked to the table where she was still sitting. She was chewing the inside of her cheek, clasping her hands on the scarred wooden top, her fingers moving restlessly against one another.

I held out my hand. "Trust me, Raven."

She stood, slipping her hand into mine, and shook her head. "That's the odd part, Damien. Given what has happened, I do trust you."

"What did your gut instinct say when you met Andy?"

Her brow furrowed. "To hold back."

"Then listen to your gut. First impressions are often the right ones." I winked, wanting her to be comfortable. "And in my case, you're spot-on."

She let me lead her from the restaurant, although I felt her tension as we stepped outside. I saw the way her gaze darted around, looking in the shadows, searching the doorways. All my senses were tuned to the area around us, my training kicking in. I wrapped my arm around her waist, tucking her into my side.

"You're fine," I assured her. "Nothing and no one will come close."

I liked how it felt when she slipped her arm around me and nestled close.

"Okay," she breathed.

When we arrived at her building, I checked out the lock, pleased to see it was decent. Not what I would install, but not easily picked. I disliked the fact that you could follow someone into the building and get to her apartment without warning, though. He'd already done it at least once. She pressed the elevator button, waiting for the old lift to arrive.

"I thought you were on the second floor?" I asked, surprised she didn't take the stairs that were directly to the right.

She grimaced. "It smells like death in the stairwell. Both of them. Old, musty, and awful. The light flickers a lot. The doors jammed once, and I was trapped in there for over half an hour. Now I wait for the elevator. It's old but reliable."

I hid my grin. "Gotcha."

I followed her into the elevator, then down the hall, laying my hand on her arm before she slid the key into the lock.

"Do you have any lights on inside?"

"No."

"Are your blinds open?"

"In the bedroom, yes. Not the living room."

"Good. Don't switch on the lights. We're going inside fast."

She frowned but didn't ask why. We walked in,

and I shut the door behind us quickly. "Can you walk me to your room?" I asked.

I was pleased when she didn't question me, instead taking my hand and heading us down a short hall. In the doorway of her room, I saw the window—the blinds open, but slanted so you couldn't really see in. I scanned the area, my eyes already used to the darkness. I skirted around the bed and dresser, lowering myself and angling the bottom slat so I had a clear view of the street below. Given the weather, the rain-soaked streets were mostly empty. She lived on a fairly quiet road, the lights along the sidewalk casting pools of illumination on the cement. There seemed to be nothing out of the ordinary until I focused on the one unlit streetlight across the street from her apartment. The doorway of the building was dark as well, and I narrowed my eyes, studying the black. I watched as the shadows moved a little, indicating the doorway wasn't as deserted as the person hiding in it believed.

I stood, easing back.

"Stay here," I instructed. "Wait thirty seconds, then go to the living room and turn on a light, but don't open the blinds. Do the same in the kitchen. Move around but stay away from the windows."

"Where are you going?"

"I'll be right back. Stay here," I replied. "Do the back stairs lead to an exit?"

"Yes. To the small parking lot and alley."

"Perfect. Where are they?"

"To the left at the end of the hall."

"Okay."

I had to admit she was right. The stairwell was dim, musty, and obviously not well used. I grimaced as I hurried down the steps, opening the door to the back of the building. I rushed along the alley, coming up the side of the building beside hers. I peered around the corner at the doorway in question. I waited a moment until I saw another slight movement.

The bastard was in the doorway, staring up at her apartment. I moved farther down the block, then crossed the street and came up beside the building, startling him when I stepped inside the doorway.

"Looking for someone?" I addressed the hooded figure.

His low curse and the way he backed into the corner let me know he had zero awareness of his surroundings. He had been too focused on trying to catch a glimpse of Raven.

"Fuck off," he muttered. "None of your business."

"Oh, but it is. The woman you followed earlier and whom you're stalking at this moment is very much my business, *Andy*."

The use of his name startled him even more and he tried to rush past me, but I blocked him.

"You are going to leave her alone. She's not interested. She's been polite about it, but not anymore. You leave her alone, or you'll answer to me."

"I don't know what the fuck you're talking about," he bluffed. "I was standing here to get out of the rain for a bit. I'm waiting for a friend to pick me up."

"It's not raining, and your *friend* is really late. As in, never coming. I suggest you fucking walk away, or you're going to find yourself in more shit than you can handle."

I held up my phone, and he cursed, holding up his hands to cover his face from the flashlight I illuminated. I got a decent look at him, committing his features to memory. "That woman you've been bothering is under my protection. Leave her alone. I'll only warn you once. I see you again, I won't hold back."

He made a noise between a huff and a snarl. I felt the hate rolling off him. The frustration. "You don't want to mess with me, asshole," I added. "Leave and don't come back. Find another hobby besides bothering women not interested in you." I paused. "Try bingo. I hear that's riveting."

With a curse, he pushed off and rushed away. I stepped away from the building, watching his retreat with narrowed eyes. I wished I had some gadgets with me. A tracker. A Taser. Something useful. I resisted the urge to follow him. I could find out more using my brain, my computer, and my hacking skills.

But first, I had to make sure Raven was okay.

Something crunched under my foot, and I looked down at the glass I had trod on. I crouched, picking up a piece, realizing it was a lightbulb. I checked out the fixture inside the door, not surprised to see the broken bulb. I made a mental note to check the cameras in the area and find out when the streetlight went down as well. I had a feeling it, as well as the light fixture, had had a helping hand in its destruction. Andy had made himself a perfect place to spy on Raven.

I returned to Raven's building, buzzing her apartment. She let me up and was waiting at her door, looking anxious.

"Are you okay?" she asked.

Before I could respond, she threw her arms around me, hugging me hard. "I was worried."

It felt natural to hold her close. I couldn't resist lowering my head to brush a kiss on her crown and breathe her in. Her hair smelled like summer—flowers and sunshine. It was light and airy, and I liked it a lot.

"I'm fine," I assured her.

"Was he there?"

"Yes. But he's gone."

She burrowed closer, and I felt her shiver.

"I scared him, and I warned him to leave you alone. He backed off, and I hope he got the message."

She didn't speak, and I tucked her closer. "I need you to show me your profile on the site, okay?"

With a small sigh, she eased back and went inside. I followed her to the table, looking around as she booted up her laptop. The apartment was small but tidy. The walls were white, the furniture older but comfortable-looking. There was lots of wicker and cushions. Blankets draped over the back of the sofa, the arm of the chair. A bookcase overflowing with books. More on a table. A pile on the floor by the armchair. Various throw rugs were scattered on the wooden floors. It was feminine and pretty. Like her. The kitchen was tiny but organized. Pots and kitchen utensils hung on the one wall from a pegboard. The appliances were old, but gleamed.

"Here," she said, pushing the laptop my way.

I studied her profile. There was no picture, just a snapshot of a sunset. Her info was basic and her memo clear. *Looking for friendship in a new city.* I lifted my gaze to hers. "Most people on these sites are not seeking friendship."

"I know, but there are a few. But I wasn't interested in a hookup."

"Just friends?"

"I didn't want a boyfriend. I didn't think I was ready."

"Ah," I said, her words explaining a lot. "Bad experience?"

"You could say that."

I nodded, letting it go for now. "So, no picture?"

"The site encourages people to chat and get to know each other, then exchange pictures."

"Did you and Andy exchange photos?"

"No. We met at Roasters Coffee Bar. I had a book, and he wore a red hoodie."

"Can you show me his profile?"

She tapped on the keyboard, frowning. "It looks like he deleted it."

"Or made a new one."

She sighed. "I'm going to delete mine."

"Leave it a couple days. Please. I'm going to use it to find out more about Andy. If that's his real name."

"How?"

I smiled. "I have my ways."

She chewed the inside of her cheek. "You've got layers, don't you, Damien?"

I chuckled. "No. I have talent. And access to information most other people don't have. I only use it for good, though."

"Okay," she said, stifling a yawn. She looked tired —exhausted, in fact.

"Are you going to be okay here—alone?" I asked.

She nodded. "I'll bolt my door, put a chair under the knob, and keep my cell phone beside me."

I held out my hand. "Let me program my number in there. I live a few blocks over. I can be here fast."

She handed me her phone, and I entered my digits and called myself. Then I saved her information. She told me she hadn't kept Andy's number when she changed phones, but she had it on a piece of paper. I tried the number, not surprised to find it no longer working.

"No doubt a burner cell," I observed. I tucked the piece of paper into my pocket. I doubted it would help, but I would take anything I could get. "I can sleep on the sofa if you want."

Her eyes widened, and she swallowed. "No, I'll be fine. The walls are thin, and Mrs. Wallace lives next door and is up all night. If I scream, she'll call 911."

I nodded but added my address into her phone. I showed it to her. "If you're frightened, you call me—or text. I'll come get you right away. Do you understand?"

She blinked but nodded.

I stood and walked to the door, turning when I got there. She was behind me, looking anxious.

"If you're scared, nervous, or can't sleep, call me. I'll come right over."

Once again, she wrapped her arms around me, hugging me. I held her tight, loathe to leave her, yet knowing she needed her rest. The urge to scoop her into my arms and carry her to her room was strong. The desire to take her to my place where I knew she would be one hundred percent safe was even stronger.

But I had no right to do either thing.

Yet.

But I would be watching her. Carefully. And I would be right there if she needed me.

I drew back, looking down at her. Her wide green eyes gazed up at me, so many emotions swirling in their unique depths. I cupped her cheeks, holding her face in my hands. Our eyes locked and held, and I lowered my head, pressing a gentle kiss to her mouth. She wrapped her hands around my wrists, a low whimper escaping. I stepped closer, kissing her again, this time a little harder, our lips holding longer. Then again, her mouth opening underneath mine. I swept my tongue inside, lost to her taste and the feel of her. I slid my hands down her throat, over her arms and around her waist, pulling her tight to my chest as the kiss deepened. I had never experienced a reaction to a woman the way I did to Raven. The need to protect her, be close to her. It was unnerving.

Yet I liked it.

Finally, I drew back, both of us breathing hard. I held her close, dropping kisses to her head.

"I want to stay," I admitted.

"I'll be fine."

I laughed lowly. "That's not what I meant."

"I know."

I released her, lifting her hands and kissing the knuckles. We both knew it was too fast. "Anything at all, you call me, you understand?"

"Yes."

"I'm not leaving until I hear the bolt locked and that chair wedged under the doorknob."

"Okay."

"I'll call you tomorrow. Keep your blinds down and stay away from the windows for tonight."

"Okay."

I hated seeing her close the door. I waited until she did as I instructed, then I left. I departed via the stairs, came out on the street a couple of structures away and ducked into a doorway and stood watching her building. Nothing seemed amiss. I doubted Andy was around, and if he was, he would think I was still up there with her. That gave me some comfort.

Finally, I turned and hurried home.

I had work to do.

CHAPTER FOUR

Damien

I didn't sleep much, heading into the office early the next day, making a point of driving past Raven's place. I parked and went to the doorway I'd found Andy in and took a couple photos, noting in the dull light how clean the glass was on the lightbulb fragments. I planned to call the building later and find out if the broken lightbulb was a one-time only thing, or if he had been using this spot for a while. The street was deserted, and I checked out a couple other places I thought he might frequent. I found some other evidence of broken bulbs swept into corners, and I had a feeling he had several locations he liked to use.

I also had a feeling, no matter how much I warned him, he wasn't going to take no for an answer.

In the office, I made coffee and poured a cup, knowing I was going to need the strong brew. I headed downstairs to my secure server room, the banks of monitors bright and showing me everything I needed to know.

After Julian left, Leo and I changed several things. Julian had run both businesses as separate entities, and I'd widened the gap even more. Leo had nothing to do with Hidden Justice. I ran all their servers and programs for Hidden Justice. No one got past my security—firewalls or encryptions. But I was no longer part of a crew. I was firmly in the background, although I knew if needed, I would step up to help, the way Marcus and Matteo had come forward when Julian needed their help to rescue his wife and daughter. Elite Security took precedence, and I expanded its clientele and staff, making us the most sought-after security firm in the city.

I tapped the keys, looking over the system I had put in place. Everything was fine, exactly as I expected it to be. Then I opened a new window and began to hack. I knew how to keep the world out of Hidden Justice, but there were few places I couldn't get into. The Real Connection was an easy one. Their firewalls and security were simple to slip through. I found Raven's profile and started going backward. I dug into their databases and found Andy's deleted profile, but nothing more. I hit dead end after dead end. I couldn't find anything but an empty profile with a stock photo and a simple match line.

Seeking friendship—a real connection, not a hookup. Are you that girl for me?

Finally, frustrated, I started digging into his name. I came up with zero. Andrew Smith did not exist. At least, not this one. I grew frustrated, yanking on the back of my neck to ease the tension in my muscles. As I suspected, his burner cell gave me no clue. It was as if I was looking for a needle in a haystack.

I grabbed my phone and sent off a text, smiling grimly when I received a reply.

On my way, was all it said.

I stood and rolled my shoulders. I had to go upstairs and attend to business there. I could keep digging, but I hoped the text I sent would give me another angle to come at this.

In my office, I sent a text to Raven.

Me: Morning, pretty lady. Hope all is well and you got some sleep.

Her reply was fast.

Raven: I'm fine. All was quiet.

I frowned.

Me: And the sleep? I asked again.

This time, there was a small delay. I could picture her sitting on her little sofa, staring at the screen, trying to decide whether she should lie or not. Finally, she replied.

Raven: Not much.

I wasn't surprised. I had spent some time on the dating site, creating a fake account and going through all the processes and looking around. I had hoped my programs here would have come up with more, but they, too, had struck out. But I hadn't been able to rest much, worry about her staving off my sleep.

Me: I would like to take you to dinner.

Raven: You took me to dinner last night.

Me: No, although I enjoyed having dinner with you, that was necessity. Tonight would be pleasure. Different thing. I want to take you out. Somewhere casual but nice. Please.

Raven: Parent/teacher night. Working late.

Me: Great. So am I. I could pick you up, we can eat, and I'll drop you home. I would really like to see you, Raven. Please.

I waited for her reply, smiling when she agreed and sent me her school address information. I smirked and didn't tell her I already knew it. Instead, I thanked her and told her to let me know when she was ready and to wait in the school for me. She replied with a smiley face.

I set down my phone, feeling pleased.

A few moments later, my door opened and Egan Vulpe strolled in. I stood and shook his hand.

"Thanks for coming."

He smiled widely. "You need a favor? I'm here to help. But first, coffee."

I studied him as he poured a large mug. Egan had been a Marcus find. An expert with explosives, a computer genius, and lethal with his training, he had been a great fit with our team. Originally from Romania, he had been in Canada for over twenty years. He worked hard on his dialect, wanting to blend in. His accent was subtle, rounding out his words—unless he was angry or upset. Then you heard the harsh edge of his accent clearly.

He was tall—well over six foot five, with dark brown hair brushed high off his forehead. His shoulders were broad, his face long, and his features bespoke his heritage. Heavy brows and a thick scruff covered his chin. His intelligent brown eyes missed nothing. He sat down across from me, sipping his coffee.

"You let your hair grow back."

He grinned, flashing his straight white teeth. "Yah." He ran a hand over his head. "Too cold to be bald here in winter, so I'm getting ready."

I laughed. Winter was months away. He changed all the time. Bald, longer hair, short. A thick beard, scruff, clean-shaven. I never knew which Egan would appear.

He set down his cup, lifting his hands. "Here I am, my friend. What do you need?"

I indicated the pad and pile of pencils on the corner of the desk. "A composite drawing."

On top of all his other talents, Egan's sketches were top-notch. I preferred them to a computer program. Especially this—I wanted nothing out there that I was searching for someone.

He frowned. "A case? I thought you were out."

Egan still worked with Hidden Justice but only took on the role as needed. He owned a gym that was highly successful. He also had a studio since his talent extended into paintings as well. I owned two of them, the detailed canvases eye-catching and stunning. He lived on the second floor, as did Sofia, my cousin, and two other former agents. I now lived in Marcus's old place. Our headquarters had been divided into apartments, the space unrecognizable. None of us wanted any reminders of what had happened the day Marcus and Missy had rid the world of a sick bastard who was after her. Marcus shut down the office, and once he left, we remodeled.

He narrowed his eyes. "The Watcher has a special interest?"

I smirked at his nickname. Because of my computer work and the security firm, I had earned the name the Watcher. All the guys used it, and I didn't mind it. It suited me as I was ever watchful of the programs and my clients.

"This is personal."

I told him about Raven and meeting her last night. He shook his head, fury etched on his face.

"Scum. I hate the ones that prey on women."

"I can't find him. I think he's using a fake name. Andrew Smith—thousands of them in the world. I thought if I had a picture, I could use one of my contacts to run it through some databases."

"Good idea." He leaned forward, grabbing the pad and choosing a pencil. He opened the pad, balancing it on his knee. "Describe him."

For the next while, I spoke, recalling everything I could about Andy. Egan would show me the sketch, and I would have him change a shape, add a mark, darken a shadow. Finally, he handed it to me. "Yah?"

I nodded, looking it over. "That's him."

Andy's face stared back at me. Decent-looking guy, slim, shaggy hair, regular features. But it was his eyes. Egan had somehow captured the slightly crazed, unstable gaze of undisguised hatred in his eyes. The pinch between his eyebrows that suggested barely concealed rage. I felt the same unease looking at the sketch as I had when we were face-to-face.

"I worry what he'd do if he got his hands on her. Or any other woman he becomes obsessed with. I don't think he's stable."

"You hack into their system?"

I scrubbed my face. "Yeah. Got nothing. Fucking frustrating. I need to dig deeper. I want to search his email addresses and his provider. Find out his real name—where he lives. I haven't been able to break the payment part to get his credit card info. Then, I could find him easily, but that is a third-party provider, and their firewalls were far more encrypted."

"I can help."

"Not on assignment?"

He shook his head. "No. Nothing to blow up. New bosses have other ideas." He shook his head sadly. "Marcus was far more fun."

I laughed. "I'm sure your other skills come in handy."

He pursed his lips and shrugged. "At times."

I studied him for a moment. "How's Sofia?" I asked with a small grin. Egan was crazy about her. She never seemed to notice, or if she did, she ignored it.

"Infuriating," he replied, confirming that he'd gotten nowhere with her.

"You know she likes to maintain a professional distance due to Hidden Justice,"

He shook his head, rolling his eyes. "I'm a consultant now. So deep undercover, no one even knows. Not even that scum we took out knew about me or my skills. I run a gym. I pay taxes. I'm perfectly legal," he said, his accent suddenly thick.

I chuckled. "Have you tried just asking her to dinner?"

"I have tried everything. I am stuck in the friend zone. Permanently."

"She is stubborn."

"Stubborn?" He snorted. "She is *încăpăţânat.*"

I laughed at his obvious ire.

"You are her cousin. You talk to her. Tell her what a great guy I am. I would treat her like a queen. My queen."

"I'll drop a word. We're having dinner next week."

"Good. All I want is a chance."

He stood, heading to the front office and returning with the sketch he made. "I took a copy. See if I can find anything. Between us, he can't hide."

"Thanks, I appreciate that."

"You like this girl?" he asked.

I huffed out a long breath. "Yeah, I do. There is something about her."

"Like Marcus?" he asked. "Julian?"

"Maybe."

"Then I will make it a priority."

I stood and shook his hand.

"Send me anything you have on this asshole," he instructed. "I'll cast my net."

"Thanks, Egan."

"You'll talk to Sofia, right?"

"I will." I met his eyes. "And I won't be lying when I tell her you're a good guy. But she's skittish. She saw what happened with all the bosses. Matteo, Marcus, Julian. How their wives became targets. That frightens her."

"She would be safe. I would make it so. I would give it all up and just be Egan. Stay home and look after *bebelusii*."

At my shocked expression, he smiled. "Sofia is a doctor. Very important. She loves what she does. I stay home with the children, and she can keep her career. I want only what is best for her."

"You might want to back it up a little, Romeo. Get her to have dinner with you before you inform her you have day care planned."

He laughed. "Good advice." He was still laughing as he walked out the door.

I shook my head. I had a feeling my cousin didn't stand a chance.

RAVEN

I checked my ponytail in the mirror in the teacher's lounge, my nerves fluttering. They had been all day since Damien texted me. While it was true I hadn't slept much, it wasn't for the reason he thought. He'd chased Andy away—I knew I was safe in my apartment. Even if Andy returned and got into the building, he couldn't get into my place. And I had called my principal and she picked me up this morning, so I hadn't worried about running into him then either. Andy was, in fact, the last thing on my mind.

What, or who, was on my mind was Damien. His reluctance to leave me. The way he took charge of the situation. He didn't know, but I had watched him confront Andy across the street. I saw the way Damien stealthily approached the building, then dragged him from the doorway. I couldn't hear them, but the difference in their postures said it all. Damien —tall, commanding, determined. Andy—hunched, hidden, no doubt belligerent. When Damien stepped closer and Andy hurried away, I felt only relief. When Damien had sat in my apartment, for the first time since moving to the city, I didn't feel as alone as I had. He was calm and collected, yet I felt his wrath at Andy's behavior.

The way he used my computer, I had no doubt the man had downplayed his skills. His fingers flew over the keyboard, and his concentration was intense. The questions he asked and his subtle way of taking control were sexy and comforting at the same time. The attraction I felt toward him was undeniable, and from the way he had kissed me before leaving, he felt it as well.

And we were having dinner, not because he felt the need to protect me, but because he wanted to. Since I'd gotten his texts, he'd been on my mind all day. I could hardly wait to see him.

The door opened, and the principal walked in. "Raven," she greeted me. "All go well with your parent interviews?"

"Yes, they did, Tracey. Except the Flynnes. They feel Aaron should be in the advanced reading class."

She rolled her eyes. "Did you point out the child can't read a full sentence yet?"

"I did. They think he's just shy. But brilliant."

She shook her head. "He's a normal student. A lovely child. I dislike it when parents push their own desires on their children. Let them develop at their own speed. It only harms them in the end."

"I assured them I would work with him one-on-one when I could. That seemed to satisfy them. For now, at least."

Tracey beamed. "That is why you are one of my best. Besides that, are you all right? I can give you a lift home."

"No, a friend is picking me up. I'm good. I'm

going to go get my purse and wait for him by the doors."

She lifted one eyebrow quizzically. "Him?"

I felt the heat in my cheeks. "Yeah. Him."

"Not—"

"No. He helped me out with Andy. Scared him away. He seems like a really nice guy. He owns a company called Elite Security."

Her eyebrows shot up. "Elite Security?"

"You know it?"

She nodded. "My husband does some hours with them. On occasion, they need off-duty cops. Mike thinks the whole organization is top-notch."

"Well, Damien seems to be."

She smiled, her eyes gleaming. "I met Damien once. He was top-notch in many ways, I think."

I had to laugh at her words. "I agree."

She laid her hand on my arm. "Okay. You go get ready. I'll see you tomorrow."

"Okay."

I went to my classroom and grabbed my purse. I shut off the lights and hurried to the front doors. Damien was waiting, leaning against the hood of a car, scrolling through his phone. I took a moment to admire him. Tall, dressed in jeans and a leather jacket, he was sexy and intense-looking. I was suddenly anxious to be close to him again, and I stepped outside. He glanced up at the sound of the door opening, tucking his phone into his pocket and watching me approach him with a wide smile.

"Damn, girl," he breathed. "Teachers didn't look like you when I was little."

I grinned. "Or maybe you were too young to notice."

"No. I remember my grade one teacher. She had a furry upper lip. I got sent to the corner the day I asked her why a caterpillar lived under her nose."

I began to laugh, and he bent down, brushing his lips over mine. "You are so beautiful when you smile."

"You make me smile."

"Glad to hear it. Did you have a good day?"

"It's better now."

"Can I take you to dinner?"

"Can I have a hello kiss?"

For a moment, he looked startled, but before I could retract my question, he pulled me in, covering my mouth with his warm lips. I wound my arms around his neck, enjoying his gentle caresses. He kept the kisses light, indulgent. A few soft sweeps of his tongue. But he held me close, and I felt his protectiveness. His desire, even as he held himself back.

He released me, taking my hand and kissing it. "Dinner," he said, his breathing deep. "We need dinner."

I nodded, feeling slightly off-kilter. "Dinner."

"More of your delicious mouth after." He paused. "Please."

"Since you asked so nicely…"

He grinned.

"I'm a sucker for good manners."

"I'll remember that. For later."

He opened the door, waiting until I slid in. He bent, handing me my seat belt.

"Later?" I asked.

"When I want more than a kiss. I'll ask so politely, you can't refuse."

"Is that a fact?"

He pressed his mouth to mine once more. "Yes, Ms. Raven. Please, Ms. Raven. I'll do anything, Ms. Raven," he murmured, his voice low and rumbly. "I'll be such a good boy, Ms. Raven. I'll make you feel so good, Ms. Raven."

Then he stood and winked, shutting the door. I watched him walk around the car, my breathing fast.

I had a feeling he would get exactly what he wanted if he talked that way.

CHAPTER FIVE

Damien

God, she was beautiful. Her hair was incredible, and for some reason, I was fascinated with it. It hung down past her shoulders in a swath of rich, ebony-colored silk. She had it in a long ponytail, and I had to bite back my groan when she released it, massaging her scalp with a satisfied sigh. The scent of it, of her, drifted to my side of the car, and I inhaled greedily. I liked her fragrance. It was light and airy, not cloying or overpowering. I had the constant urge to bury my face into her neck and inhale her where I knew her scent would be concentrated.

As well as somewhere else. Somewhere warm, wet, and musky.

Her voice brought me out of my lust-filled musings. I shifted in my seat to relieve the pressure of my cock pressing against my zipper.

"That feels better," she murmured.

"Does it hurt to wear it in a ponytail?" I asked, trying to make my voice normal.

"It's heavy, and by the end of the day, I'm glad to let it out. Not as much as when I wear it up in a bun, though. By the end of the day, my head aches sometimes."

"It's beautiful—your hair, I mean. Well, you are too, but your hair, yeah, ah, gorgeous." Internally, I rolled my eyes. That was so fucking smooth. *Not.*

But it seemed to delight her. "Yeah?"

"Yeah," I said firmly.

"Thank you."

I smiled. "You like Italian?"

"You mean you?" she teased.

I chuckled. "The food. Or we can do Chinese? Thai?"

"Love them all."

"Great. We'll do Italian tonight. Chinese next."

"You're so sure they'll be a next?" she replied, lifting one eyebrow in a sexy, quizzical look.

"Trust me, Raven, there will be." I pulled into the parking lot of my favorite little bistro.

She smiled, looking pleased.

"What?"

"I like how you say my name," she admitted.

"It suits you," I responded as I opened the door of the car and held out my hand to help her.

"It's really the shortened version."

"Oh?"

"My full name is Ravenna Jade." She smiled. "My mom loved the name. My dad added Jade because of my eyes. When I was born with lots of dark hair and my eyes were already green, which is unusual, they decided it was meant to be."

"I like it."

"My mom thought it was cool, but she shortened it to Raven. She thought it suited me and would be easier as I went through school."

"She was right. Your hair—it's so dark, it reminds me of a raven. I think they are beautiful, majestic birds."

"You certainly are a charmer, Damien DeSalvo."

I wound my arm around her waist. "You ain't seen nothing yet."

We had a corner booth and sat beside each other, our thighs pressing together. It felt intimate and cozy, and I liked her close. After making sure she had no allergies, I ordered the dinner for two. Whatever the chef made was what we would eat. I poured us each a glass of wine, and we clinked glasses. I studied her in the candlelight. She wore a pretty skirt and blouse, feminine and lacy. She had a shawl draped around her shoulders. The muted green of her outfit complemented her coloring. Her eyes looked tired, two thumbprints of blue underneath them showing her lack of sleep.

"Any contact today? I asked mildly.

"No. I haven't seen him all day." She took a sip. "Thank God."

"Good." I drummed my fingers on the table. "How did you pay for your membership to the online dating app?"

"Oh, I had a month free trial. I had to give a credit card for after it expired." She shook her head. "Andy said he always canceled and made a new profile before his card was charged. He told me once he didn't really have to pay for dates."

I snorted. "And yet there he was—on a dating site. His profile was pretty empty."

"How do you know that?"

I decided to be honest. "I hacked into their system."

She gaped at me. "You hacked…" Her voice trailed off. "Isn't that—" She leaned close with a whisper. "Isn't that illegal?"

I smirked. "Yes."

"Yet—" she waved her hand "—you did. And you told me."

"I need to know what or who I'm dealing with. Who I have to protect you from. I need to know everything I can about him."

"Maybe you should look at other sites."

I blinked. "What?"

"He mentioned he'd tried other sites as well."

I picked up my phone and sent Egan a text. He replied swiftly, telling me he would cast a wider net.

"Who did you just text?" she asked.

"A colleague helping me."

She sat back, shaking her head. "I feel as if I just stumbled into a spy movie."

I laughed, waiting until the bowls of thick minestrone soup were placed in front of us, a basket of bread set down, and cheese and pepper added to the soup before the waiter departed.

"Nothing that over the top."

"But you are, ah, connected."

I picked up my spoon, dunking it in the fragrant broth. "I am exactly what you need to protect you. To make sure this guy is out of your life for good."

"And then?" she asked breathlessly.

"Then you have time for me."

I loved how the color rushed to her cheeks. She picked up her spoon and concentrated on her soup, but I saw the smile that pulled on her lips. We both wanted that time.

"That was incredible," she murmured, setting down her fork. The meal had been amazing. Soup, salad, pasta, beef medallions in a wine sauce, a decadent cheesecake, even the lattes had been exceptional. I was pleased to see her eat and enjoy her meal. We'd sat close the entire time, exclaiming over our favorites, laughing, and talking. I stole kisses whenever I could —light little pecks on her cheek, the end of her nose, her full lips, and more than once, I'd indulged in my desire to bury my face in her neck and kiss her there. Inhale her fragrance. It was about as perfect a dinner as it could be.

We shared more information about ourselves. She talked about her brother, who worked in Alberta in the fuel sector. I told her about growing up as the only child of an Italian immigrant father and Canadian mother. I made her laugh with my imitations of my mother and father arguing over their different cultures and which was the best way to raise me.

"Are you still close?" she asked.

"My dad passed when I was twenty. He was a lot older than my mother. She lives in Florida now with her second husband. Good guy. They live in a little retirement community, and I go see them every year. I call her every week."

"What does she think of your career?"

I winked. "She thinks I run a security firm. That I push paper and assign bodyguards to famous people."

"So, she has no idea."

"I do push a lot of paper around. I have someone else who assigns the jobs," I admitted. "As for what I was trained for… No, she has no idea, and she never will."

She looked away, reaching for her coffee cup. The movement caused her shawl to fall away, and I glimpsed the sight of dark marks on the top of her arm as she reached down to pull the shawl back into place.

Rage hit me like a wrecking ball, and I reached across to stop her hurried movement.

"Did he do that?" I seethed, pushing up her sleeve and seeing the impressions of fingers on her pale skin. "He fucking marked you?"

"They don't hurt."

"Not the point. You don't touch a woman with anger. Ever. My father taught me that from the moment he could make me understand. Women are to be cherished. Protected. Cared for." My hands shook in rage as I looked at the marks on her skin. "I am going to teach him a lesson he won't forget."

She cupped my cheek. "He grabbed me yesterday and shook me. I told you that. I bruise easily. I don't want you going after him, Damien. If he leaves me alone, leave him alone."

"Why?" I asked, pressing her hand to my cheek.

"I don't want you hurt in any way. Please."

I turned my head and kissed her palm. "He can't hurt me, Raven. He doesn't stand a chance against my skill set."

"Please."

"If he leaves you alone, I'll leave him alone. If not, all bets are off," I lied.

I had no intention of letting this rest. I had a feeling she wasn't the first woman he'd stalked. But I swore, she would be the last.

She frowned, obviously unsure if she should believe me. She leaned forward, dropping her voice. "Are you in the mafia?"

I began to laugh. "No."

"Are you an undercover agent of some sort?"

"You watch too much TV."

"But you're more than a business owner," she insisted.

I inclined my head, letting her know she was right.

"Will you tell me?"

I had seen what secrets did to a relationship. They almost cost Julian his marriage, and it took them a long time to recover. I would prefer to be honest, but I didn't want to scare her away. "One day, yes."

She sighed. "Okay."

Then she yawned, and I glanced at my watch. It was past eleven. We'd been there for over three hours, talking, eating, and enjoying each other's company. I had to take her home and let her get to bed. I didn't want to, though—I wanted to stay with her and talk more. Then kiss her until I had my fill. All the sweet ones had been great, but I wanted her lips underneath mine. My tongue in her mouth. Her taste filling me up.

Her underneath me on my bed. Her voice begging me to take her. Crying out when I did.

I signaled for the check, knowing I would have to be content with good-night kisses. For now, anyway.

We walked to the car, and I waited until she slid in before heading to the driver's side. I took my time, looking around carefully. I saw nothing out of the ordinary, and I got in, driving her home. In front of her building, I was pleased to see the streetlight fixed and lights back on in the building across from hers. I had called the company that owned the building, and they confirmed the light was constantly being vandalized. I arranged a special unbreakable cover for the light and had it installed for them. Anything to make Andy frustrated enough to stay away.

I left my car parked in front of her building and escorted Raven upstairs. She left her lights off, and I checked the perimeter, pleased that the street was deserted and I saw nothing out of the ordinary to give me any concern. I swept her apartment, but it was empty. Maybe my warning last night had been enough to scare Andy, and Raven was right. We could move on and forget about him.

I was sure she would agree, but I kept that thought to myself. It was too early to relax yet.

I went back to the living room, where she was leaning on the back of the sofa.

"All okay?" she asked anxiously.

"All good."

"Thank you for tonight," she said, smiling, looking oddly shy. "It was lovely."

I stepped in front of her, sliding my fingers under her chin. Our eyes met, mossy green gazing into blue. I lowered my head and kissed the end of her nose, then her cheek. I dragged my lips to her ear. *"You're lovely, Raven."*

She whimpered, sliding her hand up my chest and gripping my shirt with her fists. "Damien," she whispered.

I dropped my face to her neck, kissing the softness. Tasting her. Inhaling her warm scent. I flicked my tongue on her skin, and she shivered, her head falling back, giving me more access. I kissed up and down her neck, nudging her blouse out of the way with my nose and pressing my lips to her collarbone. Her shawl slipped off, and I dragged my mouth to her arms, going back and forth, ghosting my lips over the dark smudges.

"Never again," I vowed. "He'll never get close enough to you to touch you again."

She moaned and cupped my face, her eyes wide and filled with need. "Kiss me, Damien. Please."

I covered her mouth with mine, our tongues stroking together. Soft and exploring became deeper. Wetter. Hungrier. I held her tightly, encasing her in my arms, delving my hand under her blouse to the warm skin underneath it. I traced the delicate ridges of her spine, our mouths never separating. I was lost in a vortex of sensation. The feel of her hand gripping my hair. The other one clutching my back, her fingernails a sharp press on my skin. The taste of her. Sweet, salty, altogether unique and perfect. The silk of her hair on my skin. The need to feel more. To be closer. My cock was hard and erect. Throbbing with desire for her. Every nerve was awake and snapping, aching with longing. Her low noises and muffled moans spurred me on. I lifted her to the back of the sofa, her legs wrapping around me, pulling me into the heat between her thighs. I swam deeper and deeper with her. Explored her with my tongue and hands. Touched her as much as I dared, wondering how much more I could take. She cupped my erection, and I groaned loudly.

We broke apart, our lips swollen, her hair a mess from my hands, her blouse askew. My shirt was wrinkled, the top two buttons missing. I was gasping for air, my chest pumping rapidly.

Our gazes locked, her eyes muddled with passion, wide with desire, and confused.

"Damien," she whispered. "You don't want me to touch you?"

"Jesus," I responded, hanging my head. "*Yes*. Yes, I want you to touch me. I don't want to rush this, Raven. I don't want you to feel pressured."

She laughed quietly. "Pressured isn't what I'm feeling right now." Then she dragged in a deep breath. "But you're right. We need to back this up a little."

I nodded, lifting my head and meeting her eyes. "I fucking hate that you're right."

She smiled and traced my cheek, running her finger over my bottom lip. "You are an amazing kisser."

I caught her finger in my mouth and nibbled the end, then released it with a kiss. "I had an amazing partner."

Our eyes held and locked. "May I see you again?" I asked.

"Yes, please."

"Is tomorrow too soon?" Then I shook my head. "Damn, I have events the next two nights. Thursday?" I asked hopefully.

"How about I make us dinner here?" she asked. "We can just relax."

"I'd like that." I helped her off the sofa, and she walked me to the door. I looked down at her, marveling at her prettiness.

"Thank you for tonight," she said, sounding shy again.

I tipped up her chin and kissed her. "My pleasure."

"Oh, I had a bit of that, too," she teased.

I kissed her again. "You'll get a lot of that. I promise."

She smiled against my mouth. "I look forward to it."

"Is it okay if I text you the next couple of days?"

"Yes."

"And if anything happens, you'll call, right? No matter what I'm doing, I'll pick up."

"Okay. I will." She paused. "Can you call me when you get home? Just so I know you're safe?"

I felt a warmth in my chest at her words. "Yes."

I listened for the locks to engage on the door before I left. It was hard to walk away, but I forced myself to do it.

I hated it, though.

RAVEN

Wednesday passed without problem. No glimpses of Andy. No discovering he'd somehow gotten my phone number again. I relaxed a little, wondering if Damien's scare tactics had worked. I sincerely wished for it, although I hoped Andy hadn't moved on to another woman. I sent the website a detailed letter describing Andy's behavior. I hadn't heard back, but I hoped they investigated and somehow blocked him from getting back on the site. I also wondered if the companies shared any sorts of lists of troublesome clients and hoped, if they did, his name was on that list.

Damien sent me some sweet texts and called in

the evening to check up on me. We talked for a while until he heard me yawning.

"I need to let you go so you can go to bed," he murmured.

"I'm already there."

His voice deepened. "You're already in bed while talking to me?"

"Yes."

"Tell me you have on some old sweats and a big shirt that used to belong to your brother. That you're swaddled head to toe and under the blankets."

"I sleep in the nude."

There was a beat of silence. "Jesus," he muttered.

I began to laugh. "I have some shorts and a T-shirt on."

"Well, damn, woman, don't blow my fantasy now. You're naked. Naked and talking to me, wishing I were there." He dropped his voice to a whisper. "Touching you, kissing you the way I was the other night."

I whimpered, rubbing my thighs together.

"Except this time, I wouldn't stop."

The ache that had started between my legs grew.

"You're going to let me soon, right? Touch you the way I want to touch you? Kiss you everywhere?" he breathed out. "Please, Ms. Raven. Please tell me you'll let me."

"I wish you were here."

I heard a dull thud. "What was that?"

"Me banging my head on the wall, wishing this stupid evening was over so I could get in my car and come there. Then you could come." He paused. "Several times."

I shivered at the pure lust in his voice.

"Soon."

"I'm looking forward— Damn, I have to go. Sleep well, Raven. Dream of me."

He hung up, and I curled up in bed, his sexy voice and dirty promises ringing in my ear.

My phone buzzed, and I looked at the text.

Damien: Call my name when you come
tonight, my beautiful Ravenna Jade. It'll be
your name I groan out later when I'm in the
shower.

I tried not to smile at his words. I failed.

And it was his name I whimpered into my pillow.

Twice.

CHAPTER SIX

Raven

I arrived at school early, wanting to get a jump start on the day. I smiled at the security guard who let me in. In my classroom, I got busy sorting some puzzles we were going to do on letters. I heard an odd thump and looked up, startled, not seeing anything. Other teachers were arriving, so no doubt, it was someone in another classroom. I finished my task, then got up to start putting the puzzles on the desks when I saw it.

On the outside window glass was a daisy. A simple, innocuous daisy that could have been picked up by the wind and came to rest on the windowsill. But this one was pressed into the glass—almost crushed, the petals broken and torn. A tremor started in my feet, and I shook my head. It was a coincidence. It had to be.

I turned my back and finished my task, sitting

back at my desk. I stared at the window. It was just a crushed daisy, I told myself. Carried here by the breeze. Nothing else.

I glanced down at my phone, running my fingers along the keypad. The urge to call Damien and hear his voice, tell him my silly concern, was strong.

"If someone crosses me, they'll end up pushing up daisies," Andy had said during one conversation. "I don't like traitors."

Something in his tone rang true and real, and his words had stuck with me.

Did he consider me a traitor now?

I glanced at the daisy again, watching as it let go of the glass and slipped off, falling to the ground.

I shook my head. I was overreacting. A flower had hit the glass and fell. It was summer, and there were lots of daisies around. That was all it was.

I heard the sound of the kids arriving, and I stood, slipping my phone back into my drawer. I wasn't going to bother Damien about a stray flower. I was sure even he would think I was being ridiculous.

I stood and went to greet my little students, firmly putting Andy and the crushed daisy out of my mind.

I was on edge all day, although nothing else untoward happened. I went to the store and bought everything I needed to make dinner, planning the menu in my head. Damien liked to eat, and he seemed to have a sweet tooth. In the grocery store, I was startled as I went around a corner and saw a man there in a hoodie, but when he turned, I let out a sigh of relief. He was a stranger. So many people wore hoodies now, and I needed to stop seeing Andy everywhere.

As I paid, something caught my eye, and I saw someone in a black hoodie turn the corner outside. The way they hurried away made me anxious, the pit of worry in my stomach growing. I took a cab home, rushing inside. Upstairs, I peered out my windows but saw nothing. I shook my head at my overactive imagination and went to the kitchen to make dinner. I loved to cook, and it always relaxed me. My kitchen was small, but I could still make a nice meal in it, and I got busy chopping and stirring, rolling, and baking.

By the time seven rolled around, the apartment smelled amazing, and I was ready to see Damien. More than ready. When he buzzed up, I let him in and waited in the hallway. The elevator door opened, and he strode toward me, looking concerned, his hands filled with flowers and wine.

"Raven? What's wrong?"

I flung my arms around his neck, letting him pull me to him. "Nothing," I assured him. "I was just anxious to see you."

Laughter rumbled in his chest, and despite the items he carried, he hugged me close, dropping a kiss to my head. "Happy to see you too."

He pulled back, bending low to kiss me. Every

fiber of my body relaxed at his closeness, and every nerve lit up at the feel of his mouth on mine. He kissed me hungrily for a few moments, then eased back with another chuckle.

"If we don't stop, we're going to give your neighbors a show."

"Right."

We went inside, and he handed me the bunch of flowers and the wine.

"Something smells incredible."

"You mentioned Chinese. I made my cashew chicken and rice. And I baked some cookies."

"Sounds amazing. I'm starving."

He opened the wine and poured us each a glass as I quickly stir-fried some vegetables and set out the chicken and rice. He filled his plate, shutting his eyes at the first bite. "Delicious."

We talked about simple things. His business, the events he'd been working.

"We do a lot of red carpets for celebrities. Toronto is a hot spot for movies."

"You don't like them?"

"I prefer to stay in the background, but some of the clients ask for me specifically. I try to accommodate."

He shared some funny stories about the movie star he'd been escorting around.

"He's a great guy. His wife is a nightmare. Constantly breaking protocol, demanding things we're not obligated to do." He shook his head. "She wasn't happy when I informed her going to the mall to get a certain shade of lipstick did not fall under my jurisdiction. She couldn't believe I was unable to get a police escort to drive me to Sephora and back faster."

"Oh my," I said with a smile.

"Her assistant took care of it. She was already out on one of at least a dozen errands she was sent on that day. The list is never-ending with her."

"He must love her."

"He doesn't discuss it, and I don't ask. They're a power couple, so I suppose it works for them."

I didn't understand that way of thinking, but it wasn't my life. He asked me about my kids, and I made him laugh when I told him about little Frank and the crayon he shoved up his nose.

"Luckily, he left enough out for the school nurse to get a grip on it and remove it. We called his mother, who just sighed and informed us he did that at least once a week lately, and to send him back to class."

He shook his head. "You must deal with a lot of parents and kids misbehaving."

"I do. And I can be very strict, Mr. DeSalvo. Be warned."

He winked. "Yes, Ms. Raven."

The way he said my name made me blush.

He finished two plates, sighing in appreciation when he finished the last mouthful.

"You can cook for me anytime."

"Sure. I don't have a lot of room, so I have to keep the meals simple."

He stood, taking our plates and bending to drop a kiss to my forehead. "You can come use mine. Marcus was a great cook, and his kitchen is rarely used now that I live there. You can bring it back to life."

"That was your old boss?"

He sat down. "One of them—yes."

"Do you miss him?"

"I miss him and Julian, even Matteo at times. But they're happy and settled. I see them on occasion."

I stood and switched on the coffee. I slipped to the washroom and washed my hands, coming back to find he had cleared the rest of the table and set out the dessert and coffee.

I sat down and poured us each a cup. He bit into a cookie, groaning at the taste.

"Oh my God."

I grinned. "My own recipe."

"You need to make these for me all the time."

"I can do that."

"You know what else you need to do?"

"What?"

He crossed his legs and studied me. "Tell me why you're all jumpy. Something happened today, and you're not sharing."

I blinked. I thought I was acting normally. At my surprise, Damien smirked.

"I notice things. And your tells are screaming.

Something upset you."

"My tells?"

He leaned forward and touched my cheek. "Your left eye twitches a little when you're upset. You keep darting your gaze to the windows. You jump at every sound." He took my hand in his. "Tell me what happened today."

"Probably just my imagination working overtime."

"Tell me anyway."

I told him about the thump and the daisy. What Andy had said to me once. The man disappearing around the corner. I shrugged self-consciously. "Probably nothing, right?"

For a moment, he said nothing, then he huffed out a long breath of air. "I think your first instincts were right, Raven. It was something." He held up his hand before I could speak. "We are going to err on the side of caution and assume it was Andy smashing a daisy against your window as a passive-aggressive warning. Perhaps he was at the store and disappeared before you could be sure." He bent forward, resting his elbows on his knees, staring into my eyes. His gaze was intense, determined, and furious. There was no doubt he was angry, yet his voice remained calm and steady. "And you should have called me. Immediately."

"I didn't want to bother—"

Again, he held up his hand. "You are *not* a bother. I would rather react to a hundred coincidences, than not be there the one instance you needed me. Do you understand?"

He cupped my cheek, stroking the skin softly. "I hate thinking of you worried when I could have sent someone to watch over you until I could get there myself."

"Someone to watch over me?"

He nodded.

"I don't need a bodyguard, Damien."

"I disagree. Until I find this asshole and get him away from you, you need someone around so he can't get to you."

"You make him sound crazed."

He sat back with a frown. "From what I saw and what you've described, he very well could be. He's a stalker, Raven. He has you in his sights."

"Today could have been nothing."

He dipped his chin in acknowledgment. "Maybe. But it could have been something significant. Promise me next time you will call."

I shut my eyes, drawing in some deep breaths. Damien moved, shifting his chair closer. "You came to me, Raven. You needed my protection that day. You need it now. I want to give it. Listen to me, please."

I relented and nodded.

"Okay, good," he said and pressed a kiss to my forehead. "I'll come up with a plan and fill you in."

"Do I get any say in this plan?"

"Sure." He grinned. "You can choose to sleep in

my guest room or my bed. Your choice."

"I am not staying with you."

"If I decide it's necessary, you will."

I stood. "Anyone ever tell you that you're bossy and high-handed?" I asked and turned to go to my room. I felt cold suddenly and wanted my shawl. But Damien caught up to me by the sofa, snagging my hand. He pulled me close, engulfing me in his embrace. I wanted to push him away, but he felt so damn good. Warm, solid, safe. He rocked us gently side to side.

"I'll do whatever it takes to keep you safe, Raven. It's become paramount to me."

"Why?" I whispered against the hard muscles of his chest.

He slipped his hand under my chin, meeting my gaze.

"I can't explain it. It's as if you settled into a space in my heart I didn't know was vacant. I think about you every spare moment." He chuckled. "Even every moment I don't have to spare. I worry about you. Wonder what you're doing. Hearing you felt scared earlier—I fucking hate it."

"I'm sorry."

"Don't be sorry, just agree with me."

"Agree with you?"

"Let me make sure you're safe. If we find out I'm overreacting, I'll admit it."

"And in the meantime, you will have gotten your

way."

A smile tugged on his lips. "Well, there is that."

He bent low and brushed his mouth on mine. Once, twice, and again. Pressed a little harder each time. Held our lips together longer. Until I couldn't take it and flung my arms around his neck, letting him kiss me the way he had the other night. Hard. Deep. Passionate and demanding. I had never been kissed the way Damien kissed me. Each press of his mouth, every sweep of his tongue, I felt claimed. Possessed. Desired. Every taste of him left me wanting another. More. I wanted all of him.

With a groan, he gathered me up, turning and lifting me to the back of the sofa again. Moments passed as our mouths moved, tongues stroked, and whispered words passed between us.

Until the window behind me shattered, the glass screeching with the intensity of the blow it took. The blinds made a deep metallic sound as if it were being torn apart. One moment, I was in Damien's arms. The next, we were on the floor, his body covering mine defensively.

My frightened gaze met his furious one. He pulled me to my feet, and we looked at the rock lying on my rug, slivers of glass all around it.

"I don't think we can put this down to coincidence," he scowled. "You're coming home with me. Tonight."

I didn't argue.

CHAPTER SEVEN

Damien

"Stay here," I instructed Raven. "Call the police and lock the door behind me, and don't open it for anyone but me. You understand?"

She nodded mutely, her face ashen.

"Don't touch the rock, don't go near the window. Turn on the hall light and pack some things if you can. You are coming home with me."

I rushed out the door, pleased to hear the snap of the locks behind me. Downstairs, I stood on the sidewalk, staring up at Raven's window. There was no doubt Andy was behind this. The super of the building came out, looking confused and upset.

"What the hell?" he muttered, glancing up. "I heard glass break. How the hell did that window get smashed?"

"With a rock and good aim."

"Why? And who are you? How do I know you didn't throw it?"

"I was having dinner with Raven." I introduced myself. "She can vouch for me," I added, handing him one of my business cards.

He looked at my name, his eyebrows lifting.

"Okay, now the question is why? And how did they throw it up that high?"

I glanced behind me at the van parked on the street. "I have a feeling he stood on top of that."

He followed my gaze and grunted.

"As for the why, this goes back to the man Raven told you about."

"He's still bothering her?"

"Yes."

I looked around, wondering what set him off. I looked across the street, glancing behind me. I jogged to the other side and leaned against the building. The way the blinds tilted, you could see shadows. On one window the blinds were a little more open. With binoculars, you could see inside. There was no doubt in my mind he had seen me kissing Raven and lost it.

I glanced down at the rock garden in front of the building. One rock was missing. I knew exactly where it was.

Fuck.

Now, he was angry.

Angry, crazed, obsessed people were not good.

I had to find him. Fast.

Officer Canbury snapped his notebook shut. He met my eyes, his own frustrated. "Not much to go on. No witnesses, nothing tying him to being here. No idea who he is."

"It was him," I stated firmly.

"I can't bring someone in for questioning when they don't seem to exist."

"I know." Exasperated, I ran a hand through my hair.

"I know this is upsetting. And I agree it sucks, but all we can do is give a report for insurance and canvass the neighborhood." He met my eyes again. "Not that it will help much."

"I have a sketch I can send you. It's at the office."

"That might help."

I wanted to punch a wall. Scream at the injustice. Women, anyone, shouldn't have to put up with this sort of behavior. But Andy had covered his tracks. The police could do nothing.

But I could.

I glanced at Raven. She had gone from ashen to ghostly, her gaze never staying in one spot, her knee bouncing. She gripped the arms of the chair she sat in so tightly, I was surprised she had any blood circulation left in her fingers.

The officer and I exchanged cards. After examining the scene outside, agreeing with my hypothesis, he had come upstairs, talked to Raven and me. After he left, promising to keep in touch, the super brought a piece of wood upstairs, and I helped him cover the window.

"I'll get it fixed as soon as possible."

"She's staying with me for a while," I informed him.

He glanced at Raven and nodded. "Good idea."

He left, and I turned to Raven. "Did you pack?"

"Um, yes."

I looked over at the kitchen. She had cleaned it up as well.

"I'll get your bag."

Her voice stopped me before I went down the hall. "Why is he doing this? He agreed to friendship. He's the one who crossed the line and changed the rules."

I kneeled in front of her. "He never wanted friendship, Raven. He uses sites to find lonely women and take advantage of them. He locked on to you and became obsessed."

"But I'm no one. Nothing special. And I never encouraged it. I asked him to leave me alone."

"You did nothing wrong. It's him. Not you. He's at fault." I tucked a lock of hair behind her ear. "I'm going to be blunt here, Raven. You're in danger. He's fixated on you. He saw us kissing tonight, and now he's angry. So until we find him, you need to stay with me."

"Or you need to walk away and forget you met me," she shot back. "When he doesn't see you anymore, he'll calm down. You can move on with your—"

I laid a finger on her mouth, silencing her.

"Not happening. You know that. You know I feel something for you. And you for me. I am not walking away. I'm going to protect you." I smiled, moving my finger to her cheek and stroking the skin. "And you're not no one. You're special."

"And who will protect you?"

Her words were my undoing. She was more worried about me than herself. I stood, taking her with me and wrapping my arms around her. "I can protect myself, and I have friends. I promise I'll be fine. And as long as you're with me, you will be too. Don't fight me on this. Come home with me."

I felt the fight go out of her. "Okay."

I pressed a kiss to her head. "Okay, get your things."

———

She was tense in the car, clutching her bag, her shoulders stiff. Her eyes were in constant motion, looking at the streets. I reached over and covered her hand. "Everything is fine."

"How do you know he's not following us?"

I chuckled lowly. "Because Egan is following a few cars back. If Andy is around, we'll spot him."

I pulled into the secure, underground parking lot. The door rolled shut behind us, and by the time I parked, Egan's car came in, the sound of the heavy door descending again echoing in the garage.

I got out and opened Raven's door, taking her bag and holding out my hand. She let me pull her from the car, and we waited until Egan joined us.

"Nothing," he said.

"No, the asshole made his statement and took off like the coward he is."

Egan smiled at Raven, holding out his hand and introducing himself. Raven smiled at him, and he grinned at me with a wink.

He whistled softly. "*Frumos.*"

Raven looked confused, and I shook my head. "He said he's tired and is leaving."

Egan threw back his head in laughter, clapped me on the shoulder, and headed to the elevator. "I'm around if you need me. I only have one building to blow up this week."

Raven gaped at me. "He blows up buildings?"

"He works for a company that implodes buildings. They call him in when needed. He also works at Elite on occasion."

"Ah. That must be cool."

I tugged her toward the elevator. "Working with me, you mean?"

"Um, sure, but mostly, blowing up a building. I've seen those shows."

"If you get him started, he'll talk your ear off for hours. Show you videos."

We stepped into the elevator, and she pursed her lips. "Hearing him talk in that accent wouldn't be a hard thing."

I scowled at her, and she giggled. I liked hearing that sound.

"Keep it up, and you'll sleep in the bathtub," I threatened.

She shrugged. "I'll roam the halls until I find Egan. I'm sure he'll let me borrow his sofa."

I crowded her into the corner. She peered up at me, mischievous and adorable.

"He's in love with my cousin."

She sighed heavily. "Oh well. Bathtub it is, I guess."

I lowered my head, pressing my mouth to hers. "I can think of somewhere else far more comfortable, my lovely Ravenna Jade," I murmured against her soft lips.

"Oh, okay," she replied, her breath floating over my skin. "Whatever you think is best."

"Good answer."

Inside my place, she looked around with wide eyes, her gaze taking it all in. I hadn't changed a lot since Marcus lived here, although the kitchen wasn't used as much. I had painted the walls, brought in my own furniture, and turned his workout room into an office since we'd added a big workout area on the second floor where Hidden Justice used to be located and I didn't require my own workout space.

"It's so open," she said. "I like it."

"Yeah, it's comfortable."

She headed for the kitchen, running her hand along the gleaming counters and eyeing up the large stove. "I suddenly want to cook something."

I laughed. "Tomorrow. Tomorrow, you can cook to your heart's desire."

"I have to work tomorrow." She turned to me. "I'll have to get an Uber to work or leave earlier and walk."

I shook my head. "Neither. I'll drive you to school and pick you up afterward."

She frowned, but I didn't let her speak. "Yes. That is exactly what is happening."

"Where is Egan's apartment?" she asked. "I don't think he's as bossy as you are."

I glared at her, then before she could move, bent and flung her over my shoulder, snickering at her indignant gasp. I carried her down the hall, listening to her protests and demands to be set down. In the guest room, I threw her bag on the bed, swatted her butt playfully, then carefully lowered her to her feet, letting her slide down my torso slowly, feeling every inch of me.

"Then he has you fooled. He's way bossier."

"He's not as sexy as you either," she whispered.

I grinned. "Pleased to hear it."

She looked around. "Is this, ah, your room?"

"No, it's the guest room. I'm not going to pressure you, Raven. We have lots of time. You can stay here and be safe. That's what really matters right now. I'm right down the hall if you need me."

She reached up and cupped my cheek. "Thank you."

I turned and pressed a kiss to her palm. "Anything you need, you just have to ask. Okay?"

"Okay."

RAVEN

The bed was comfortable, the room quiet, but I couldn't sleep. The events of the past days played over and over in my head, keeping me awake. The strange, almost violent look in Andy's eyes as he cornered me in the alley. Running into Damien. His sweetness and caring, his intense protectiveness since that day. It was overwhelming. And tonight. The sensations, the emotions kissing him brought out. I had never reacted to another man—even my ex—the way I did to Damien. Together, we were an inferno, and I was lost the moment his mouth touched mine.

And then the rock. The way Damien took charge.

Dealt with the cops. Called Egan for backup. Brought me here.

He'd been sexy, thoughtful, and worried since we got home. Fussing that I had enough blankets, insisting on leaving my door open and a light on in the hall, worried I would wake up and be confused where I was. Bringing me a glass of water. Then an extra pillow. He poked his head in a short time later, asking if I was hungry. I grinned at him from the bed. "I can't sleep if you don't stop coming in here, Damien. Not hungry, thirsty, or cold."

"How about lonely? Are you lonely?"

"Impossible to be lonely when you pop in every five minutes."

"Right. Okay, I'm just down the hall if you need me."

"I might have heard that already."

He strode in and bent, pulling me up by my shoulders and kissing me soundly. "Okay, woman, enough. Go to sleep and stop calling for me to constantly come in here so you can kiss me. I can only take so much."

Then he left, leaving me turned on and suddenly lonely.

I knew if I called, he'd be here in a moment. If I lifted the blanket, he'd slide in with me and kiss me again. Until we couldn't stop. Until we were naked and joined together—and it was too soon for that.

I rolled over and burrowed under the blankets.

Right?

A short while later, I opened my eyes and peered at the clock. It was almost three, so I had obviously fallen asleep. I looked at the door, surprised to see it closed, the room pitch dark. Damien must have checked on me and shut the door when he saw I was sleeping. I sighed and shut my eyes, when a sound had me opening them again. The mattress dipped behind me, and I tried not to laugh.

"Determined, aren't you?"

"I told you."

I froze. That wasn't Damien's voice. Rough hands grabbed me, rolling me over, and I was pinned into place by a heavy body. Wearing a hoodie. He pressed a knife to my throat, holding up his phone so I could see his twisted smile. Blood was splattered on his hoodie and across his face.

"You didn't listen, and now everyone has to suffer. Your boyfriend is dead, and you're next."

I started to whimper.

Andy's voice dropped. "Once I'm done with you."

He pressed the knife harder, and I felt the slice of the blade in my throat. He smiled, evil and malevolent.

"Scream while you can, bitch. Your tongue will be gone soon enough. It'll keep you quiet until I'm done with you."

My cry echoed off the walls.

CHAPTER EIGHT

Damien

Her shriek jolted me out of the half sleep I was in. I was too anxious, too worried about her to fully relax.

The terror in her bloodcurdling scream woke me fully. My feet hit the floor before the next one pierced the air. Her begging and pleading were loud. Fervent. Her sobs wild in fear. She cried my name repeatedly.

"Damien!"

"No, please, don't! Not him! Don't!"

"Don't hurt him!"

"No! Damien!"

I rushed through her doorway, the light from the hall filling the room. She was upright in her bed, braced against the headboard, fighting off an invisible intruder, crying and out of control.

I grabbed her shoulders, desperate to wake her. I shook her gently, speaking loudly, calling her name.

"Raven, baby, open your eyes. Baby, it's me. I'm here." I shook her again, speaking louder.

"Raven—look at me!"

Her eyes snapped open, the panic and fear striking at my heart. Tears poured down her cheeks. I cupped her face. "It was a nightmare. A bad nightmare. I'm right here, baby. Right here."

Her gaze bounced everywhere, her body shaking. She gripped my wrists, gasping for air.

"D-Damien?"

I pressed my forehead to hers. "Right here, Raven. You're safe. We're both safe."

"He—he was here. He had a knife. He said he killed you." Her hand flew to her throat. "He had a knife right here. He cut me—I was bleeding."

I gathered her into my arms. "No, Raven. A nightmare. It was a nightmare."

She began to sob, burrowing close, her entire body racked with shudders. Her skin was clammy and cold. I stood, carrying her from the room and into mine, cursing myself. I should have known leaving her alone in a strange place wasn't a good idea.

I slid into my bed, keeping her in my arms. I pulled the blankets over us and rocked her, making hushing noises, saying her name repeatedly so she knew she was awake.

My phone chimed, and I grabbed it. It was a text from Egan.

Egan: Nightmares or SOS?

Me: Nightmares

I responded and set the phone aside. It didn't surprise me he had heard her. The screaming had been intense.

I stroked my fingers through her hair, pressing her face to my chest. "Raven, I need you to calm down, please."

"He—he said he killed you." Another long tremor went through her. "He said you—you were dead."

I shut my eyes at the agony in her voice.

"I'm not. I'm right here, holding you. It was just a dream. A terrible dream. He's not here. You're safe, I'm fine. We're fine. Please relax."

"Don't let go."

"I won't."

She let out a long, shuddering breath, going limp in my arms. Slowly, the sobbing stopped, and she became quiet. I held her close, running my hand up and down her back, cupping her head, playing with her hair. Letting her feel me. She warmed up, the earlier coldness of her skin returning to normal. The frantic breathing eased off, small stutters of air escaping her mouth. I pressed a kiss to her head. "Raven," I murmured. "Look at me, please."

Her eyes met mine, the red rims and tears making my chest hurt. "He can't get to you here. Ever. This building is the safest place for you to be. He can't get to you out there either, because I won't let him. You're safe, do you understand? So safe, Raven. I promise."

She nodded, her exhaustion and the emotion wearing her down.

"Can I stay here with you?"

"Yes."

"I, um, I have to…" She trailed off, and I let her slide off my lap, indicating the door to the left.

"Use my bathroom. I'm going to get you some water."

"Okay."

I hurried to the kitchen, filling a glass with ice and water, and came back to find her at the end of my bed, looking around. I pressed the glass into her hand and watched as she drank deeply. With a smile, I refilled it from the tap in the bathroom and set it on the nightstand. I lifted the blankets.

"In you go."

She crawled in, and I slipped in beside her, pulling her close. She settled her head on my chest, snaking her arm around my torso. I pressed a kiss to her crown, stroking her hair. I turned off the light and spoke quietly.

"Sleep, Raven. I'm right here."

"I'm sorry," she replied.

"Nothing to be sorry for. I understand. But I want you to sleep, knowing I'm watching over you and everything is fine. Okay? We'll talk about it in the morning."

"Thank you," she whispered.

Slowly, she relaxed, and I kept up my light caresses until I was certain she was asleep.

I mulled over what had just occurred. In her nightmare, Andy killed me. She was screaming for me, not herself. She feared for my safety more than her own.

Which meant she felt this draw as strongly as I did. It had been instant between us.

Something I didn't believe would ever happen to me.

I tried not to groan when I thought of what all my old bosses would have to say about this.

Chip off the old block. Following in our footsteps. Other such catchy phrases came to mind.

They were going to have a field day with this when I told them.

And they were going to find out soon. I needed as much advice as I could get.

Raven was quiet and withdrawn in the morning. She sipped a little coffee, pushed away the plate that had toast on it for her, and barely spoke. She didn't meet my eyes.

"Raven."

Finally, she lifted her pretty eyes to mine, the green dull and muted today. She was pale and looked as exhausted as I felt. She had only slept in short periods, waking with a start, anxious and worried. I hadn't slept at all, worried and concerned about her.

"Can you call in sick?"

"No, it's too late."

"I could send Egan in. I bet he'd do great with a roomful of kids. By lunch, they'd all know how to build a bomb," I said with a smile, hoping she would laugh.

Her lips quirked. "Probably not a good idea."

"Andy can't get to you. I'll walk you into the school and pick you up later. I'll have someone watch the building. I already contacted Tracey and told her."

"How?"

"I called her husband, and he handed her the phone. I explained what needed to happen and gave her the heads-up about my plans. Mike was off, so he is going to sit on the school for me. She feels better knowing he is around. The kids are used to seeing him on occasion so no one will ask, and I'll feel better."

"I see."

I studied her. "If that's all right with you."

"Do I really have any choice?"

"You could stay here today."

"So Andy wins? I have to hide?" She shook her head. "I hate that I have to be watched. That my personal life is impacting so many people. I just *hate* it."

"We all care about you, Raven. Your boss wants to help. So does her husband. And Egan." I paused, reaching over to clasp her hand. "And me. Especially me."

"I bet you wish you'd stayed home on Sunday. That I'd run into the bar and kissed someone else."

"Not in a million years. You were supposed to kiss me. I firmly believe that. And I'm going to look after you. If you allow that."

She opened her mouth to speak, and I smiled. "Yes, Raven, I have people to look after me too. We'll both be safe, all right?"

She blew out a long breath. "Okay."

I pushed her plate closer. "One piece. Eat one piece. Please."

She lifted the toast and bit into a piece, chewing slowly. It pleased me to know she would at least have something in her stomach.

"I'm going to get dressed. Then I'll drive you to school."

She nodded.

I stood, stopping to drop a kiss to her head. "We'll get through this."

"Then what?"

I smiled again. "Then we're gonna spend a lot of time getting to know each other. I'm looking forward to it."

I felt her gaze on me as I left the room.

I had a feeling she was looking forward to it as well.

RAVEN

The day was surreal. Damien driving me to school. A quick meeting with Tracey and Mike. The lingering remains of the nightmare that flitted through my mind. I tried not to think of it too much. I had a lot of glimpses of Mike in the morning as I taught my class, surprisingly calm given the turmoil my life felt like at the moment.

Dark clouds gathered most of the morning, matching my mood. My little charges helped to distract me from everything outside the classroom. We started a new book, each child getting a chance to read out loud. I encouraged them, gently correcting the wrong words, helping them sound out some bigger ones. Around eleven, the rain started, and just before lunch, the lights flickered, and the power went out. It was an older building, and it happened a lot. I saw Mike standing outside my door, and he gave me the thumbs-up to let me know it was nothing out of the ordinary. A few moments later, the decision was made that, due to the fact that the power would be out for the rest of the day, school was going to be canceled for the afternoon. It happened on occasion. Giving the class a snack, I sat down and contacted the parents, arranging pickup. I was busy over the next while, parents showing up to pick up their children. I wished them all a good weekend, and when the last of my charges were gone, I sat at my desk with a sigh. The building was heating up without any air circulation, and I was too worried to open my windows. Damien called, his voice warm over the line.

"I hear school's out early."

I chuckled. "For some. I'm going down the block with some other teachers and will work at the coffee shop for a while. They have power. I can do my lesson plans. Mike said he would drive me there." I paused. "I'll be with others. He doesn't have to stay."

"Okay," he agreed—far too easily for my liking. "But stay there until I pick you up. Do not leave, Raven. Understand?"

"Yes."

"I'll come around four to get you. That gives you three hours. Enough time?"

"Yes," I said suspiciously.

"What?"

"You're agreeing to this very calmly."

"I know you're covered. That's all that matters."

"Okay."

"I'll see you then. Don't leave without me. Even if someone offers you a ride."

"I won't."

He hung up, and I pursed my lips. He was acting far too agreeable. But I stood, took my bag, and met Mike in the office. He drove me to the coffee shop and walked inside with me, going to the counter to get some coffee to cover the reason he was here. He left with a wave once I sat with a couple of my coworkers. I felt oddly vulnerable. I hated the feeling intensely. Even moving from a small town, I had never felt this worried or scared. I disliked Andy for taking that away from me and, for an irrational moment, resented Damien for opening my eyes to the fact.

Except I realized I was being stupid. He had done nothing but help me. And he was amazing. I was lucky he had been the man who had met me at the door of the bar.

With a sigh, I stood up and got a coffee and a muffin. I noticed a man in the back, meeting his eyes briefly. He didn't appear interested in me at all, yet for some reason, he made me nervous. He sipped his coffee, worked on his laptop, and ate a sandwich. He got a refill, not even sparing a glance in my direction, yet I felt his presence somehow. I shook my head at my worries, then got to work with my fellow teachers, all of us sharing ideas and talking about our students. Chelsea taught grade one and Meghan taught the other kindergarten class, so we often swapped plans and thoughts. Chelsea left about an hour after we got there, and Meghan and I chatted for another while until her husband texted her, saying he was headed home early. She smirked at her phone.

"Guess I know what he has on his mind," she mumbled, not looking put out. "You want a lift home?"

"No, I'm good," I replied, suddenly anxious.

"Okay. See you Monday."

She left with a wave, and I glanced around. The coffee shop was quieter than when we arrived, most people leaving due to the rain. The man was still in the back, but his laptop was closed, and he was staring out the window. He looked relaxed and at ease, but somehow that made me even more uptight.

I texted Damien.

Me: Hi.

He replied quickly.

Damien: Raven—okay?

Me: Will you be coming soon?

Damien: What's wrong?

Me: Probably nothing, but there is a man here, and something is making me nervous. He isn't even looking at me, but I feel as if he is.

For a moment, there was no reply. I saw the man look at his phone, chuckle, then pick up his laptop, stand, and walk toward me. He stopped at my table and smiled.

"Check your messages," he requested.

I looked at my screen.

Damien: That's Leo. He's with me, so you are safe. I'll be there soon.

I glanced up and met Leo's eyes. They were kind and warm.

"May I sit?"

"Sure."

"What gave me away?"

"Nothing. I just am so tense, I think I noticed things that weren't there."

"And you made me."

"Sorry."

"No, it's all good." He held out his hand. "I'm Leo. I work with Damien at Elite. We run the company together."

I gaped at him. "He sent his partner to babysit me?"

He chuckled. "He had meetings this afternoon, and I was free. It was nice to get out of the office for a while. And I wasn't babysitting. I hire babysitters for my kids. I was watching over you as a favor."

"That explains why Damien was so laid-back about me coming to a coffee shop."

He steepled his fingers under his chin and studied me. "He was concerned. We are all aware of the situation, Raven. Andy is a man on the edge. None of us wants you around should he decide to cross that line. Damien would do the same for me. Any of us who work with him would."

"He said he would be here shortly. I'm sure—"

He held up his hand. "Don't insult me by finishing that remark. I am not leaving until the man himself shows up. It's a great opportunity to get to know the woman who has driven my normally calm friend into a tizzy." He grinned. "It's kind of fun to watch, although I wish the circumstances were different."

"You know him well?"

He nodded. "We've been coworkers a long time."

"Do you have any dirt on him?"

He looked shocked. "I would never betray—"

"I bake cookies."

His eyebrows flew up.

"I also love kids and would babysit."

He covered his mouth with his hand, muffling his laughter. "Is that the way it's gonna be?"

"I bake awesome cookies. And your kids will love me."

He leaned forward. "One time in the office…" He paused.

I moved closer. "I'm all ears."

CHAPTER NINE

Damien

I walked into the coffee shop, spying Leo and Raven at a table. They were chatting, laughing, both looking relaxed. I rolled my shoulders, feeling relief that Raven was fine and grateful to Leo for being there. I studied her for a moment before heading to the table. She looked tired, but her spirits seemed to be good, so I was pleased.

She saw me walking toward her, and she smiled. Bright, wide, not hiding the fact that she was happy to see me. My heart thumped fast in my chest in reaction to her delighted expression. I bent and dropped a kiss to her cheek, then sat, extending my hand to Leo. "Thanks," I said.

He grinned. "My pleasure. We had a great visit. Your woman is clever. She made me right away, not that I was trying to hide," he added with a wink.

I glanced at Raven, who was shaking her head. "I was concerned," I admitted. "Better safe than sorry. Even sitting with friends, Andy might approach you."

She held up her hand. "I'm not upset. I appreciate it."

"Good."

"Besides, Leo is right. We had a lovely chat."

"About?"

She tilted her head. "We were talking about his family."

"And?"

She shrugged. "Maybe a few other things. That is private, Damien," she said in her best teacher voice. "You don't ask such personal questions."

I grinned. "Yes, Ms. Raven."

She blushed, standing. "I need to use the restroom."

I watched her walk away, grateful I could see the door from the table where we sat.

"She is awesome," Leo enthused. "Funny, articulate, pretty. The whole package."

"I know. You saw nothing?"

His face darkened. "Once. Across the street. I was sure I saw a guy in a dark hoodie in the doorway of the office building. A semi rolled by, and when my line of vision was clear, no one was there. It could have been nothing."

I shook my head. "In this case, I'm sure it was. He's obsessed with her. I need to find him."

"Egan working on it?"

"Yeah. I'll double down now that all the meetings are done too." I stroked my chin. "I have a feeling he knows his way around computers. How to erase his trails. He's good."

"You're better. Between you and Egan, you'll find him. I'm sure the sketch he did will ping off something."

"I hope so. In the meantime, she'll stay with me. I'll keep her safe."

"Not much of a hardship, I'm sure," he murmured, sounding amused.

I watched Raven walk toward us, the light gleaming on her dark hair, her hips gently sashaying as she moved. My body tightened at her subtle sexiness.

Her company wasn't a hardship at all. My cock, the desire I felt for her—that was going to be the problem.

"Nope," I agreed dryly. "Not at all."

———

Raven became visibly nervous as we headed outside to my car. I tucked her close, opening her door and closing it firmly. I noticed she kept her gaze on me as I walked around the front of the vehicle. I slid inside and started the car, then reached over and took her hand.

"You're perfectly safe with me."

"I know," she said with a small smile. "I'm just—"

I shook my head. "You don't have to explain. I understand."

"Thank you," she murmured, and I squeezed her fingers. "Could we stop by the grocery store?"

"Sure."

I drove us to the large one by my building, and we went in. We both added some things to the cart. I hid my smile at all the baking ingredients she added. I needed some basics, and I stopped at the butcher counter, looking at steaks. It was supposed to be a nice weekend, and I thought I would grill our meals.

She let out a sudden giggle, and I glanced at her. "What?"

She shook her head. "Nothing. I, ah, I just have to go there." She pointed toward the pharmacy. "I'll be right back."

"You're okay?"

She nodded. "I can see you, and I'll only be a moment."

My number was called, so I moved forward, asking for the steaks I'd chosen, watching as Raven moved to the pharmacy, picking up something, and heading back toward me. I turned back to the butcher, asking for some chicken, my attention diverted for a moment. Raven appeared beside me, setting a couple of things in the basket. We finished the shopping and headed for the cash register. I began to unload onto the belt.

"Damn, I forgot sour cream," I muttered.

"Go get some. I'll unload."

I hesitated, and she looked at me. "I'm surrounded by people," she pointed out.

She was right, so I hurried away, returning just as our order was done. I added the container and frowned as she scanned her card before I could get mine out.

"Don't argue with me," she said. "I'm inconveniencing you enough. I'm paying for the groceries."

I held up my hands and added the packed bags to the cart.

I didn't say a word until we parked and got into the elevator. I set down the bags I was carrying and rested my arms on either side of her, caging her in.

"You, Raven, are *not* an inconvenience."

Then I kissed her.

By the time the elevator door opened, we were both breathless.

"We clear on that now?"

Her eyes were wide in her face, her lips wet. She nodded wordlessly. I pressed my mouth to hers again. "Tell me when you need reminding again."

A smile pulled at her lips.

"I will."

"Where will you grill the steak?" Raven asked.

I indicated she should follow me, and I took her up the steps that were only accessible from this floor that led to the rooftop. She gasped in wonder at the pots of flowers and herbs and the small grassy area.

"This is amazing!"

"Marcus was big on gardening. Grew all his own herbs. I don't have as many, but I try to keep some, plus the flowers. I added the gazebo and the grill. I like to sit outside."

"It's awesome." She sat down at the table. "You would never know this was up here."

I sat across from her. "I know. It's private and high enough to be fairly quiet. Once the neighborhood slows down in the evenings, it's quite peaceful." I studied her body language, seeing how her shoulders relaxed and some of the tension left her face now we were ensconced in the building. "You can use it whenever you like."

She glanced over my shoulder. "I assume you aren't taking me home after dinner."

"You assume correctly."

"Or in the morning."

I sat back, bending my leg over my knee. "Nope. Until I have a handle on this asshole, you're stuck here with me."

"Unless I insisted."

I sighed, running a hand over my neck. "I won't keep you here like a prisoner, Raven. But you're safe here. He can't get into the building, throw something through the window, or even see you. If you insisted on returning to your apartment, I would go with you. Assign a bodyguard to you as well as stay. Your place is a little small, but I'd make do."

"And if I refused all that?" she asked quietly, testing me.

I shrugged. "Then you'd find security detail following you everywhere. Me included. I won't give him the chance to get to you."

I saw the wonder in her eyes. The relief. Then she smiled and sat back. "I guess I'll stay, then. Especially if you're going to grill. I can't have a barbecue at my apartment."

I laughed, pleased to know she wasn't going to fight this. I meant it. I wouldn't force her to stay here—that would make me no better than the asshole I was trying to find—but I wouldn't let her be alone either. Here, I knew exactly how to protect her.

"Do you want to eat out here?"

"I'd like that."

"Okay, you relax, and I'll bring the stuff up."

She stood, suddenly looking nervous again. "Oh. No, I'll help."

I wrapped an arm around her. "He can't get to you here. Not a chance."

"I just feel better when I'm closer to you," she admitted.

My chest warmed at her words. I kissed her softly. "Okay, then. Come help."

We returned downstairs, gathering everything, filling a tray. I wasn't a cook like Marcus, but I could grill well. We'd bought a premade salad, and Raven had picked up a fresh baguette, admitting to a slight addiction to bread. We returned up to the roof and soon were sitting down to eat. The food was delicious, the wine helped us both relax, and I teased Raven about her downplaying her bread addiction. She almost growled as I reached for the heel of the bread, making me laugh before handing it to her. The other end was already gone. When we'd gotten back to the apartment, I had pulled the bread from the bag with a frown.

"Jesus, someone bit off the end. How did I not notice that in the store?"

She had tried to hide her grin but failed.

"You took a bite out of the bread? In the store?" I gaped at her.

"Once I paid for it. It was still warm, Damien. Warm," she repeated. "I couldn't resist."

All I could do was laugh. She was completely adorable, and I didn't want her any other way. I liked her just like that. Free-spirited bread-stealer that she was.

I encouraged her to tell me more stories of the

kids she taught, enjoying the way her eyes softened when she spoke of her students.

"You'll make a great mother one day," I said without thinking.

She stared at me, her mouth forming a silent O.

"I mean, if you wanted kids," I added.

"I would love a couple of them," she admitted.

"It seems so natural to you," I observed. "But I didn't mean to overstep."

"No, it's fine." She waved off my concern. "I love children. I love being part of their lives. Watching them learn and discover the world around them. I would like to have my own one day." She paused. "What about you?"

I finished my steak, chewing slowly. I pushed away my plate and took a sip of wine.

"Given my occupation, at one point, I would have said no. But now, I think so."

"Your occupation?" She eyed me over the rim of her glass. "You've said a few other things. You mentioned your training and your background. Your assurances I couldn't be any safer. I assume you didn't always operate a security firm?"

"No."

She pursed her lips. "Are you a spy? An undercover agent? 007?"

I chuckled. "Nothing that impressive. In fact, I was never a field agent. I have no machine guns in my car or a pen that will explode when needed."

"Damn."

"Sorry."

"It's fine. I can live with that."

"I can, however, protect you better than anyone else in this city."

"There is a story there."

"Yes."

"You said you'd tell me."

"When the time is right."

"Okay," she agreed and dropped the subject. "What do you have planned for the weekend?"

"Whatever you want. I'm at your beck and call."

She grinned. "I've never had a beck-and-call guy."

"Well, here I am. I assume you plan on making cookies from the items I saw you put in the cart?"

"Yes."

"Then whatever you want. As long as I get to be taste tester for said cookies, I'm your guy."

A mischievous look passed over her face, and she tried to hide her grin. I narrowed my eyes. "What are you up to?"

"Nothing."

"I think you are."

"Well then, Mr. Super Spy, you'll have to find out." A breeze stirred her hair, and she shivered a little. I glanced up at the clouds that had gathered while we were eating, surprised at how quickly they were coming in.

"We should head in," I said. "We'll continue this discussion inside."

She stood with a smile. "Or not."

I grinned as I followed her down the steps. I was looking forward to getting her secret out of her.

Any way I had to.

CHAPTER TEN

Damien

Back in the apartment, Raven curled up on the sofa with her Kindle, and I sat across from her, using my laptop, checking emails. Every so often, I would feel her eyes on me, but when I would lift my head, she would drop her gaze back to her e-reader, a small smile tugging at her lips. She was up to something, but I hadn't figured it out yet.

Outside, the wind was stronger and the clouds darker.

"Are you afraid of storms?" I asked.

"No. I love to watch them."

"Me too. The skylight in my room is the perfect place for it."

She lifted one eyebrow. "Is that a fact?"

"It is."

"Trying to lure me into your bed, Damien?"

"Is it working?"

She giggled, and I grinned at the sound.

"You like the sunlight best, though, I assume."

"Why would you say that?"

"You seem like a sunshine kind of girl."

"I enjoy the sun and summer, but I actually love the darkness. You know most people hate the winter and how short the days are? I love it. The nighttime. The inky skies and the stars. Winter is my favorite season. Fall, second."

"You are one odd girl, Raven."

She laughed again.

I enjoyed teasing her. I liked hearing her laugh. I liked being the one to make her laugh.

I looked back at my laptop, unhappy with Egan's latest message. He still had come up empty trying to find Andy. He was convinced Andy was a hacker and had deleted every trace of himself from the site. I had to agree. We were going to start delving into other sites, although there was a chance Andy had used a different name or had erased himself there as well. Egan informed me he was shocked at the number of dating sites there were. I had to agree with him, especially given how much harder that would make our job of finding this slimeball. But I was determined.

I shut my laptop and looked over at Raven. She shifted in her seat, rolling her shoulders.

"Um, could you hand me that pillow?" she asked, indicating the other end of the sofa she was seated on.

"Sure."

I placed the laptop on the table beside me, stood, and picked up one of the toss cushions to give her. Unexpected movement caught my eye as I picked up the pillow, and I gasped in disbelief as a mouse scurried under the other cushion.

"Fuck," I swore, jumping back.

"What?"

"A mouse," I said through gritted teeth. "A goddamn mouse."

"Oh."

"I hate mice."

Suddenly, it appeared again, and without thinking, I backed up, hitting the other sofa and falling on it. "Damn it!" I yelled. "There's more than one!"

A strange noise hit me, and I looked at Raven in a panic. Her hand was covering her mouth, and she was laughing.

Why the hell was she laughing?

We were being overrun by rodents, for fuck's sake. Scurrying little vermin were in my apartment.

My gaze went back to the mice. Then I frowned. They hadn't moved. One was still under the cushion, its ass peeking out, the other sitting in the middle of the seat. Perfectly still.

I stood, staring. Something wasn't right. Raven's laughter grew louder, and I glanced her way then at the mice.

And spied the thread attached to them.

I snapped my head in her direction, glowering at her. I thought about how chummy she and Leo were when I arrived at the coffee shop earlier. Laughing and joking when I walked in, talking about something amusing.

That fucker had sold me out. Told her about how much I hated mice.

"Think you're funny, do you?" I asked.

She could only nod, her laughter still loud.

I reached down, pulling the mice off the sofa. Fake, stuffed mice. It hit me. At the store by the pharmacy was the pet aisle. There had been a display of toys. She had distracted me. Twice.

Played her funny little joke. Now it was payback time.

I glared at her, holding up the mice. "You are going to pay for that little stunt, Raven."

She scrambled off the sofa, standing behind it. "Nope."

"Yes."

"I had to. It was too easy."

I stepped closer. "Catching you will be too."

Her eyes widened, her gaze roaming the room, looking for her escape. Except she didn't have a chance. Her gaze gave her away, focusing on the route she planned to take. She lunged to the left, and I was behind her instantly, still holding the damn mice. She had one in her hand and turned, flinging it at me, half laughing, half scared. I caught her before she could get far, throwing her over my shoulder, swatting her behind. "I warned you."

"Put me down."

I carried her to my bed and flung her on the mattress, following her down, pinning her to the bed.

"Gotcha."

She giggled and held up another mouse, tapping it on my nose. I had to laugh. "I can't believe Leo told you how much I hate mice."

She nodded. "I had to bribe him."

"With?"

"Cookies."

I laughed. The bastard had a major sweet tooth, and his wife only allowed him a treat on occasion. Of course he couldn't resist the lure of cookies.

"I found it hard to believe," Raven mused. "The man who chases after bad guys, makes me feel safer than I ever have, and seems larger-than-life, is frightened by mice?"

"I'm not frightened. I just dislike them."

"You looked as if you were going to pass out when you saw them."

I slid my hands down her arms, tossing the mouse in her hand over my shoulder. I entwined our fingers, lifting her arms over her head and lightly holding them in place.

"I was startled."

"You were adorable."

I shook my head, lowering my face to her neck, kissing the soft skin. "You're the adorable one."

She shivered, and I grinned against her throat.

"Scared now, my Ravenna Jade?"

"Yes."

"Of what I'm going to do to you, my beautiful girl?" I asked, tracing my lips over her ear, capturing the lobe and tugging on it with my teeth.

"Of how you make me feel."

I pulled back, meeting her wide-eyed gaze.

"How am I making you feel?" I asked in a low voice.

"Needy," she breathed. "Achy with want."

Her words hung in the air between us. The playfulness evaporated, desire building around us.

"I can ease that ache," I murmured. "I *want* to ease that ache."

"Please," she whispered. "Damien, please—"

I cut off whatever she was about to say. Our mouths melded together seamlessly, moving and caressing. I slid my tongue inside her mouth, meeting hers, twining and tasting. I swallowed her breath, filling my lungs with her essence. She pulled on her hands, and I released them, grunting in approval as she wound them around my neck, tugging on my hair and keeping me close. I slid mine under her back, lifting her, dragging her to the middle of the bed, our mouths never separating. I swam in the sensations she brought forth in me. The need and want. The feel of her under me. She tugged on my shirt, and I pulled back, my mouth protesting being apart from hers. I tore my shirt over my head and threw it behind me with the discarded mouse. I helped her pull hers off, groaning at the sight of her pretty, lacy bra, the dark blue of it contrasting with her skin, making it look creamy and inviting. But as pretty as the bra was, I was far more interested in the beautiful swells it hid from my eyes, and I slid my hand around her back, unhooking the bra and pulling it down her shoulders, baring her to me.

"Fuck, you are beautiful," I whispered, tracing her breasts, running my fingers around her nipple that hardened under my touch. I took her mouth again, lowering her back to the bed, kissing her until she was shaking. I dragged my mouth over her throat, across her collarbone, and slowly drew one nipple into my mouth, playing with and teasing it as she whimpered. I showed the same attention to her other one, smiling at her low gasps and pleas. I traced my hand over her stomach, stopping at the waistband of her skirt. I looked up, our eyes meeting, mine pleading for permission, hers heavy-lidded and filled with passion.

She lifted her ass and popped the button on the side. I slid off the material, adding it to the growing pile on the floor. Then I drank her in. She wore a wisp of lace between her legs, the same deep blue as her bra. Two tiny bows beckoned my fingers, and I tugged, the material giving way easily. I heard her sharp intake of air as I gazed at her, naked, beautiful, and on my bed. I traced a path between her hip bones, drawing lazy patterns on her skin with my finger.

"You want this, Raven? You want me? Us?"

"Yes."

"You have to know something. Once we do this, once I make you mine, I'm all in. I'm not a player. I'll be yours." I paused. "I'll consider you mine." I dropped my voice. "I protect and cherish what is mine."

She sat up, grasping the back of my neck and bringing my mouth back to hers. "So do I."

We became a mass of quivering limbs, seeking mouths, and desperate pleas. The rest of my clothing was discarded, our hands working together to rid me of the material that separated us. Her skin rubbing on mine was soft, the feel of her wrapped around me intoxicating. I slid my hand between her legs, finding her warmth, feeling her desire, the wet of her like silk on my fingers. She gasped as I played with her, widening her legs when I slipped one, then two fingers inside her. Her breathy little moans and whispers were pure erotica to my ears.

"Yes, Damien. Oh God, like that. Yes, touch me like that."

"Harder, please. More, give me more."

I groaned as she wrapped her hand around me, stroking me from root to tip. She used her thumb to spread the precome around the crown and traced her fingers along the vein that protruded under the thin skin. She cupped and stroked my balls. We kissed endlessly—deep, passionate ones; gentle, adoring presses of our lips; long, languid strokes of our tongues. I learned her dips and curves. The feel of her hips filling my hands. The taste of her everywhere. Sweet, salty, musky. She made me groan when she took me in her mouth, her tongue discovering everything she'd explored with her hands, this time the sensations wet and hot. Finally, she hovered over me, our gazes locked.

I blindly reached into the drawer, pulling out a condom. She ripped it open with her teeth, sheathing my rigid cock, then slowly lowered herself on me. I groaned as her pussy engulfed me. Blistering heat pounded down my spine, my cock gripped inside her body. She stopped when we were flush, her cheeks red, her eyes wide.

"Oh my God," she whispered. "You feel so good."

"So do you." I grabbed her hips. "I need you to move."

She rolled her hips, and I cursed. She did it again, rising up and lowering herself, smiling at the low groan she pulled from my chest.

"Jesus, baby."

She leaned forward, the angle changing. She was close enough, I kissed her. Swallowed her cries of delight as she began to move. She undulated over me, whimpering, wrapping me in her heat. I slid my hand between us, stroking circles on her hard clit, feeling her orgasm beginning. I pressed harder, smiling as her muscles locked down and she flung back her head, riding me harder. I lunged up, taking her down to the mattress under me, thrusting into her. I kissed and licked at her lips, her neck, her breasts. Sucked her hard nipples. Drove into her mindlessly, my orgasm beginning to bear down on me. She sobbed out my name, coming again, pulsating around me. I lifted my head with a long, loud groan and let the pleasure take me. I spiraled down into the ecstasy, my body shaking, the frenzy so great I could only try to keep up. I lost myself for a moment, finally rousing enough to realize I was pinning her to the mattress, my head buried in her neck, my body satisfied and exhausted. I eased from her, quickly disposing of the condom, then rolled over and pulled her into my arms.

We were silent aside from our heavy breathing, wrapped around each other as tightly as possible. I pressed a kiss to her forehead, sliding my fingers under her chin and tilting up her face.

"Okay, Raven?"

"You really have to ask?"

I chuckled. "I was pretty rough near the end."

She frowned. "No, you were exactly what I needed. You made me feel wanted."

"You were. You *are*."

She snuggled closer. "That was the most beautiful thing I've ever experienced, Damien."

"I think so too."

"So, it was okay for you?" she asked, her voice suddenly shy.

"We were amazing. You were perfect. You *are* perfect."

"I'm hardly perfect," she scoffed.

"Well, for me, then. You're perfect for me."

She traced a lazy circle on my chest. "I like that."

"Good." I pressed a kiss to her messy hair and rested my head on the pillow, surprised to find how much I enjoyed holding her. I was never one for cuddling after sex, yet with Raven, it was different. I had a feeling everything about her was going to be different.

Her voice broke in to my inner musings.

"Should I apologize for the mice?"

I shook with silent laughter. "No, you're good. I didn't even see you put the package in the cart."

"I hid it under some lettuce."

"And I assume that is why you encouraged me to go get the sour cream?"

"Yep. I had her scan the mice, and I shoved them in my purse."

"You thought of everything. I'll have to keep a better eye on you, troublemaker."

She chuckled, pressing a kiss to my chest. I liked how her mouth lingered.

We were quiet for a moment. "Leo mentioned you hate snakes too."

I burst out laughing. I had a feeling this girl was going to keep me on my toes.

I rolled her over, staring down at her. Her eyes were soft, her mouth swollen, hair messy, and her cheeks flushed. She looked freshly fucked and completely satisfied.

"Will you punish me like this again?" she asked, looking impish.

I lowered my head and kissed her.

"Bring it on, Raven. You'll see what happens."

She grinned. "I look forward to it."

"Me too."

CHAPTER ELEVEN

Raven

I woke with Damien wrapped around me. I wasn't sure of the time, although the shadows in the room let me know it was fairly early. My back was nestled against his front, one heavy arm draped over me, our legs entangled, and his breath hot on my neck. The position was protective, his entire body against mine. And although he was asleep, not every part of his body was at rest. His cock was pressed between us, hard and ready.

And my body responded.

Last night had been unexpected. Everything about Damien was that way, but I knew neither of us had planned for our relationship to get physical so quickly. But it felt amazingly right. As if it was supposed to be that way. Being with him was easy. He was funny, sweet, charming, yet his darker side was present as well. Always watchful, on alert, ready to defend. I had a feeling when he told me his background, I wouldn't hear stories of police training. I was certain, if needed, Damien could be lethal. Strangely enough, the thought brought me comfort, not worry.

But with me, he was gentle. Passionate and loving. And sex with him was unlike anything I had ever experienced in my life. He'd had me again, taking his time, drawing out our pleasure. Then in the dark of the night, I'd woken up to his mouth on my neck, his whispered words of needing me in my ear. It was intimate and slow, our bodies locked together, rocking gently, his lips on mine until I came with an intensity that brought tears to my eyes.

And even now in his sleep, he wanted me. No one had ever desired me this strongly before. Not even my ex. And we were supposed to get married.

I shut my eyes, forcing away those memories. I wanted to stay here, in the present, with Damien.

I shifted, and he clutched me tighter, his breathing stirring the hair around my ears.

"Stay, baby. Don't go," he mumbled, moving his leg behind me and pulling me tight to his body. "Like you here."

He slid his hand from my waist, lower, his fingertips ghosting over my center. "Hmm," he sighed, still mostly asleep. "Nice." He pressed his lips to my neck. "Mine."

Wondering how asleep he was, I lifted my leg up

and back, draping it over his hip. His cock slipped into my folds, and I tried to stifle my groan at the feel of him. Hot, hard, ready—nudging at my entrance. Unable to resist, I moved, and he slid inside, his hips moving with mine. I felt him wake, already moaning.

"Raven, holy shit, baby, what—" The words were cut off with a low, guttural groan. "Fuck, you feel good." He tilted his hips, going deeper, sliding his long fingers to my clit and rubbing it.

"Is that what you want, Raven? My cock? My fingers?"

"Yes," I moaned, pushing back against him.

He grabbed my leg, opening me more and sinking in totally. He began to move, hard, powerful strokes, his fingers never ceasing their teasing.

"Take it, then. Take all of me."

I cried out as he slid my clit between two fingers, using his thumb to tease it as he massaged my flesh. I was already so close, it tipped me over the edge, and I succumbed, crying out, my back arching as Damien held me close, still moving, setting off another small orgasm within me, then pulling out and gripping me close, coming all over my back.

"Damn it, Raven, you felt too good bareback."

I shut my eyes, realizing we hadn't bothered with a condom. I'd been caught up in the moment with him.

"I get the shot. I just had one last week, so we're covered."

"I still want you to feel safe." He sighed heavily into my neck, kissing the damp skin. "I haven't been with anyone for over a year, so I'm clean."

"I haven't been with anyone since my fiancé dumped me. That was well over a year ago, and it had been a while since we'd been together. He said he wanted to wait until we were married. Make it more romantic if we were desperate for each other."

He held me tighter. "And?"

"He wasn't as desperate for me as he was for my best friend. I caught them screwing each other in the room at the back of the church when I arrived to marry the bastard. The whole church heard us yelling. Turned out they'd been having an affair for months."

"Fuck, Raven, I'm sorry," he murmured.

I shrugged, surprised to find it no longer upset me. Meeting Damien had helped me move past that hurt.

"Is that why you moved?"

"One reason. I hated that my mom had to witness that too. She was sick and never recovered. It's hard to get past two such personal losses when everyone keeps wanting to talk about them. I got tired of the pitiful looks. I hated it that conversations stopped when I walked into a room. When I'd hear snippets of gossip involving me. Being called 'poor Raven.' I had to get out. It was too much." I sighed. "His defense was that he didn't love me and was only going through with the wedding because of my mom being ill. He planned on divorcing me once she died. I saved him the trouble."

"What a bastard."

"Everyone heard him too. I heard they got married and moved. I wonder if he'll cheat on her as well."

He held me tight. "You didn't deserve that, Raven. But I'm glad you didn't marry him." He lifted my chin, meeting my eyes. "I would never cheat on you. Ever. I meant what I said last night."

It was impossible to look away from his intense gaze. Truth blazed from his eyes.

"I know," I said quietly. I patted his arm. "But we're okay, um, coverage-wise. I won't get pregnant or anything."

"I'll keep using a condom until you tell me not to."

His declaration made me smile.

"I need a shower," I whispered. "I'm covered in you."

He chuckled. "I like you covered in me." But he threw back the covers, getting out of bed. He held out his hand. "Come with me, Raven. I'll clean you up." He winked as he pulled me from the bed.

"For now."

The shower was long, hot, and we somehow got messy again and had to start all over. I tried not to giggle as Damien aimed the showerhead at the tile wall, washing away the evidence. After we got out, I tried not to ogle him as he moved around, a towel tucked at his waist, his broad shoulders and well-toned torso still glistening with water from the shower. He caught me eyeing him up and stopped in the process of pulling a T-shirt out of the dresser. He lifted one eyebrow, teasing and confident.

"See something you like?"

I shrugged. "Meh."

He laughed and advanced toward me, looking dangerous and far too sexy after what had occurred in the shower. And the bed. And last night. I backed away, realizing my mistake as my legs hit the mattress and I fell backward. Instantly, he was over me, his smile wide.

"I like what I see," he murmured, tugging on the towel wrapped around me. "Even if you're hiding it." He traced his finger along my collarbone. "Not *meh* at all." His gaze darkened. "Sexiest damn thing I have ever encountered."

Our eyes locked and held. My breath stuttered in my throat. He began to lower his face to mine when his phone rang out. It was a familiar ringtone, and I lifted my eyebrow. "Is that 'Eye of the Tiger'?"

He chuckled. "Egan. He's fixated on Rocky." He

stood, looking regretful. "And if he's calling, I need to take it."

I nodded. The moment had passed. It was fine—I was already feeling the effects of him having had me so many times. My lady bits could use a rest.

He wrapped his hands around my shoulders, pulling me into a sitting position. He bent and kissed me. Long, slow, sensuous. I felt it in every molecule of my body. Even my lady bits woke up, deciding they weren't that sore after all. He gazed down at me in wonder. "You bewitch me, Ravenna Jade."

"I like how you say my name."

"I like saying it."

"You're pretty addictive yourself."

He kissed me again, a fast, hard press of his mouth on mine. "Good."

He picked up his phone. "I need to go downstairs and see Egan. You okay here?"

"You said I was."

"I meant it. The building is secure. So is the rooftop if you want to go sit in the sun for a while."

"I might. I'll be outside a lot soon. Might as well get used to it."

"What are you talking about?"

"School is out soon. I work at a day camp in July. Well, three weeks of July, with a friend of mine."

"You don't take the summer off?"

"No. I enjoy being with the kids. We have lots of fun. Deb and I did the Easter break one, and we got along well. So, I agreed to do the July one. The pay is decent, and I still have all August off."

He frowned.

"What?"

"We'll discuss this when I get back. Relax and enjoy some downtime. Keep your phone beside you, and if something feels off or you get nervous…"

"I'll call."

"I won't be too long, I hope. I'm just downstairs in Egan's apartment."

"Okay."

He disappeared into the walk-in closet and emerged in shorts, grabbing the shirt he'd taken from the drawer earlier. He pulled it over his head and ran a hand through his short, dark hair. He held up a pass. "Use this to open the door for upstairs and swipe it to get back into the apartment."

"What about you?"

"I got this one for you last night. I have my own."

"Okay. Thank you."

"Anything. You call. Don't hesitate."

"I will."

He studied me and then, as if liking my response, nodded. I heard his footsteps head down the hall and the door close behind him.

"Good thing I hadn't planned on leaving the building," I muttered, then shook my head. I was being petulant. I had zero interest in leaving the safety of the building or being far from Damien right now.

The garden upstairs called my name, and I dressed, put on some sunblock, found a baseball hat of his to use, my Kindle, and a bottle of water. I put everything in my satchel and headed upstairs, sighing in pleasure when I got to the roof. It was sunny and warm, but there was a nice breeze, and the high walls gave a sense of privacy. I headed to the gazebo and sat in a lounger, looking around. It was a lovely space, and I could smell the flowers and even the fragrance of some of the herbs growing in the pots. I settled back and opened my Kindle, deciding, of all the places I could be today, this might be my favorite spot.

DAMIEN

I looked at Egan, shaking my head. "Nothing? At all?"

"No," he huffed out. "Nothing. It's like he's invisible. The sketch didn't get a hit in any of the databases. I searched other dating sites, although I'm not done yet." He looked at me in wonder. "Do you have any idea how many there are?"

"I know. It's a different world."

He snorted. "The firewalls on some of them are so simple to get through. People have no idea how easily they could be compromised."

I frowned. "I wonder if he only creates a profile

128

once he zeroes in on a target. Maybe he hacks into these sites, finds his targets, and then builds a profile to match it."

Egan nodded slowly, pursing his lips. "Have you considered this is possibly the first time he's done this? Maybe it is an attraction gone awry on his part?"

"I had, before the rock through the window. The smashed daisy. I saw the crazed look in his eyes. I recognize it."

He held up his hands. "Just checking, Watcher."

I rolled my eyes.

"I think you may be onto something, though," Egan mused. "We need to come at this from a different angle. Instead of searching the actual site, we need to dig into the back end. See if he left a trail."

"If he's as clever as we think, he's probably rerouted through a ghost VPN."

Egan smirked. "Even the cleverest people make mistakes."

"I'm going to use the Hidden Justice software and search police records. See if anyone filed a report against this fictitious Andy Smith, or someone with the same MO."

"Good plan." He sat back. "We should concentrate on the slightly less popular sites. The bigger ones are harder to get into and tend to have safety checks in place. I think he'd haunt the ones he knew he could get in and out of easily. The Real

Connection isn't huge. I think that might be our starting point."

"You sure you have time for this?"

"Absolutely. I want to help." He lifted a shoulder. "I am a little bored at the gym. Nothing exciting about sweaty people. This is far more interesting."

I laughed, not surprised. Egan loved computers as much as I did and was talented when it came to hacking and investigating. "Okay."

We drew up a list, dividing it. Tossed around some more ideas.

"I was thinking of calling Marcus and Julian. With their experience, they might have ideas."

Egan reached into a drawer and handed me a laptop. "Encrypted," he said.

I used my own program to video call them. Marcus answered, his voice a familiar rumble, his smile wide.

"Damien. How are you?"

"Well, Marcus. I'm well. You alone?"

He turned the laptop he was using so I saw who he was sitting with. "Actually, I'm with Julian and Matteo. We're having a drink and relaxing. Do you need me to be alone?"

"No, the more, the merrier. I need to pick your collective brains. Egan is here as well."

"Hold on. Let me get us set up." A moment later, I could see all three of them. They looked healthy and relaxed. We chatted and exchanged news, laughing over some antics their kids had been up to, offering congratulations on yet another baby for Marcus and Missy. Then Marcus paused. "What's going on?"

"I have a situation."

Instantly, they became the men I knew best. Intense, fierce, ready to lend a hand.

"Talk to us," Julian stated, leaning forward, assuming his role as Commander.

I took in a deep breath and told them everything, leaving out the newer, private parts of my relationship with Raven.

They asked questions, listened carefully. Viewed the sketch that Egan scanned and sent them. They all looked a bit surprised when I described our first meeting and the fact that Raven was now ensconced in my apartment, but they didn't comment.

"What can we do?" Marcus asked. "What do you need?"

"I could fly out and be another set of hands," Julian offered.

"No," I replied. "I don't want to take you away from your families. I need your contacts. I was the IT guy—behind the operations. You had the more, ah, personal relationships with the law enforcement agencies." I cleared my throat. "Those known and not known to the public."

"You need to see if they have anything," Marcus stated. "If there are any similar cases. If the guy in this sketch is known to them."

"Yes. They might have reports I haven't accessed yet. I would rather do it with a phone call than start hacking. I'll save that for a last resort."

Julian rubbed his chin. "You said Raven moved to Toronto in the last while?"

"Yes."

"Maybe this perp did too. Check other provinces. Some of the dating sites are locally supported. Maybe he moved recently too and has done this elsewhere."

"Good idea."

"We'll get on to our contacts right away," Marcus assured me. He met my eyes. "This girl– Raven. She's important to you?"

I ran a hand through my hair. "Yeah, she is."

Marcus tilted his head. "How important?"

"It's early, Marcus."

He studied me.

"Tell me something," he replied. "How do you feel when you think about her in danger?"

My fists curled of their own accord. "I want to rage and burn down the city to find whatever it is that is putting her in that situation. I can't stand the thought of her upset or hurt. Of being alone and vulnerable. It makes me crazy."

He sat back, a smile playing on his lips. He shared an amused glance with Matteo and Julian.

"Sound familiar, my friends?"

They all chuckled, and Julian shook his head. "Lightning," was all he said.

Matteo, who had been fairly quiet the entire time, leaned back with a smile. "Should I draw up plans for another house on the island?"

Egan barked out a hoot of laughter, and I shot him a look. "No thanks, Matteo. I don't think Raven is an island type girl." I paused. "I mean, I have no idea what our future holds. That is, we haven't talked…" I trailed off, realizing I had nothing.

They all laughed, finding my bumbling answers amusing.

"Let me know," he said. "You can always use the guesthouse and come for a break. She'd certainly be safe here."

Marcus glanced at Egan. "How's Sofia?" he asked with a wide smile.

Egan's face fell. "With all due respect, Marcus, fuck off."

"Still resisting your charms, is she?"

Egan scowled, then sat back, nonchalantly rolling up his sleeves. "Victory will be all that much sweeter."

Everyone, including me, laughed.

"You could put in a good word for me," Egan said to Marcus. "She trusts your opinion. You chat me up."

I smacked his leg. "Wrong expression. You want to chat her up. You want Marcus to talk you up."

He rolled his eyes and flicked his hand. "Your language kills me. Even after all these years. Talk—chat. What is difference?"

Marcus smirked. "The difference is how riled up you get, which makes you sound as if you just got off the boat."

Egan huffed and Marcus chuckled. "I'll put in a word next time we talk."

Then he focused on me. "You take care of your lady. We'll make some calls, and you keep digging. We'll find him. Eliminate the threat, and you can move on to the good stuff."

"Sounds like a plan."

I signed off and sighed, grateful for friends in high places. I would call in any favor I needed to in order to help Raven.

In the meantime, I'd been gone a while, and I needed to get back to her.

CHAPTER TWELVE

Damien

Raven was still upstairs, sitting on the lounger, her Kindle open but ignored. She was on the phone and offered me a smile as I approached.

"Sounds good, Deb. I'll see you tomorrow."

She listened for a moment. "Yeah, I'm excited too. We'll plan it all out."

She hung up, dropping her phone into her satchel. I bent, kissing her mouth, then sitting across from her.

"Tomorrow?" I questioned.

"Deb's plans changed. She asked if I could meet her tomorrow afternoon."

At my frown, she shook her head. "We're meeting at a coffee shop I've been to with her before. You can check it out first if you insist."

I chuckled. *If I insisted*. "What is the name of this place? And what time?"

"The Arbour. Two o'clock. We'll probably be there a couple of hours."

I nodded. "I'll sit a few tables away."

"No. You can look around and leave. It's a public place that Andy knows nothing about. It's down the street from her apartment. I'll take a cab back afterward."

"I'll pick you up when you're done." I didn't add that I would send Egan in to scope out the place before we went. Or that I would hang around for a while. I quickly texted Egan, who informed me that it was no problem and to send him the address.

She watched me, not saying anything. She shut her Kindle and stretched. "How was Egan?" she asked, trying to sound nonchalant and failing.

"Frustrated," I admitted. "Andy seems to be a ghost. And I have a feeling he's a hacker and deletes every trail he might have left behind."

"He told me once he was brilliant and could have any job he wanted within the computer world," Raven informed me. "I wasn't sure if that was true. He liked to brag a lot."

I ran a hand through my hair. "In this case, he might have been telling you the truth. So, anything you can remember, tell me, even if it seems insignificant. You think of something, let me know."

She looked troubled. "I will."

I reached over and took her hand, wanting to

distract her. "Anything you'd like to do today? Go for a walk? A movie? Errands you need to run?"

"Really?"

"Of course. As long as I'm with you, you're safe, Raven. We don't have to stay here." I sat back, ogling her, then winked. "Unless you prefer that."

Color bloomed on her cheeks, and I laughed softly. "After last night and this morning, I can still make you blush?"

She shrugged. "It—sex—is still pretty new to me. My fiancé was the only guy I had ever slept with, and I had the feeling I wasn't exactly very good at it."

I hid my surprise at her confession. "Why would you say that?" I asked quietly, feeling anger start to build.

"Why else would he have an affair with my best friend?"

"Because he's an asshole with no morals. I don't think much of your friend either. But that's not on you."

"When we fought in the church, he said I drove him to it because I was so indifferent."

I barked out a laugh. "You are *not* indifferent, Raven. You're passionate and warm. He was just turning the blame on you—guys like him do that. *She* made me unfaithful. *She* didn't give me what I needed. It's all bullshit, but that's how they rationalize it. It's not you, though."

"Is that what Andy does? Does he blame me for his obsession?"

"Probably."

"That makes him even more dangerous, then."

I didn't sugarcoat it. "Yes—which is why there will be eyes on you tomorrow."

"Wow, I sure can pick them."

I leaned forward, meeting her eyes, making sure she saw the truth in mine.

"Third time's the charm, my Ravenna Jade. You got me."

She smiled, glancing down.

I slid my fingers under her chin, making her look at me. "Listen to me, my beautiful girl. You are amazing. We are fabulous together. Don't let your ex or his stupid remarks get into your head. He was lacking, not you. I want you so much it boggles my mind."

"Oh. I was worried…" She trailed off.

I had to chuckle. "What? That I didn't enjoy myself? Was my constant hard-on not proof enough? Did the loud moans and the way I was all over you not give you a clue?"

Her color deepened. "I'm not very experienced."

"And that in itself is a turn-on for me. Knowing I can show you, that we can learn together. That you trust me enough to tell me. All of that is such a treasure. *You* are such a treasure. And you did everything right,

Raven. I love how you touch me, want to explore me. What you call your inexperience, I call a gift. Knowing I get to share all that with you? There are no words for it."

"Oh," she breathed out.

"Leave that asshole where he belongs—in the past. Soon, Andy will be a distant memory too. Then there'll be us. Moving forward, growing, finding our future—together."

Her eyes widened. "You sound so certain."

"I am. My old bosses all fell hard and fast. They compared it to lightning. You get struck hard and fast, and it changes you forever. I never understood what they meant until I kissed you." I stroked my finger over her smooth cheek. "Immediately, I knew how important you would be to me. And I'm right here, Raven. Not going anywhere, happy to be with you, until you catch up."

She blinked, and a smile curled her lips. "I think I already did. I felt it too."

My own smile broke out, wide and thrilled.

"Good. Then we keep going forward. Together."

"Together," she repeated.

I kissed her, our mouths brushing in long, slow movements. It was a kiss that promised, that spoke of a trust between us, a future we both wanted.

And as fast as it had happened, we both knew it. Felt it.

And I knew that one day in the near future we'd

say the words. But not yet. For now, we were content in the knowledge we shared the emotion.

I drew back with a smile.

"Come on, my beautiful girl. Let's go enjoy the sunshine."

She nodded happily and let me tug her from the lounger. I wrapped my arm around her, hugging her close for a moment. She nestled into me, fitting against me perfectly.

"Okay," she agreed.

RAVEN

"I don't think you put enough butter on the popcorn," Damien said dryly. "Was that an entire package?"

I laughed as I tossed the bowl, spreading the butter around the fluffy kernels. I *had* used a lot. But he was exaggerating. "Barely a quarter."

"Hmmph."

"Never mind your sass. Is the movie ready? Did you get drinks?"

He laughed, gripping my hip and lowering his head, pressing his mouth to mine. "Yes, Ms. Raven. I got drinks and Twizzlers. Some chocolate. Blankets. Pillows. I even lit a couple of candles, and the movie is ready." He grinned as he kissed me again. "I can't believe you have never watched the Avengers or any of the other movies in the series."

"Well, we're going to fix that now, aren't we?"

"We are." He grabbed the bowl of popcorn and my hand, tugging me behind him. "Come on, woman, we have a lot of movies to watch. You're lucky I'm an expert."

I sat down, and he draped a blanket over my knees and settled the huge bowl between them. He sat down, flicking off the light and starting the movie. "How many are there?" I asked around a mouthful of popcorn.

"Twenty-seven."

I gaped at him. "Holy shit."

His eyes widened. "Ms. Raven, you just swore. Do you talk to your students with that potty mouth?"

I grinned. "No, but I kiss you with it."

He laughed and kissed me hard, plunging his tongue into my mouth and making me whimper. He drew back, licking his lips. "Buttery, salty, and Raven. A great combo. Now stop attacking me and watch the movie."

Three movies later, I turned to him. "I liked one and three best so far."

"The movie or the actors?" he asked, amused.

I sniffed. "The movies, of course."

"Uh-huh." He eyed the mess around me. "You know you eat like a bird most of the time. Had I known junk food was your thing, I would have taken you to a movie the first night."

I laughed. "I don't eat like a bird. I eat very well. But movie snacks are my weakness." I winked. "And handsome, protective men." I eyed him in appreciation. "You could have your own hero movie."

He grinned. "Oh yeah? Tell me more, Ms. Raven."

"I don't think so. You'll get a swelled head."

He pushed away the bowl on my lap, leaning into me. "Trust me, Raven. My head is already swollen. It is whenever you're this close." He nipped my neck. "I told you that earlier." He kissed the skin behind my ear, making me whimper. "Do you want to watch another movie, Ms. Raven? Or can I take you to bed?"

"Um…"

"Please, Ms. Raven." He dragged his lips over my cheek, lightly pressing them to mine. "I'd show you my hero moves. I'm harder than Iron Man or Captain America." He ground into me. "Let me show you how I can fly to new heights. I'll take you with me." He hovered over my mouth. "Please, ma'am. Let me make you feel good."

I dragged his mouth to mine, and he chuckled as he slid his tongue along mine. We kissed endlessly, him tugging me to his lap. Our lips were slippery from the butter, sweet and salty from the snacks. Eager and desperate to taste each other. He spread his legs, pulling me down, and I felt his desire, hard and unyielding, between my thighs.

"Please," I gasped. "Damien."

He stood, his hand cupping my ass, his mouth ravishing mine.

And he showed me everything he promised.

Twice.

We pulled up to the coffee shop, and Damien slid the car into park. He looked at me, peering over the top of his sunglasses.

"Rules?"

"I walk into the shop, and I don't leave without you being there."

"If you get nervous?"

"I call you."

He nodded, looking through the window. "Is she here?"

"The girl in the booth. With the light brown hair."

"Couldn't you sit farther into the restaurant?" he asked, tapping his thumbs on the steering wheel.

"The tables are twos, and there are some couches scattered around. We need the booth to work on."

He huffed, and I laid my hand on his arm. "Egan was here ten minutes ago. You said he was around."

"He is."

"If you watch me walk in, then I'm covered."

He nodded, the set of his shoulders stiff. I hated seeing him upset. I much preferred the laid-back, teasing, sexy man who kept me up most of the night. The one who woke me up this morning by carrying me to the shower and doing wicked things with his tongue that made me scream his name. I knew he hated letting me out of his sight, but I also knew if he was in the restaurant, he would distract me. But watching his distress mount, I relented.

"You can walk me in if you want," I offered. "Stay and meet Deb, have a cup of coffee."

He glanced at me with a frown, then sighed. "I'd feel better if I walked you in, but I'll get the coffee to go, and I'll leave."

"Okay, that's a good compromise."

I waited until he came around to my door, holding it open and helping me out. His old-fashioned manners were a lovely change from a couple of the men I had met online. He carried my bag with one hand, his other keeping me close to his side. I felt his tension ease a little when we went inside and Deb stood, hugging me. I introduced them, and he shook her hand, polite and friendly. He set my bag on the booth bench and smiled. "I'm going to grab a coffee. Can I get you something, Ms. Raven?" he asked, keeping his voice teasing and light.

"I'm going to get a sandwich and coffee with Deb."

"And one of their pieces of fudge cake to share,

right, Raven?" Deb asked. "It's wicked good, and we feel a bit self-restrained when we share instead of getting our own."

Laughing, he pressed a kiss to my head. "Okay. I'll leave you to your self-sacrifice. Call me when you're ready to go."

He sauntered to the counter, waiting patiently as the child in front of him took forever to choose the donut he wanted, then ordered a coffee. Damien chose a double chocolate donut and paid, then stopped by the table. "I'll be going. I paid for your lunch, ladies, so enjoy." Then he leaned down and kissed me again.

"Remember the rules," he murmured into my ear, straightened, and walked out. I watched him get in his car, make a call, then slowly pull away. His gaze locked on mine as he drove by, his lips pulled down in a frown. I sighed and met Deb's curious gaze.

"You have a story to tell me. I need to know when and where you met Mr. Tall, Dark, and Intense in the Lexus and why I haven't heard about him until this moment. My God, he's dreamy. And romantic—he walked you in and paid for our lunch. Girl, you better start talking!"

I laughed and picked up the menu. "Let's get lunch, and I'll fill you in."

I glanced at the list of sandwiches, buying myself some time. I couldn't tell her everything, but I could tell her something. I just had to figure out what.

DAMIEN

I circled the block, keeping my eye on the area, seeing nothing unusual—and no one in a hoodie hiding in a doorway. I parked the car, walked back toward the coffee shop, and headed up the ramp of a parking lot across the street. I found Egan in his spot, surveying the area. I settled beside him, handing him the donut.

"Anything?"

"Nope. No one loitering, looking in the windows, nothing. The only person to go in since you left was a lady with a stroller."

"Good." I took off the baseball cap I was wearing and ran a hand over my head. "You can go. I'll sit it out until she calls."

Egan lifted his shoulders. "I got nowhere special to go. Sofia is working nights, so she is asleep. I've got a bunch of programs running to find this ghost. I'm happy to stay. I can keep you company."

"Great."

I trained the binoculars on the coffee shop, zooming in on Raven's table. They were eating lunch, their laptops open, papers on the table. She was listening to something Deb said, her brow furrowed, then she began to laugh, dropping her head to her chest and covering her eyes. Obviously, it was something personal. Probably about me. That made me grin. I would have to ask.

I looked around, stiffening at the sight of a man walking toward the coffee shop, his head down, wearing a hoodie. I made a noise, and Egan grabbed his binoculars, looking to see what I was reacting to. But I relaxed when the person lifted his head and I saw it was just a kid.

"I freaking hate those damn hoodies," I muttered. "Everyone wearing one looks like a suspect."

Egan chuckled. "I know."

We were quiet for a while, then he turned to me. "Have you added any trackers to her things? Her purse or phone? In case…" He trailed off.

"I plan to do that today. I want to tell her first. She gets riled up if she thinks I'm taking unnecessary actions without consulting her."

"She's stubborn."

"Remind you of anyone?"

"Sofia had dinner with me last night."

"That's progress. How'd you convince her?"

He trained his binoculars at the shop, shrugging. "I showed up with food, walked in, and sat down. She didn't have much choice."

I began to laugh. "I'm shocked she didn't kick you out."

"It was Thai. Her favorite. I knew she wouldn't be able to resist."

"And?"

"It was good. I kept it light. Just buddies."

"Uh-huh. Buddies."

"Baby steps. Like you said," he agreed. "I am patient man."

I tried not to laugh. Egan was patient when it came to building a bomb, setting a timer, planning a building demolition. When it came to my cousin, patient wasn't the word that came to mind.

I trained my binoculars on the street. It was getting busier, but no one stood out. A man with dark hair in a suit went into the coffee shop, holding the door open for a woman and child coming out, but otherwise, there was nothing. I scanned her table, seeing Raven's laptop closed and a piece of some sort of dessert between them.

"Go home, Egan. They're almost done, and Raven will call soon. I'll handle it from here."

He stood and stretched in the shadows. "Maybe he'll give up. He knows she has someone."

"I hope so. I still want to find out who he is. Stop him from doing this to someone else. Someone who doesn't have a partner to protect them."

He laid a hand on my shoulder. "And I will help."

"Thanks."

I watched his retreating figure, smirking as he appeared on the street, his camo gone, just another guy wearing jeans and a T-shirt. I checked on Raven, frowning when I saw Deb was alone. Assuming Raven was in the washroom, I scanned the front of the coffee shop, shocked to see her out on the sidewalk. She turned and headed to the right, stepping into a cheese shop. Cursing, I shoved the binoculars into my pocket and rushed down the steps and out of the parking garage, not even sparing a glance at the coffee shop. Fury burned through my veins. I told her to stay put. She knew the danger. The precautions we were taking. Was she planning on a shopping spree where Andy could step up behind her or drag her into an alley again? Did she have any sense?

I took a deep breath and entered the cheese shop, spying her in the corner, a basket over her arm. I stepped behind her, my fists curled to keep my anger in check.

"Why are you never in the place I leave you?" I asked, my voice low in irritation.

She chuckled, not at all put out. She turned to face me. "I saw Egan stroll by. I knew if he was leaving that *you* were watching me. I also knew you would follow me in here. I had zero doubt I was in danger." She patted my chest. "I knew you were watching me, Damien."

"How?" I asked.

She smiled. "I felt your eyes on me. You were close the whole time."

I felt my ire begin to slip.

"And what if you were wrong and I didn't follow you in here?"

"I would call you." She shook her head. "You

agreed to this too easily, Damien. I already figured out when you say yes, you have a plan. And a backup."

I took her basket, looping my arm around her waist. "Think you know me so well already, Ms. Raven?"

"Yes."

"And what do you think is going to happen next?"

"You're going to let me pay for my purchases, then take me back to the loft and show me who is really in control here."

I dropped my head to her neck, nibbling on the soft skin. "And then?" I murmured.

"You're going to fuck me hard just to prove it."

"Shopping time is over," I growled.

She laughed. "Good thing I'm done, then."

She was right.

CHAPTER THIRTEEN

Raven

Resting my chin on my hand, I stared out the window. Rain pelted the glass, the trees bending under the fury of the wind. I sighed, wondering how long the storm would rage. Surprisingly, the school hadn't lost power, and my little students had all been picked up. Damien was running late, and I was in the staff room waiting for him. Across from me, Tracey was working, Mike sitting at the table, doing something on his phone.

"You two can leave. I'm perfectly safe in the building," I said for the third time. "It's locked, and there are a few teachers left."

They ignored me the same way they had the last two times I had offered.

I went back to my calendar, looking over the summer. I had planned on playing tourist in August. Going to Niagara Falls, spending a few days touring around wine country. Maybe doing the CN Tower, the aquarium. But it would be hard, given everything happening. Unless, of course, Andy disappeared. He hadn't been seen since the rock incident on Friday, and it was now Tuesday. I was hoping his absence was permanent.

The only good thing about the situation was staying with Damien. Living with him was like a dream, even considering the circumstances. He was larger-than-life to me. Sexy, sweet, caring. Intense, stern, and demanding. Always gentle, yet ready to defend at a moment's notice. He had told me his name with his team was the Watcher, and I understood why. He was incredibly focused, his eyes seemed to take everything in, and he saw things no one else noticed. We had cooked supper together last night, and I had baked cookies, slapping his hands as he tried to taste the batter, steal chocolate chips, and informed me he had to taste test every batch as they came from the oven. He had pouted hard when I informed him the cookies were for Leo. He pinned me against the cupboard, kissing me until I admitted some were for him.

"The lion's share, right?" he demanded, moving his mouth up and down my neck, licking and kissing. "For me, right, Ms. Raven?" He slid his hands up my legs, teasing me with one long finger, slipping the digit under the lace of my underwear. "Right, Ms. Raven?"

He bit down, sucking my skin between his teeth. "Mine."

I gasped as he touched me, stroking lightly, the feel of his fingertip soft enough to tease but hard enough to make me want more.

I clutched his shirt, fisting it in my hands. "Yes."

"Oh, good answer," he murmured, pressing harder, stroking me. "I feel you, my Ravenna Jade. I love feeling how much you want me. I love hearing your noises."

Then he brought me to a fast, shuddering orgasm.

He got the bulk of the cookies. I was saving Leo's for him tomorrow since he had been off today on a personal errand.

My phone ringing brought me out of my lust-induced fog. I saw Deb's name and answered brightly.

"Hey, you."

"Hi!"

"How are you?"

"Awesome. Was wondering if we could meet and do the shopping Thursday after school?"

"I think so." I hedged a little, knowing I had to check with Damien. "I think my dentist appointment is next week," I lied. "I'll check when I get home."

"Great."

"How's your week going?"

"Oh my God, Raven. Your luck must have rubbed off."

"What?" I asked, puzzled.

"After you left, a guy came over and introduced himself." She giggled. "We went out last night, and I'm seeing him on Friday."

A shiver of cold went through me. "A guy in the coffee shop?"

"Yeah, he said he was watching me."

"Deb, you shouldn't go out with guys who pick you up in a coffee shop. Especially if they say they were watching you." I felt the stirrings of panic. "What did he look like?"

"You didn't notice him? The guy in the business suit?" Then she snorted. "Of course you didn't. Not with an intense and sexy guy taking over your brain. Suit guy is gorgeous. Tall, short brown hair, eyes a dark brown. Great shoulders. He came in after we did and sat in the corner. I kept staring at him, and he came over after you left."

I relaxed at her description. Andy had shaggy light hair, his eyes were a washed-out blue, and his shoulders were narrow. He was thin, and he told me once he didn't own a suit. Hated the "big man." Still, I worried.

"What does he do?"

"Relax. He's a financial guy. Gave me his business card. I checked him out. Stewart Anderson is his name. Thirty-two. A VP. He was charming. Both on Sunday and last night. Drove a nice car, took me to dinner. A gentleman. He kissed my hand at the end of the evening—both nights. Asked to see me again.

Informed me he wanted to take this slow. Then he kissed me softly. No tongue. It was so romantic."

I blew out a long puff of air. "Ah, okay."

"I think meeting him in a coffee shop he often frequents is safer than my usual online dating anyway."

"I guess so," I admitted.

"Why did you sound so upset?" she asked.

"I, ah, had a bad experience with an online guy. Strangers make me a little nervous now."

"I'm sorry," she replied.

"No problem. So, I'll let you know about Thursday night."

"Okay. Sounds good."

She hung up, and my phone buzzed again with a text from Damien.

Damien: Five minutes. Stay inside. I'll bring an umbrella.

I stood. "You two are sprung. Damien is here."

They laughed, and Tracey shook her head. "I have two more reports to write up."

Mike began to stand. "I'll walk you to the door."

I shook my head. "I know the way, and I am perfectly safe. Damien is already outside, waiting for me."

He sat down. "Fine."

I left the staff room and walked toward the door,

noticing how my footsteps echoed in the building. The hallways going off the main one were dark, the rooms all empty. As I passed one hall, a sound came from the darkness, and a chill raced through me. Panic hit me hard even though I knew it was the sound of the plumbing or the building settling. Perfectly logical explanations for a noise I wouldn't have given a second thought to a couple of weeks ago. Now I jumped at every little noise and shadow. I began to hurry, almost running, bursting through the door outside where Damien stood, umbrella in hand, waiting for me. I barreled into him, and he wrapped his arm around me.

"Raven? What's wrong?" he asked anxiously.

I shook my head, not wanting him to know how easily frightened I felt. If he suspected, I would have someone glued to me twenty-four hours a day. I lifted my face, smiling. "Just anxious to see your face, handsome. I missed you today."

His smile was wide. "Is that a fact, Ms. Raven? As it just so happens, I missed you too, so I'm glad to see you." He captured my lips with his, kissing me deeply.

"You ready to go home?" he asked.

"Your home?" I replied.

He kissed me again. "Feels like home, now that you're there," he said, then walked me to the car and waited until I got in. He bent and kissed me again. "You can stay forever if you wanted."

I had no idea how to reply.

And I had no idea how to tell him forever sounded good.

It was just too soon.

Wasn't it?

"You're jumpy again, Raven," Damien said after dinner. "Mike said nothing happened today, you said everything is fine, so which one of you isn't telling me the truth?" He sat back, lifting his wineglass to his lips and taking a sip.

"I am?" I asked, stalling for time.

He lifted one eyebrow, waiting for me to speak.

With a sigh, I told him about the dark hallway and my unfounded fear. He listened, then nodded. "Thank you for telling me. What else?"

I was shocked how well he knew me. That it wasn't just my momentary panic that was on my mind. "Deb met someone at the coffee shop."

He leaned forward, intent and serious. "Tell me everything."

I repeated the conversation, and he didn't interrupt. "I saw a guy walk in not long after you did in a suit, carrying a messenger bag. Deb was smart to check him out. You didn't notice him, I assume?"

"No."

He sighed. "No doubt just a random meeting. I'd feel better if I could check it out myself."

I grinned and handed him my phone. "I had Deb tell me the name of the company he works for. This is the link he gave her."

"Smart girl." He scanned my phone, his finger swiping the screen quickly. He paused a few times, then shrugged. "Looks legit." He sighed. "Should I leave it alone?"

"If his picture matches and it looks legit, I think we need to leave it. It's Deb's business, and she really likes him. If this thing with Andy hadn't have happened, I wouldn't have given it a second thought. They met in a coffee shop."

"You're right, I suppose. If she wants more info on him, I can dig and find out his background."

"How?" I asked. "How are you able to do that, Damien?"

He set down his glass. "I always loved computers. I taught myself a lot, plus I went to school. Law enforcement fascinated me, and I thought I wanted to be a cop. A CSI, actually. I started studying it. I also took lessons in weapons. I excelled in the firing range. I could hit any target, no matter the circumstance. But I was frustrated when I realized I could spend years studying to be a CSI and never work in that field, and although I was a great shot, I had no desire to be a cop and work the streets." He flashed me a grin to make me relax. "Or be an assassin."

Recalling the time I'd asked him if he was an assassin, I smiled back. He continued.

"Then one day, I was approached about a different job. One that would put my computer skills to use. My gun skills as well."

"Oh?" I asked.

"A private agency known as Hidden Justice."

"I've never heard of it."

"That's the point. Most people haven't or won't ever know of our existence."

"What was the mandate of this, ah, agency?"

I met her eyes. "To seek out, locate, and eliminate the scum of the earth. Those who prey on the weak. The poor. Women and children, especially. Sex trades, drug rings, child porn. You get on our radar, you're done. There is no trial or second chance. Your fate has been determined."

I felt my eyes widen. "What if you're wrong?"

"That has never happened. Not once. It is a very specialized agency. Run by an elite group of men."

"You said you owned a security company."

He sat back. "I do."

"I don't understand."

"I'll tell you, if you want to know."

"I do."

"Okay, then. Get comfortable, Raven. This will take a while."

I shook my head. "So, Matteo, Marcus, and Julian all now live on an island somewhere with their families."

"Yes."

"Leo was badly hurt and works with you now."

"Yes."

"Egan really blows up buildings plus, ah, other things and still works on some projects where his specialist training is needed. Your cousin helps out medically if required. You run all the computer systems in this country, keeping the agency hidden and the people safe?"

"I think you followed me pretty well."

"And most of the security people are ex-agents?"

"Not all, but some."

"So, you are all trained killers."

"I told you that you kissed the right man, Raven. But no one can protect you better."

I blew out a shaky breath. "I think I need to sit down."

He smiled. "You are sitting, baby." He held out his arms. "Would you feel better on my lap?"

I scrambled to my feet and dove onto his lap. He wrapped his arms around me, holding me close. I greedily inhaled his scent and felt the comfort of his embrace. It warmed me, grounded me.

He pressed a kiss to my head. "Trust me, Raven. You are safe."

"I already trusted you. Now my mind is in overdrive."

He chuckled. "I am a consultant with Hidden Justice. Way deep in the background. So is Egan. I run the agency. He does some work, but his name isn't associated with the agency or anywhere but his gym and a couple other businesses."

"Like?"

I grinned. "The master explosive expert loves to paint pretty landscapes, and he has created a very popular line of cologne and perfume he works closely with a company on. Apparently he has a gifted nose for fragrance."

"Oh, ah, wow. And you?"

He glanced down, cupping my cheek. "I hang around pubs hoping to find a damsel in distress. I hit the jackpot last week."

I sighed, looking down. "Can I ask you some questions?"

"You can ask me anything you want."

I looked up, meeting his blue eyes. "Have you killed people?"

CHAPTER FOURTEEN

Damien

I wasn't surprised by her question. And I wanted to be honest with her. I had seen what omissions and withholding the truth had done to relationships. I didn't want my past to be an obstacle for us. I didn't want her frightened of me either.

"Yes," I replied. "I have killed people. People who bring great pain and suffering to others. It's part of the mandate."

"How many?"

I shrugged. "I never counted, Raven. I did what I had to do to protect innocent lives. I saved far more than I ever killed. They were the lowest of the low. The dregs of humanity that preyed on others." I scratched my head. "I was never a full-time field operative. I preferred the background. The recon and planning. It's where my talent was best used. I only went on some missions. Not all of them."

"Why did you stop?"

"It takes its toll on a person. Matteo knew what he wanted to do from a young age because of something that happened to his sister. Marcus sought revenge for the death of his parents. He wanted to save others from losing someone they loved. Julian was a natural leader who had nothing to live for but the job. Then they all found something more important." I shifted, running my hand up and down her arm, hoping she understood what I was saying. "I did it as a job. A service. But I saw my friends shot, hurt, almost lose whom they loved the most. And my reasons were different. I never wanted to move up in the ranks, run a team. I am a strong part of the cause with my computer skills. I protect those who have the calling by keeping their identity safe. I can step in when needed, but when Julian left, I knew my loyalty was to my bosses more than the calling. You have to be one hundred percent invested. I wasn't. I help if needed. I give them information to aid the cause. But I am not good as a full team member anymore. I like running Elite. Helping other guys like me who needed to get out but have a lot to offer. Julian was smart to open the firm. I'm proud to keep it going."

"Are you in danger?"

"No."

"Egan?"

I huffed. "That's up to him. He takes on assignments when needed. But he has never been a front man. Marcus brought him on board, and when Marcus retired, Egan became freelance. He runs his gym. Paints. He does actually work a legitimate job for a company that demolishes buildings. If needed, he steps in for HJ. And he works on occasion for Elite. He likes to dress in a tux and look fierce," I said, hoping to make her smile. She seemed okay with what I had told her, but she was pale.

A glimmer of a smile appeared, but she was still processing.

"So that's why you were so confident you could find Andy?"

"I still am. We're digging deeper. He can't hide forever. One thing I've learned is perps always slip up. They get overconfident. Make mistakes. He knows how to cover his tracks, but we'll find a glitch and follow it."

"And in the meantime, you're stuck with me. I've turned your life upside down. Caused you so much trouble."

I frowned. "That's not how I see it, Raven."

She pursed her lips, and I lifted her chin, stroking the soft skin while holding her gaze.

"I hate that he frightened you. But I'm grateful it was me you ran into. Our connection is very real, Raven. Don't you feel it?"

She bobbed her head in agreement.

"I like having you here. I hate that I have to

protect you, but I like doing it. I like being the guy you turn to. And I love having you here with me. Don't doubt that. I meant what I said before. If you stay forever, I'm good with that. More than good."

Her lips quivered, and I felt the shudder go through her body. I pulled her closer, my mouth close to her ear. "I'm falling for you, Raven. Hard. I'll keep going slow until you catch up with me, but know I'm right here. With you. And I'm not going anywhere."

Her pretty green eyes were wide, glistening with tears under the lights. "I'm here too, Damien. I just can't stand the thought of you hurt because of me."

"Not happening. We're going to find Andy and get him out of your life and stop him from doing this again. He won't get to me or you. Understand?"

She nodded, but I saw her worry. Felt her tension. She stood, leaving my arms, walking around the apartment, stopping at the window and staring into the darkness and the streets below. I could almost feel her mind racing, trying to come to terms with what I had told her, understand the life I had led. Still led. She turned and looked at me.

"Did you like it?"

"Like what?"

"Killing people."

Her question surprised me. It also explained her withdrawal from my touch. I stood and crossed the room, standing in front of her. "I did what I had to do to protect innocent lives, Raven. Did I enjoy pulling the trigger? Ending someone's life? No. Did I get satisfaction that they would never be able to hurt another human being? That by killing them, I saved countless other people? Yes, I did," I stated honestly. "I have never, nor will I ever, kill someone I didn't one hundred percent believe deserved it."

"Would you kill Andy?"

"If your life was in immediate danger, yes," I answered without hesitation. "If I had to protect you, I would."

She didn't say anything, looking conflicted.

"Have I frightened you now, Raven? Are you scared of me? Disgusted?" I felt a pang of pain flex in my chest at the thought of losing her trust and affection. "I would never hurt you. Ever."

"I know that," she whispered. "You don't frighten me."

"Then what is it?" I lifted her chin, making her meet my eyes. "Why do you look so upset?"

"Because part of me says I should be afraid. I should be upset."

"And the other part?" I asked gently, cupping her face.

"Is so grateful that you have that past. That I feel so safe with you." She blinked at the moisture I could see building in her eyes. "I know you would never hurt me, Damien. All I feel from you is protection and gentleness. Even when you're furious at what is happening around us, you treat me so carefully." She turned and kissed the palm of my hand. "I think you're amazing. Thank you for trusting me and telling me."

I lowered my head and kissed her. She wrapped her hands around my wrists, rising on her toes to get closer. I drew back, meeting her gaze. "I want to take you to my bed and make love to you, my Ravenna Jade. Tell me I can do that."

"Yes," she said simply.

I lifted her into my arms, carrying her down the hall, our eyes locked on each other. In my room, I stopped by the bed and set her on her feet, our mouths meeting again. Clothing fell to the floor as we kissed endlessly, dropping to the mattress in a mass of entangled limbs. We touched and caressed. Kissed and teased. I traced my fingers over her skin that was like silk, and she let her hands roam over my muscles. Neither of us was in a hurry. I kissed the soft indent of her elbow, trailing my lips down to her wrist and back, discovering a ticklish spot on her left arm. She made me whimper as she teased the skin below my navel with her lips. The sensitive spot behind her ear made her moan when I nuzzled it, flicking my tongue on the warm area. I loved it when she ran her fingers through the back of my hair, her touch light and indulgent. She blushed as I spread her wide, gazing at her, whispering praises about her perfection. Groaned when I used my tongue to show her how perfect. Cried out as she climaxed and I pushed inside her, feeling her orgasm crest, then rise again as I moved within her. I slid my hands up her arms, holding them over her head, our fingers entwined as I rode out the pleasure, our eyes locked, silent words flowing between us.

I will protect you.

I trust you.

You'll never be alone again. Let me take care of you.

Keep me.

Stay.

Raven arched her back, once again crying out my name as she orgasmed, the feel of her setting off my own release. I dropped my face to her neck, groaning in pleasure, the sensations rippling through my body, sending waves of ecstasy throughout me. Raven wrapped her arms around me, holding me tight, her voice a quiet hum in my ear. "Damien," she breathed. "Oh my God, Damien."

I lifted my head, kissing her. Saying with my mouth what I couldn't speak out loud yet.

I love you.

Slowly, we separated, then I gathered her in my arms. She sighed, resting her head on my chest. I felt the wetness of her tears on my skin.

"That was intense," she whispered before I could ask.

"It always is with us."

She glanced up, meeting my eyes. "It felt even more so this time."

I wiped my fingers under her eyes, taking away the moisture. "Because *we're* more."

"We're moving fast, Damien."

"Are you with me, Raven?"

Her voice was quiet in the dim light. "Yes."

"Then we're moving along just right for us."

With a sigh, she snuggled back into my embrace. "Okay."

In the morning, she handed me a container before she got out of the car. "Can you give these to Leo?"

I shook my head. "I have a better idea. Why don't I pick you up and take you to the office after school? You can see where I work, meet some other people, and give Leo his cookies yourself? He'd love to see you."

"You have time?"

"I'll make time. Besides, those are so damned good, not sure you can trust me to give them to him. I want to eat them myself."

"You have lots in the apartment."

I leaned over and nipped her neck playfully. "I want all of them. Just like I want all of you."

She shook her head, using her best teacher voice on me. "You have to learn to share, Damien."

"Maybe the cookies. You, *never*, Ms. Raven."

"Okay. Pick me up. I'd like that."

"Okay. Four?"

"Yes."

I glanced around. "All right. You can go inside. You're under surveillance. Remember anything makes you nervous, you call me or that other number I gave you. You aren't alone."

She looked around, seeing what I saw, but not seeing anything. She nodded. "Okay." She opened her door, stopping when I called to her.

"Aren't you forgetting something?"

"No. I have my satchel and my phone. My laptop."

I reached over and traced her lips. "How about a goodbye?"

"Oh. Oh!" She leaned over the console.

I cupped her cheek and kissed her. Softly. Sweetly. "I'll see you later, Raven."

"Have a good day," she murmured, slipping from the car and hurrying to the door, using her pass to get in. I waited a bit, making sure nothing seemed out of place. My guy was right there, raking the grass, ignoring me. He would stay outside her windows for the day, working on a repair project we'd constructed. Every day, it was different. If Andy was around, he'd have no idea someone was watching over her. But there was someone outside, inside, or both. It was never the same person and never the same task. I wanted to wire up the school, but it was too difficult given privacy issues if it was discovered. So instead, I had a tracker on her phone and laptop that she'd watched me install. She carried her phone everywhere, so I always knew where she was. And she had eyes on her constantly. Andy couldn't get to her.

I only hoped we could get to him before he ever had a chance to do so again.

In the office, I was busy with the never-ending paperwork when Egan strolled in, looking pleased with himself.

"How was dinner with Sofia the other night?" I asked dryly. "Successful?"

"She didn't kick me out. She ate the dinner I made her, and we shared some time afterward." He smiled widely. "I gave her a large brandy, and she fell asleep."

I sat back with a laugh. "That's how you plan on seducing her? Feeding her and knocking her out with alcohol?"

"No," he replied, disgusted. "I want to show her how I care for her. I fed her, let her relax, then when she was asleep, I tucked her into her bed and made sure she was comfortable." He grinned. "She said my name in her sleep."

He sighed. "She kicked me out in the morning when she found me on her sofa. But she made me coffee first." He pulled a face. "She makes horrendous coffee."

"She's a doctor. She's used to drinking tar."

"I offered to remake the pot properly. That's when she kicked me out."

I shook my head in silent amusement. His caveman ways would not impress Sofia. She was strong, independent, and fierce. She had to be. He would have to learn the hard way.

"Anything to report?"

He leaned forward. "Yes."

I set down the file I was holding. "What?"

"How would Elite Security feel about adding a new arm to the company?"

"A new arm?"

"Cybersecurity."

I frowned. "That would draw too much attention."

"Not if it was only for one client."

"Who?"

He grinned, sitting back. "The Real Connection."

"What have you done?"

"I paid a visit to their office. Spoke with the owner. Showed him how flimsy his firewalls are. How quickly I got in. Told him why I did it."

"Jesus, Egan. I said discreet."

He shrugged. "This asshole is good. I need an in."

He was right. I had tried several ideas this morning, coming up empty-handed. Whoever this guy was, he covered his tracks well.

"And what good is them tightening their firewalls now going to do? How does that give us an in?"

"He told me a little tidbit. He does a daily backup."

"We know that. So does Andy. We checked them. He erased everything."

"No. He does a second daily backup. It's stored off-site. It's not in their system."

I sat up. "Are you telling me we can have access?"

"Jeff, the owner, was horrified to hear someone was in danger because of his site. He said he had Raven's letter and was about to investigate it and see if they had any other complaints."

"He should have moved quicker."

"He's been away. He only got back today. The letter was waiting for him. She mailed it." He smirked. "Smart girl was worried Andy would find the email and delete it."

"So, we get access?"

He nodded. "We're meeting him tomorrow. In exchange for his cooperation, I promised him that Elite would tighten his security. The company he paid did a shit job."

"This is the break we needed."

He sat back, looking smug. "Yep."

"I owe you, Egan."

He regarded me silently.

I glanced at my watch, seeing it was almost time to pick up Raven. The hours had flown by today. "I'll sing your praises to Sofia when I see her."

He nodded sagely. "Then we're even."

CHAPTER FIFTEEN

Damien

Raven was waiting inside the door of the school and hurried out to the car as I pulled up. I studied her face. She looked calm and happy.

"How are you?" I asked, leaning over for a kiss.

"Good. No trouble at all again."

"Great."

In the car, she chatted, telling me about the antics of her kids, her list for shopping on Thursday, the fact that Deb had texted her, excited.

"Her businessman sent her flowers. She's never received flowers before."

The businessman had slipped my mind, and I hadn't delved into him as I had planned to. "I see. So, you want me to leave it alone?"

"Yes. I don't think you have to worry. She isn't." Raven chuckled. "She wants us to double-date one night."

"Even better. I can check him out in person."

I parked underground, and we took the elevator up to the main floor. I took her to Leo's office located in the back of the building, and she gave him the cookies she made him. She entertained him with the story of the mice she hid under the cushions, exaggerating my reaction and making him laugh loudly. He was thrilled with the cookies and winked at her. "I got more. My wife wants an evening out without the kids," he whispered, loud enough for me to hear.

Raven nodded and winked back. "We'll talk," she mouthed.

She stood, lifting her bag and rounding the desk to hug Leo. As she went by his handheld scanners, a constant ping went off. She stopped frowning. "What is that?"

I met Leo's eyes, slightly shaking my head.

"A door alarm that needs fixing," he said. "It's been going off all day, driving me nuts."

"Oh, annoying," Raven replied and hugged him. "Thanks again."

"Anytime."

I took her elbow, heading upstairs. In the elevator, I turned to her, pressing a finger against my lips, indicating she needed to stay quiet. She frowned as I slipped her bag off her shoulder, carrying it. I led her into my office, then into the back, shutting the door firmly behind me.

"Okay, you can talk."

"What's going on?"

"You walked past one of the extra scanners we use to search for bugs. It went off," I explained.

Her eyes widened. "Bugs?"

"Listening devices. Tracking devices. If you had walked through the detectors at the front door, they would have gone off as well."

"But…" She looked around wildly. "You know about them. You added them."

"No. Ours would register with the scanner. Whatever this is wasn't from me. They're blocked in this room—there are extra precautions taken here so nothing gets through, even the most sophisticated devices. Leo will be up in a minute, and we'll find where they are."

"How?" she asked.

"Let's find it first and figure that out."

Leo came in, grim-faced. It only took us a minute to figure out there were two bugs. One listening and one tracking. Both were on a little fuzzy animal Raven had clipped to the outside of her satchel. I held it up, showing her the tiny devices.

"Did you leave your satchel behind at some point when you were out with Andy?"

She frowned and thought it over. "Yes. He spilled his coffee the first day I met him, and I went to get napkins. The bag was on the seat between us. Would that be enough time? I was only gone a moment."

"Yes. He would have had them ready and reached over to press them into place. He only needed a few seconds." I sat down, studying the small devices. "This explains how he knew where you were and could follow you."

"He could hear me all this time?" Her voice was garbled, thick.

I lifted my head, shocked at her expression. Tears were running down her face, and she was white as a ghost. She covered her mouth, her hand shaking.

"He listened—he listened to *everything*?" she gasped, her breathing fast.

I stood. "Leo—"

He picked up the little stuffed animal and headed for the door. "I'll come back."

I crossed the room, kneeling in front of her. I cupped her face, shaking my head.

"No, baby. Not when you were in my apartment complex or my home. Not inside this office building. If we had come in the front door, you would have walked through a security checkpoint that would have shut down the trackers and alerted us to their presence. Because we came up inside the building already, the machines by the front door didn't pick them up. Leo's extra scanners did."

"But before today…?"

"He may have tracked you to my street, but he would lose all capabilities to hear or track you once you're inside the apartment complex."

"So, he didn't—he didn't hear us? When we were together?" she whispered, her voice heavy with tears.

I stroked her cheek in gentle circles. "No, Raven."

I pulled her to me, wrapping her in my arms. I sat in the chair she had been in, holding her tight.

"Those were *our* moments. Our intimate, private moments," she sobbed. "To think he'd stolen that from us…"

I kissed her head, something tender and new unfurling in my chest. "No, Raven. The only one who hears how you sound when we make love is me. I'm the only man who will ever hear that sound again."

She shuddered and buried her face into my neck. I stroked up and down her back in long passes, marveling at her sweet, worried thoughts. But I hated to see her so upset. She calmed, releasing a pent-up breath of air.

"Why didn't you turn them off when you discovered them just now?"

"I didn't want to tip him off that we had discovered them if he was listening."

"That makes sense," she agreed.

"He'll assume they are being blocked right now, but not discovered. We want him to keep thinking that way."

She nodded, silent for a moment before speaking again.

"He heard us in my apartment."

"It depends where your bag was compared to

where we were. Leo is probably testing the devices to figure out their capabilities. I assume he heard enough."

"All this time," she whispered. She looked up, her red-rimmed eyes doing something to me. I wanted to find this asshole right now and eliminate him. Permanently.

And this time, I would probably enjoy it.

"The roof?" she asked. "When we were talking? When I was on the phone with Deb?"

"He might have heard you, but he might not have. I've never tested it. But he, no doubt, knows you are living in my place. He still can't get to you, Raven. He can't get in the building."

"But if he heard me, he didn't show up at the coffee shop."

"No, he didn't."

"Maybe he's given up?" she asked hopefully.

"Maybe. Or maybe he knew you were being watched. Or the scanners prevented him from hearing."

She sighed and wiped under her eyes. "Sorry, I shouldn't have gotten so upset."

"Hey, you have every right to be upset. This dickhead has invaded your privacy, frightened you, and stalked you. Don't hide that from me."

"What do we do now?"

"I'm going to keep your little bunny here and see if it can help us find him."

"Will I get him back? Emery, one of my favorite students, gave him to me."

"Yes. I'll take good care of it. But for now, it stays with me."

"Okay." She was quiet for a moment, and Leo returned, knocking before he came in. He set the bunny down. "The range is good. They aren't like what we use, but they're not run-of-the-mill either."

"Can we find him, using the manufacturer?" I asked.

"I don't know. I'd probably be able to figure it out. But I have to take them apart."

"Maybe we could test my theory before you destroy them," Raven said quietly.

"Test how?" Leo asked, ignoring me as I began to shake my head.

"You think he knows something in the building is blocking him."

"Or thinks the bugs are malfunctioning."

"But he doesn't know that you know about the bugs."

"I don't think so," I replied. "What are you thinking?"

"So, once we leave the office, couldn't we use that to our advantage? Let him think there are glitches, but the bugs haven't been found? Let him know where I will be and when? Like when I go shopping tomorrow? Or go somewhere on the weekend? See if he shows up?"

I stared at her in surprise. As much as I hated the thought of exposing her, it was a good idea. And she was incredibly brave to have suggested it.

"He'll know we're watching," I pointed out.

She shrugged. "Or maybe make him think you're backing off a little. That you think your scare tactics worked on him."

"I am not backing off."

"I know. Use your guys. Ones he doesn't know. Send them ahead." Then her eyes widened. "Why don't we go for a walk and have a fight?"

"What? A fight?" I asked. "Why?"

"He'll see me walk away from you. Maybe he'll approach me."

Leo met my frowning gaze. "That's not a bad idea."

"Maybe I should go back to my apartment," she added. "Be easily accessible."

"That isn't happening." I snapped, tightening my grip on her hip. "I'll think about the other idea."

She stood, smoothing down her skirt. She was pale, upset, and fierce. She settled her hands on her hips, glaring at me. "The bottom line here, Damien, is it is my decision. I could walk out of this building right now, and you can't stop me. I think we need to see if he is still hanging around. This seems the best way to do so. You can arrange your men. We can play things up. I know I'll be safe. Maybe he isn't even bothering anymore."

"And if he is?" I said, furious she was insisting and knowing she was probably right.

"Then you nab him. Take him to the police. Find out who he is."

Leo spoke up. "She's right, Damien. If he is around, still following, he may take the chance."

I stood. "I'll think about it, and we'll discuss the logistics in the morning."

Raven didn't budge. "We'll discuss it now."

I rubbed my eyes, tamping down my temper. I recalled how often Missy defied Marcus. The time Evie went on a lone shopping spree and drove Matteo mad with worry. I had laughed at their frustration. Their overreactions. I hadn't expected it from Raven. I supposed I should have. They would laugh at me right now.

"We will have rules. Boundaries." I pointed my finger at her. "You will adhere to them."

"You figure it out, and I'll bring in the men," Leo offered. "We'll make sure she's safe."

I nodded, and he left with a quiet assurance that he would contact me later.

Raven and I stared at each other.

"We have to do this, Damien. I have to do this. If we let him, we could still be wondering and worried a month from now. I can't put my life on hold forever."

I exhaled hard. "I know. I hate the idea, but I know."

She stepped in front of me, laying her hand on my

chest. "You'll keep me safe. If he approaches me, you'll get him. But maybe he listened to you. Walked away when he realized he wasn't getting near me and I was serious when I said no."

I covered her hand, not telling her how dubious I was. That men like him didn't stop until they got what they wanted, or the woman they were after literally disappeared to get away from them. And even then, sometimes, it didn't stop. I had seen it.

"You will do everything I tell you."

"Yes."

"No deviations."

"No."

"Fine. I'll work it all out with Egan, Leo, and the men. Tomorrow, something will delay me when you go shopping, and my lazy, good-for-nothing man will sit on his ass in a car outside. You will be inside with Deb."

She smiled. "Better not let them hear you say that."

I laughed. "Nope. But that's what I want Andy to think. See if it draws him out."

"If it doesn't?"

"Saturday, we'll take a walk and have an argument. You'll storm away and jump in a passing cab and go home. You'll let him see you're alone in the apartment."

"But Egan will be inside my place?"

"Yes."

"And it will be your man who drives me home?"

"Yes."

"And there will be some of your people in the store?"

"Of course."

She smiled at me. "Then I'm safe."

"You're coming back to mine on Sunday." I lifted her hand and kissed it. "If I last that long."

"Okay," she agreed easily.

"I hate this. The thought of you being out of my sight makes me want to rage."

"But you won't. You'll do it for me."

"Yes. Now I guess I had better take you out to dinner, so he hears us if he is listening."

She nodded, her eyes dimming. "Okay."

I wrapped her in my arms, knowing how brave a front she was putting on. "We'll figure this out, Raven. I won't let anything happen to you."

She lifted her head, the trust in her gaze humbling me. "I know. That's why I can do it."

CHAPTER SIXTEEN

Raven

As we left Damien's office, he held a finger to his ear, reminding me that Andy might be listening. I still felt sick to my stomach at the breach of privacy. Knowing he'd listened to me in my apartment. At school. While I had coffee with Deb. Some intimate moments with Damien when he kissed me, comforted me, outside the safe zones. I was angry at Andy. Furious with myself for ever having joined a dating site. Deb may have had a lot of enjoyment with it, but my experience was vastly different. Then again, we were very different people. She was outgoing and fun. Loved going dancing and to parties. Always up for a weekend away. I preferred to stay home, read. Cook and bake. I was more comfortable with a small group of friends than a roomful of strangers. I was best one-on-one. Deb loved being in a crowd.

I nodded at his reminder, and he squeezed my

hand, drawing me close and dropping a kiss to my head. I waited until we were in the car, the gate had rolled up, and we were pulling onto the street to talk.

"I mean it, Damien. I'm going shopping with Deb tomorrow, and we're heading out for a drink after at Rockies. Just the two of us," I stressed, acting as if I were returning to a conversation from earlier.

We weren't sure if Andy knew I was being watched by someone other than Damien, if he knew who Damien was. Damien assumed he did, but we decided to act as if we had no clue.

"I said I would come. I'm not comfortable with you out on your own."

"I'll be in the Dollar Store. So will a hundred other people. Deb will drive us to the bar, we'll have a few drinks and dinner and do some more planning."

"Raven—"

I interrupted him. "You are not coming, Damien. Case closed."

"And when Andy approaches you?"

"I will have Deb there, plus lots of other people around. Stop obsessing. You are almost as bad as he is."

I saw the flash of hurt on his face, and I reached over, squeezing his hand and shaking my head. He squeezed my fingers back, but I had a feeling he was actually hurt by my words.

"Can I pick you up, at least?"

"Yes, when I'm done, you can pick me up. I just

want to feel normal again, Damien. We haven't seen or heard from Andy since the rock thing. I really think he's moved on. Life can go back to normal soon."

Damien's only response was a grunt. We were quiet for the rest of the short trip, and when we arrived at his place, he held up his finger again, then unclipped the bunny from my satchel and dropped it into a cylinder.

"Okay."

"I thought both of your buildings were protected?"

"They are, but I thought you'd feel better knowing the bunny is encased in a place that, no matter how sophisticated a device it is, he can't hear us." He took the case and put it in the cupboard and shut the door. "I'll reattach it before we leave."

I stepped close and wrapped my arms around his waist. "I didn't mean it, you know. What I said."

"I know. You were very convincing, though."

I looked up. "I love how you look after me. How protective you are."

He bent and kissed me. "Good. Because that's not going to change."

"Good."

———

Deb was chatty and happy when she picked me up the next day. We drove to the store, spending an hour picking up things for activities. Chalk, watercolor paints, cardboard, colored pencils, glue, glitter, and all sorts of other items went into our baskets. I didn't see any familiar faces, but I trusted Damien and I knew there were people in the store keeping an eye on me, and I relaxed and enjoyed the excursion. Deb and I laughed and joked, came up with new ideas, and my excitement for the day camp grew. The area I taught in wasn't a wealthy one. Many of the parents both worked, and the day camp helped them have a safe, fun place for their kids to be during the day. The children loved it, and I had enjoyed working the one at spring break. It was part of the school, so I would still be in my classroom some of the time. We were outside a lot as long as the weather wasn't too hot.

"Oh!" Deb exclaimed. "I forgot to tell you! We can take the kids to the zoo one day."

"Oh, they will love that!"

She grinned. "I know. And it's all covered."

"That's amazing—how did that happen?"

She grinned again. "Stewart's company. I was telling him about it, and he just did it. Arranged it all. Got someone to donate the bus, the tickets, even a picnic for the kids."

"Seriously?"

She looked dreamy. "He is wonderful, Raven. Quiet. Calm. But I get the feeling he sees everything, you know? I told him how restricted our budget was and how I wished we could do something special for the kids like a trip to the zoo, and the next thing I knew, he sent me an email with all the particulars in it."

"That is very generous."

"He told me he grew up poor. He knows what a day like that would mean to a kid. It's the Wednesday of the first week of camp. I already have the permission forms for the parents to fill out and have asked for some volunteers."

Knowing he'd want to be there, I smiled. "I'll ask Damien."

"Great. Stewart is away that week, so he can't come. I told him he'd already done enough."

"I'd say so."

"And he reminded me he wants to meet you. Maybe next week for a double date?"

"Sure. I'll check on Damien's schedule."

We cashed out and went to her car. I glanced around, not seeing anyone, but certain I wasn't as alone as I thought. We headed to the bar, grabbing a table with enough room for our laptops. We ordered drinks and some munchies to share and had just taken a sip as a group of businessmen walked past us on their way out. One of them stopped, staring at our table. "Deb? What are you doing here?"

She looked up, a huge smile on her face. "Stew?"

He smiled and bent, brushing a kiss to her cheek. He waved at the men leaving and smiled down at her. "Having a drink with some associates. It's been a day."

Then he turned to me, offering me his hand. "You must be Raven. Deb talks about you all the time—I feel as if I know you already."

I shook his hand, shocked at the dampness of his palm and the odd feeling I got when his fingers closed around mine. I put it down to my nervousness of being out in public without Damien beside me or seeing a familiar face.

"Deb told me about your generosity for the kids. Thank you."

"Happy to do so. Kids are a soft spot for me."

I studied him. He was tall, his shoulders broad, contrasting with his lean build. He had brown eyes, short dark hair, and glasses. A beard. He was as attractive as Deb had stated, but there was something about his expression that bothered me. It was pinched. Disgruntled. Then I shook my head. I was imagining things. Again, I put it down to nerves. Maybe he was wishing I weren't there. He had barely looked at me, seemingly only having eyes for Deb.

"Join us?" Deb asked.

"Can't, I'm afraid. Heading to another meeting. But I'll see you tomorrow, right, dollface?"

She grinned. "Yes."

He bent and kissed her again. "Sorry, I have to catch up with the crew. One of them is part of the next meeting." He touched Deb's shoulder and offered me a wave.

"Nice to meet you, Raven. Cool name, by the way. I look forward to seeing you again."

Then he was gone, Deb's gaze following him. He stopped by the two men from the group who were outside and said something. One of them pointed, and he nodded, clapping them on the shoulder. Then he headed that way, and a moment later, they followed. I looked over at Deb, seeing her watching him.

"Dollface?"

She grinned. "He calls me that all the time."

"You really like him," I stated.

She nodded. "I do. He's like a dream come true."

It was on the tip of my tongue to say something about dreams becoming nightmares, but I stopped. What was wrong with me? It had to be my recent experience. Deb was happy, and I needed to be happy for her.

Our nachos arrived, and Deb rubbed her hands. "Let's eat, then we can work."

"Sounds like a plan."

DAMIEN

"Stop fidgeting."

I glanced at Egan.

"Your leg is bouncing. Relax."

I blew out a long breath. "Sorry."

"Worried about Raven's shopping trip later?"

I was honest. "Yes."

"You got it covered?"

"Yes."

"Then trust your people."

He was right.

"How long are we going to be waiting here?"

He shrugged. "I told you. He got caught on a phone call. He'll be out soon." He glanced around the off-site space where The Real Connection housed its backups. "Pretty spiffy."

I nodded. "It is."

"Remember what I told you about this guy. Don't take offense."

"Right. No handshakes, stay out of his space, don't get personal."

"Yeah, he's a bit jumpy."

A moment later, the man himself appeared. Jeff Drew was tall, the word rotund coming to mind. Heavyset, his scalp gleaming under the bright lights, he shuffled his way over. His hazel eyes were large behind thick glasses, his scruff helping hide a thick chin. He nodded at us. "Gentlemen."

I nodded back, not offering my hand. "Damien DeSalvo. Thank you for your cooperation."

He ran a hand along his bald head, his thick wedding band catching the light. "I built this site so people could find their soul mate. Get to know someone without seeing them first." He smiled ruefully. "My wife and I met online years ago. We talked for weeks before meeting or exchanging pictures. She didn't care about my appearance. She cared about the man she had come to know. I used that idea to develop this app. To think someone is using the site to stalk women? It's horrifying. Of course I want to help." He shook his head, his eyes sad. "Please follow me."

We entered a room filled with equipment. He sat down in front of a monitor, the chair squeaking under his weight. "Let's see what we can find."

"I have no idea what has happened. How is this possible?" Jeff's voice was incredulous. Confused. Anxious.

"It's possible because he knows what he is doing. Somehow he is in and out, getting what he wants and deleting his trail before your backups are done," Egan mused. "He's good. Better than I thought."

Jeff passed a hand over his head. I noticed it was something he did when upset or nervous. He did it a lot, and I had a feeling being in this room with us made him extremely anxious. He also cleared his throat a great deal and constantly had a candy in his mouth. In the closed-in space, despite the cool air, I could smell his cologne. The overtones were heavy, musky, and somewhat unpleasant. I tried to keep my breathing shallow.

I had to wonder how deep his tension ran. If he had been diagnosed with a disorder. He certainly showed many of the signs.

He turned and faced us, his eyes anxious and damp. "I am sorry, gentlemen, there seems to be nothing I can do to help you find this man. I have, however, instructed my team, and they have implemented more safety features and have added some functions that will alert us immediately if a profile is built using any of the words this Andy person used. It will log every keystroke, and regardless of what he does, they will not be eliminated. If this happens, I will forward you the information right away."

We stood, hearing the dismissal in his tone. "We are happy to provide you with some extra cybersecurity we can implement," I offered.

He stood, shaking his head. "I have looked into it and spoken with the company I had hired. They have fixed the firewalls. Tightened them. Anyone will have trouble getting in now. Thank you for bringing it to my attention."

"It's the least we can do. Let us show you what we can offer."

He wavered. Jeff stepped to the side as I approached him. I laid my hand on the computer Jeff had been working on. "I think this Andy is very talented. He might find a way in."

"Could it not happen with your solution?"

I sat down. "Can I show you? It will only take a moment."

Jeff nodded, not looking happy. He obviously didn't like the fact that we had discovered the weakness, but I was grateful he was setting aside his pride.

My fingers flew over the keyboard, moving so fast that no one could keep up—even Egan. Screens appeared and disappeared. I double-checked and nodded. "They have tightened it well," I admitted. "But I think I could get in with a few more moments." I hit some more keys. "Ours would stop them the first time it was attempted. Lock them down completely."

Jeff peered at the screen from a safe distance. "Send me the parameters. I will look them over… shortly."

His unspoken words were clear. Once we were gone. I sensed his uneasiness growing. The sweat was beading on his forehead, and he dabbed at the dampness several times with a handkerchief he took from his pocket. His dislike of being close to strangers was evident, and I knew we had to leave before he decided not to help us at all.

I stood. "I will."

Jeff shifted, clearly uncomfortable.

"Thank you for your time," I said.

"I'm sorry I couldn't help your friend. But we will keep searching," he assured us, opening the door and walking ahead of us.

I could smell his cologne, the scent hitting me again. Less concentrated, I realized I had smelled it before. I wasn't sure when, but there was something familiar about it. Jeff offered us a tight smile then waited until we left the building. He hurried away, at least as quickly as he could hurry. His shuffle was more obvious the quicker he tried to move.

In the car, Egan shook his head. "That man has some major personal boundary issues."

"Big-time. I wonder how his wife got past them."

"Maybe she has the same ones. Perhaps they somehow are comfortable with each other."

I shrugged.

"That Andy bastard is smart."

"Or knows more than Jeff thinks."

"What do you mean?"

"Jeff writes code and developed the software, but he has a team, so he isn't proficient in every area. He hired out for security. How big a staff does he have?"

"The website employs quite a few frontline people. Customer service, help lines, and all that."

"We need to check into the employees. Jeff can't be the only one with access to the software."

"You think it's an inside job?"

"Yes. But we have an insider now."

"What did you do?"

"Put a tracking program in. I could only plant it, not activate it with him watching. Next time Jeff uses that machine, it will start, and we can access the system and delve as deep as we want. But it has to be that machine. I didn't have time for anything else. Not with him watching."

"Brilliant."

We were quiet for a moment. "Anything bother you about him?"

He shrugged. "He's odd. Many computer geniuses are."

"His anxiety was evident."

He nodded. "He was a little friendlier yesterday. I think you made him uncomfortable."

"Really?"

"You are kinda intimidating. All tall, silent, and brooding."

I chuckled. "I see."

"I think our presence did that. I also think he doesn't like the fact that we found a weakness."

That made sense. "Agreed."

"Maybe we'll find something now. Or he will."

"Do you think he'll share?"

Egan scratched his chin. "I think so. I think he also feels badly, which is why he was so nervous."

He was probably right.

Egan clapped me on the shoulder. "Now you can buy me lunch."

"Okay."

I spent the rest of the afternoon and early evening worried, pissed off, and anxious. I failed at finding any trace of Andy on another site, here or in any other province. I even dug into the dark web, finding nothing. He was like a ghost.

When Raven texted, saying she was ready to come home, I was already in the car, on my way to get her. I had internally shaken my head at my behavior.

She was right. I was as obsessed with her as Andy. But in an entirely different way.

I was pleased to find a spot, and I parked outside the bar and went in, surprised to see her alone at the bar, sipping from a tall glass. Beside her, a man was talking to her, and she seemed to be ignoring him. He crowded into her space, and she frowned. I headed over, calling her name. She looked over her shoulder, surprise etched on her face. Reaching her, I slid my arm around her waist, tugging her close possessively. I bent and kissed her. "Hey, baby," I breathed out. "Sorry I'm late."

She blinked, then smiled. "You're forgiven."

I lifted my gaze to the man beside her, meeting his eyes with a glare. He shook his head and mumbled something under his breath before moving toward the end of the bar and his pack of friends waiting for him. They all made jokes about his failure, slapping him on the back and offering him another beer to "douse the flames."

"That's right, asshole," I muttered. "Keep moving."

Raven followed my gaze. "He was harmless. He asked me if I was lost."

"Lost?"

She picked up her glass and took another sip. "He said he assumed I'd fallen from heaven and was looking for a way to get back." She winked. "He offered to help."

"Motherfucker," I swore, turning in his direction.

"Oh, stop it, Damien. He was just looking for a bit of fun. I have been propositioned in bars before, you know. I can handle myself."

"Oh yeah?" I took her glass and drained it, grateful it was just water. I leaned on the bar, resting my hands on either side of her stool, caging her in.

"How was your night?"

"Productive."

"Good."

"I met the infamous Stew. He was leaving with a group of businessmen when we sat down. She introduced us."

"And?"

I shrugged. "It was fast, but he seemed nice. Deb certainly likes him."

"Where *is* Deb?"

"She left."

"You're not supposed to be alone."

She rolled her eyes. She knew I had someone in the bar. He was, in fact, just walking out the door, not even glancing our way.

"How'd you get here so fast?" Her eyes narrowed. "You were already on the way, weren't you?"

I lifted one eyebrow in acknowledgment. "You want a proposition, Ms. Raven?"

She batted her eyes at me.

I leaned close, well aware that asshole Andy was probably listening in. "You. Me. Our bed. Me tasting you everywhere. You riding me hard. You screaming my name when you come." I drew a finger down her neck. "At least three times. Maybe four."

She shivered. "That's quite the proposition."

"It's all yours," I murmured, nuzzling the soft skin at the base of her neck. "I'm all yours."

My car alarm went off.

Frowning, I took her hand, and we hurried outside. Splintered and shattered glass was all that was left of my windshield. It was like an intricate cobweb, but the spider that made it sat in the middle. A rock thrown with deadly accuracy, and from the location and force, I would say from above. I pulled Raven back to the awning at the door of the bar, sending a quick text.

Me: Don't move. Keep your eyes open for perp. Scan the rooftops around us.

If Andy was watching, which I was sure he was, I didn't want him to know I had two others looking out for Raven.

Raven stared at the destruction as I turned off the alarm and called CAA. A crowd was gathering around the car and I studied them all, but Andy wasn't among them. I was certain he was crouched on the rooftop overhead, wanting to see my reaction. Or gone by now. He was such a coward, it was probably the second. Raven turned to me, and I laid a finger on her lips, shaking my head. I knew why Andy had thrown the rock. I had pushed to see if he was listening.

His response was loud and clear.

He was. And he used his weapon of choice well again. First, the window of Raven's apartment, now, the window of my car. He was telling us he didn't like what he saw or heard.

CAA arrived, and I dealt with them and the garage where I had my car serviced. Egan showed up, and Raven slid into the back seat of his car while Egan came over, whistling at the damage to my car.

"Sending a message?" he asked quietly.

"Yes. I taunted him." I tapped my ear, knowing Egan would understand.

"I take it he has no sense of humor."

"Nope."

"He's dangerous, Damien. More devious and dark than we thought. I fear he's more than just a stalker."

I looked over at his car, seeing Raven staring at us from the back seat. She'd barely said a word since it happened, and she was pale and obviously distraught.

"I have to find him."

"We will, brother. We will."

My car was towed away, and I shook my head as he clasped me on the shoulder. "Let's get you home where you can talk to your lady in private."

In the car, I sat beside Raven in the back seat. We were quiet, although I slipped my hand around hers and held it. Her grip was tight, and I knew she was upset. After a few days of silence, she had been hopeful Andy was gone. He wasn't.

At my place, I shoved the bunny in the cylinder by the front door and followed Raven to the kitchen. She poured us each a glass of water, the cold condensation immediately covering the outside of the glass.

"I'm sorry about your car," she said quietly.

"It will be repaired."

"What if he had thrown the rock while you were in the car? What if he hurt you?"

"He didn't. He was angry. I shouldn't have said what I did to you in the bar. I knew there was a chance he was listening. The problem is, I had no idea he was so close."

"I'm going home tomorrow."

"I don't think we need to test the theory that he is watching, Raven. Obviously, he is."

"No, I meant I'm going home. Alone. If he doesn't see you around, he'll leave you alone."

I tilted my head, studying her. "You really think that will work? I'm not around, and he'll just move on?"

"I don't know, but I can't let you get hurt on my account, Damien. I can't. When I think of how that could have been you. How he could have hit you with that rock. All I could see standing there was you lying on the ground, bleeding and hurt because of me."

I set down my glass and crossed the kitchen. I took her glass from her tight grip and pulled her into my arms. She was as stiff as a board, her anxiety obvious. "He's not that good a shot, Raven."

"He's two for two."

"Through a large window and a car directly below him that he dropped a rock on. He could have been aiming for the hood, for all we know. That would have caused more damage and inconvenience," I soothed.

"He might have a gun."

"So do I. I assure you, I am a far better shot."

"I can't let you get hurt."

I lifted her chin, meeting her worried eyes. "I can't let you get hurt either. Don't ask me to let you go alone, Raven. I can't do that."

"What do we do, then? Keep letting him attack us? I hide and let him rule our lives?"

"We stick together, and you give me time to find him. We don't hide. We do what we want as long as we're careful. The one thing I know right now is that he is listening and doesn't know we know he is. I have to somehow turn that to our advantage."

"Then we fight on Saturday. Just like we planned."

I hated that she was right. "Yes."

She worried her lip. "What about your other plans?"

"Other plans?"

She slipped her arms around my waist, pressing herself close. "The ones for tonight. That you told me about earlier. You still want to do those?"

I grinned, pleased and surprised she was wanting to ignore the asshole as much as I did. "As long as you're up to it, Ms. Raven. I certainly am." I ran my hands down her back, cupping her ass and grinding against her. "Nothing has changed there."

"I guess you have some work to do, then."

I lifted her in my arms, and she laughed, wrapping her legs around me. I headed down the hall. "It's a dirty job, Raven, but someone's got to do it."

Her voice was a whisper in my ear, her breath hot on my skin. "Make it really dirty, Damien."

I lowered her onto the bed, following her down to the mattress.

"Whatever you want, Ms. Raven."

Friday morning, I borrowed Egan's car and drove Raven to work. I wanted to ask her not to go, but I knew she would refuse. I walked her into the building, knowing without a doubt Andy was still around, then once I knew she was safely inside, headed to the office. I called the garage, made arrangements for my car, then called Julian directly, bringing him up to speed on the situation. He listened, not interrupting, then mused in silence for a moment when I finished speaking.

"He's escalating, Damien. He's angry. When unstable people get angry, get denied the one thing they want, they get desperate—which makes him more dangerous."

"I'm hoping he gets sloppy."

"So he's slipped under the radar on the website, even with the extra backups they do," he said, thinking aloud. "Have you thought of an inside job?"

"Yes. I was going to contact Jeff today and ask for a list of employees. Or I'll get Egan to do it maybe," I replied. "I seemed to make him nervous."

"How?"

"I don't know. Egan noticed how tense he was around me. I put him on edge. He's, ah, already really introverted, and I was rather insistent."

"Have you checked him out?"

"Quickly. He's intensely private and stays out of the limelight. Opened the company four years ago. No complaints aside from some disgruntled people who didn't find their connection, but the same as on any site. He's late forties, heavyset, married. Clean record. Not a suspect at all."

"Okay. Get Egan to request it. If he refuses…" He trailed off.

"We'll hack in."

"You might have to. He wants to help, but handing over his employee list might not sit well. I'll do a little digging here too. None of our contacts matched up the sketch with a known entity. Their searches got no hits on the name. I think you're right in assuming it's fake." He was quiet for a moment. "Proceed carefully. Don't make him angry again."

I told him about Raven's idea for an argument. He hummed in agreement. "Not a bad idea. Might flush him out. With the right precautions, you might nab him and keep her safe." He paused. "She's brave, your lady."

"She is."

"And you really care about her." It was a statement, not a question.

"She is it for me, Julian. I can't imagine life without her now."

He chuckled. "And another one bites the dust."

"Big-time."

"All right. Let me see what I can do. I have a couple more calls I can make."

"Thanks."

I hung up and walked to the windows, staring down on the street.

"Where are you, asshole?" I muttered.

I needed to find him.

Soon.

CHAPTER SEVENTEEN

Raven

Hiding my anxiety, I smiled at Damien. "It's all pretend, right?"

He nodded, the tension around his eyes obvious. Neither of us had slept much the night before, and this morning, we had both been quiet. Damien had made love to me in the middle of the night, his movements slow and gentle, his voice a low hum in the dark. I had lain in his arms after, trying to hold back my tears, feeling vulnerable and silly.

It was just a pretend fight. Egan was already in my apartment, having swept it for bugs. Damien had decided, during our fight, he would reach for the satchel and accidentally tear off the bunny. If Andy was watching, he'd think it was an accident. But not being able to track or hear me might spur him to follow me to the apartment. Meanwhile, Damien was going to disable the bugs Andy had planted and try tracing the manufacturer to find out who they were sold to if he could.

"Are you sure you want to do this?" he asked.

"Yes. If it brings him to us, then yes."

He blew out a breath, dragged me into his arms, and kissed me. Hard. His tongue, his touch, everything about it was possessive, claiming. Perfect.

He drew back, cupping my face. "Just for show."

I shook off Damien's hand. "You're holding me too tight."

"Stop whining."

"Stop breathing down my neck. You're suffocating me," I hissed.

"Forgive me for trying to watch out for you," he snapped.

I shook my head. "Did you hear anything I said to you last night, Damien? I'm tired of this!"

"You're tired of this? You're not the one having rocks thrown at her car or trying to help someone who keeps insisting they can look after themselves." He sneered at me. "We both know you do a shit job at it."

"I managed quite well before I met you."

"Does the name Andy ring a bell?" he spat. "Jesus,

you're insufferable at times. You act like a spoiled brat."

I turned and faced him in the park. We were close to the road and visible, yet there were lots of trees around us. Not knowing if we were being watched, listened to, or both, we made sure to keep our voices low, not wanting to attract unwanted attention. The last thing we needed was someone to come over and interrupt us.

"I act like a spoiled brat?" I repeated. "I'm living in reality. You're running around acting like you're James Bond. You run a security firm, Damien. Ex-cops who are too old to do much good but drink coffee, and mall security guards high on their own power. You're not that big a deal. And I think you're making the situation worse."

His eyebrows shot up at my remark. I could tell he was trying to stay in the moment and not laugh at my description of Elite. We both knew it was anything but mall security guards.

He leaned closer, dropping his voice to a furious pitch. "Why don't you show a little gratitude instead of attitude, Raven? You have completely lost touch with reality. You think you can keep yourself safe, little girl? You can do better on your own than with me? Be my guest."

I crossed my arms. "You are just as bad as he is. You want to take over my life."

"So you've said before. You want your life back to

what it was before you ran to me for help? Go for it. I'm sick of being your knight."

I scoffed. "I never thought of you as a knight, Damien. Maybe the court jester."

"You ungrateful little…" He trailed off.

"Bitch?" I finished for him. "You keep calling me that. I'm tired of your orders, your overbearing attitude, and your scowling face. I'm done."

"Meaning?"

I glanced around, hoping I looked surprised and pleased to see the taxi idling at the curb not far from us.

"Like I said," I snapped. "I'm done. Leave me alone."

I turned, and he reached out, grabbing at my bag. The bunny tore off in his hand, and I half ran to the cab, bending at the window. "Are you available?"

"Yep," she replied.

I slid into the back seat, but before I could shut the door, Damien was there.

"Don't do this, Raven."

I grabbed the door handle. "Leave me alone, Damien. I'll send for my things."

I slammed the door, looking back to see him throw down the bunny and stomp on it in his rage.

I sighed and leaned against the back seat.

"Address?" The "driver" prompted. I was surprised to see it was a woman. We had agreed to pretend until I was in my apartment, even though Damien's person knew exactly where I was going.

"Ah," I said, worried. But she winked and touched the rim of her glasses, a signal Damien had told me meant I could trust the person.

I gave it to her and shut my eyes.

I already missed Damien.

My apartment smelled musty. The window had been repaired, and there was dust everywhere. All the blinds were shut tight. Egan relaxed on my sofa, a cup of coffee in his hand.

"How'd it go?" he asked.

"Fine." I sighed. "I hated every minute of it."

He shook his head. "Don't worry. It was needed. You both know it's not true." He stood. "But for the record, I have never been a mall cop." He glared at me. "That was low."

I began to laugh, and he grinned.

"You were listening?"

"No, Damien told me. You did good."

I sat down. "I don't know what to do now."

"You have to act normal. Like you are angry. What would you normally do?"

"Clean the apartment."

"Okay. You clean one room at a time. Open

blinds, so if he is looking, he sees you. I will go in the other room."

"Okay." I stood. "Was Damien all right when you talked to him?"

He patted my arm. "No worries, girl. He knows, eh?"

I sighed, looking around the room. It felt strange to be back here. I had never loved the place, but it was my home. Or at least, I thought it was. It was odd how at home I felt at Damien's. It felt right being there with him. Here, I felt like a stranger, even though the things around me were mine.

My phone rang, interrupting my thoughts. I answered Deb's call, my melancholy evident in my voice.

"Hey, Deb."

"Hey. What's wrong?"

I couldn't tell her, so I pretended. "Nothing. Just one of those days."

"Ah, okay. So, Stew and I were wondering about doing dinner on Monday?"

"Oh." I paused. "Can I call you back tomorrow to confirm?"

"Everything okay?"

"I just have to check with Damien."

"Oh, you're not with him?"

"No, I'm cleaning my apartment right now. He's, ah, he's busy today."

"Okay. Call me later and confirm. Stewart has

reservations at Rustic Alley for seven. If you can't go, we'll do another night."

"Okay, sounds good."

I hung up and shook my head. I was acting as if Damien and I had really had a fight. Broken up. I was being silly. I tossed my phone to the table, opened the blinds, and got to work.

My apartment gleamed, and my body ached. I looked around, satisfied. I had scrubbed every inch. Opened my windows with the music playing. Made sure I could be seen. Egan stayed in the next room, occasionally making a comment, but stayed busy with a sketchbook in his hand. Finally done, I closed the windows again, shutting the blinds, and turning on the small air conditioner. I showered, changed, and sat down. Egan was across from me, his head still bent over his work.

"What are you drawing?" I asked.

"Something for Damien."

"Ah."

I had discovered he was a man of few words.

"Are you hungry?"

He lifted a shoulder. "I could eat."

"I don't have much here, but we can order in."

He nodded. "Soon."

"Okay."

He kept his eyes on the pad. "So, you are a woman."

"Last time I checked."

"Do you find me attractive?"

"Um…" I hesitated.

He looked up with a wry grin. "I mean in general. I know you are Damien's lady."

Damien's lady. I liked the sound of that.

"Yes, Egan. You are very good-looking. Sort of exotic."

He frowned. "Exotic?"

"You can tell you're a different nationality. Your features are bold. Your voice is unusual. The accent makes you sound, well, sexy."

He paused, rubbing his chin. "And that is good, yah?"

I smiled. "Yes."

He sighed. "My woman. My lady. I cannot get her to give me day time."

"Um, the time of day?"

He nodded. "Yah. That. We have dinner, we talk, I make sure she is safe. She smiles, she laughs—" he sighed again "—but no more. No kisses, no love. I thought maybe I am too ugly."

"You are anything but ugly, Egan. This is Sofia, right? Damien's cousin?"

"Yes." He put his hand on his chest. "My heart."

"Have you told her?" I asked.

"In words, no. I try to show her. I know she is

worried because of my job. She avoids personal—" he waved his hand "—situations with me."

"Sounds as if she is worried about what she feels for you, Egan. Maybe she worries about losing you because of what you do. If she admits she cares, it makes it scary. You need to be honest with her. Tell her."

"And if she walks away?"

"Then you have to accept and move on."

He blew out a long breath. "Yah."

He went back to his sketchbook, a frown marring his features.

"Sometimes love is worth the risk," I said quietly.

He looked up, silent, then smiled. "She is. I will tell her."

"I hope she responds the way you want."

He lifted a shoulder. "One way to skin a cat."

I laughed. "No, the expression is there is more than one way to skin a cat. But I think you meant only one way to find out."

He smiled. "I like cats—and I will tell her."

"Good."

My buzzer went, and he grinned. "Perfect timing."

"Who is it?"

"Pizza."

"I didn't order pizza."

He winked. "I did."

He went to the door, hitting the enter button. In

the kitchen, I got some plates from the cupboard and took them to the table. A moment later, I heard footsteps, and a delivery man walked in, his hat pulled low.

I felt a frisson of nerves until he lifted his head and I was met with warm blue eyes.

"Pizza," Damien said with a wink. "Hot and ready."

———

Damien handed me the pizza box, which I slid onto the table. He shrugged off the jacket and hat, handing them to Egan, who slipped them on. I noticed they both wore jeans and dark sneakers.

"Thanks."

Egan shook his head. "All good." Then he turned to me, lifting my hand and kissing it. "You are lovely woman for my friend. Thank you for advice."

He left, and Damien shut and locked the door. He turned, holding out his arms. "Come here, Raven."

I flung myself into his hard embrace, the worry and stress of the day fading away.

"You're here," I breathed.

"I'm here, Raven," he murmured back. "Right here."

"How?" I asked into his neck.

He pulled back, cupped my face, and kissed me gently. He took my hand and tugged me to the table.

"The pizza place close to my building was having trouble last year. Constantly being robbed. Egan and I set up a sting and caught them. We suspected an inside job, and we were right. Idiot was even depositing the money in a bank account, so we got the owner all his money back. Frank was, is, very grateful. On occasion, we borrow his pizza delivery car. Egan said you were feeling pretty low, so I got us a pizza, brought it here. Egan will drive the car back and head home. Anyone looking will see a pizza guy go in and a pizza guy come out. Hiding in plain sight."

I reached for his hand. "I felt terrible about this morning."

He chuckled. "I knew it wasn't real, Raven."

"Still, saying those words. It felt awful."

He leaned close and kissed me. "You're almost forgiven."

"Almost?"

He lifted one eyebrow, regarding me with a serious expression.

"Oh, the old policemen and the mall security cop thing?"

"Low blow, Ms. Raven."

"Egan didn't like it either," I said, trying not to laugh at his stern expression.

"Shannon, your driver, found it amusing."

"I didn't know you employed women."

"Of course I do. I have several on staff. A couple have even been in the school with you.

Women make great security detail. They are capable, smart, agile, and, frankly, lethal if needed. And to be honest, unexpected, which throws people off."

"Huh," I replied. "Are any of them ex-Hidden Justice?"

"No, but there are women operatives there as well."

"Well, I guess you learn something new every day."

He winked as he opened the lid of the pizza box. "Leo was listening. He was shocked at your behavior. Shocked."

I began to laugh. "Does that mean I need to bake some cookies?"

"Yes." He grinned. "But pizza first. Frank makes a great pie."

"Okay."

He looked around, noticing the new window and the cleanliness. "Egan says you scrubbed all day."

"I clean when I'm upset."

"No need to be upset, but the place is spotless. Did you do anything else but clean?"

"I talked to Egan. Oh, and Deb called and asked if we'd do dinner with her and Stewart on Monday. He has a reservation at Rustic Alley."

"I hear that's good. Eclectic." He shrugged. "I'm game. What time?"

"Seven."

He nodded. "We'll get there a little early so I can scope the place out."

I texted Deb to say we'd go. She replied with a smiley face.

Deb: See you there!

We began to eat, Damien polishing off his first piece quickly.

"Did you not eat today?" I laughed.

"No. I wasn't hungry."

"Me either."

"Looking forward to dinner Monday?" he asked after his second slice.

"I suppose."

"You don't seem very enthused."

"Deb really likes this guy." I paused.

"But you don't?"

I shrugged. "I don't know him. He gave me a bit of a weird vibe when Deb and I ran into him."

He paused between bites. "How so?"

"I don't know. I felt wary."

"Given what has happened to you lately, that isn't surprising. Your guard is up when it comes to strangers."

His words made sense.

"Anyway, you'll meet him on Monday too. Maybe once I spend a little time with him, I'll feel different."

He nodded around a mouthful of pizza. He

chewed and swallowed, wiping his lips. "I'll be there too, so maybe you'll be more relaxed."

I smiled at him. "Probably."

He told me he'd spent the day wandering his place, doing some work, then wandering some more.

"I missed you today," he confessed. "My place felt empty."

"It seemed strange to be here," I admitted. "I felt displaced, which seemed odd since this is my home."

"Or maybe it's not," Damien replied.

Our eyes met, and I had to look away from the intense gaze that he focused on me.

I stood and took the empty pizza box to the kitchen. Damien followed. He stood behind me, his arms on the counter, caging me in. His heat soaked into my back, his voice a low hum in my ear.

"When Egan said you were upset, I couldn't wait to get to you. I knew I wasn't going to be able to sleep without you beside me."

Relief flooded my chest. I turned and met his eyes. "So, you're staying?"

"Of course I am. Did you think I'd leave you alone overnight?"

"I hoped not," I replied. "But I thought, with someone else watching, maybe it would be okay."

"Someone else isn't good enough. It's my job to watch over you."

I frowned, and he slipped his fingers under my chin. "What?"

"It seems to me I'm a lot of work. I don't know if I'm worth all the trouble."

"I disagree."

"All this time, all the stress. What do you get from all this, Damien? It feels so one-sided."

He studied me, lifting his hand and tracing a finger over my cheek. His touch was gentle, his voice filled with affection when he spoke. "What do I get, Raven? You want to know what I get?"

"Yes."

He smiled, his blue eyes warm and tender. "I get you. Despite the worry, the stress, despite everything, the bottom line is, I get you. You mean so much to me, I find it hard to express it." He took my hand and laid it on his chest right over his heart so I could feel the steady thump under my palm. "I get to love you, Raven. You're mine. It's a gift I never thought I would have."

I blinked, my own heartbeat picking up. "You— you love me?"

His gaze locked on mine. "I love you. Totally. Completely. Without end."

His words, spoken so simply, with so much emotion underscoring them, went straight to my heart, healing the ragged edges still left from the betrayal I had suffered. Tears filled my eyes as I saw the emotion his eyes held. Love. Love for me.

"I love you too," I murmured. "I think I have from the first time you held me."

He wrapped me in his embrace, his strength surrounding me. "I'll hold you for the rest of my life, Raven."

His promise stitched the final tear and made me understand something.

It wasn't a place I had been looking for. It was Damien. In his arms, I was home.

Damien was my home.

And I never wanted to leave.

CHAPTER EIGHTEEN

Damien

The restaurant where we met Deb and Stewart was upscale. Busy. We got caught in traffic, so they arrived just as we did, and I greeted Deb then shook hands with Stewart. His grip was firm. Too firm, as if he were trying to prove something. I brushed it off but didn't like the way he stepped forward as if to kiss Raven hello. She held out her hand and he shook it as if nothing was wrong, but I saw the flash of annoyance cross his face. I tucked her closer to my side and pressed a kiss to her hair. We were shown to a booth, and I let Raven slide in first. Deb began to slip in across from her when Stewart stopped her, tapping his ear.

"Oh, right," she said.

At my confusion, she smiled. "Stewart is deaf in his left ear."

"If I sit on the outside on this side of the booth,

I'll be asking you to repeat yourself all night," he explained.

"We can trade sides so you can have the outside," I offered.

He slid in, shaking his head. "I'm fine."

Deb sat beside him, nudging his shoulder. "Let's hope we don't get attacked. You won't be able to defend me."

He laughed, the sound unusual. High-pitched compared to his somewhat low, gravelly voice. "I doubt there will be any perps around here. If there are, my friend Damien here owns a security firm. You carrying?" he asked.

I was caught off guard by his casual term "friend." I was also surprised by his question, his use of the words "perp" and "carrying." He obviously watched too much TV. "No, I don't carry a gun."

"Ever?" he asked. "Even when you're on the job?"

On the job?

Yep. Definitely too many police TV shows.

"No."

"Hmm. Interesting."

It was another unusual remark, but before I could respond, Deb spoke.

"This place is so amazing," she enthused. "I heard reservations are hard to come by."

"The owner is a client. I called in a favor," Stewart said. "You have a financial plan, Damien?"

"I do."

"Good man. You can never start too early. What about you, young lady?" he asked Raven.

"Um, no."

"You come and see me. I can help you start one."

Deb slapped his arm. "This isn't a business dinner, Stew. Stop it."

He winked. "I just talked business. Now it's an expense. I guess dinner's on me." Then he laughed. The sound grated on my nerves, and I felt Raven shiver beside me. Stew, however, thought he was hilarious, and Deb seemed to agree. I reached under the table and found Raven's hand, squeezing it. The waitress came over and asked about drinks. I decided to have one. I had a feeling I was going to need it.

The drinks didn't help.

Stewart was cordial, affable, friendly.

And it felt like an act to me. Forced. He name-dropped. Offered unsolicited advice. Knew something about everything. Talked money a lot. The whole time laughing. Every time he did, Raven stiffened. Deb hung on his every word. He liked to talk. He also liked to stare at other tables often, and he tapped his deaf ear a lot. It was disconcerting. I noticed a device in the ear and asked him about it. He tapped it again.

"Oh, the affliction left me with no hearing, but a ringing in my ear. This helps stop it. A little tap sends a signal that cancels out the ringing. Lifesaver, I tell you. I would go crazy otherwise."

"Ah."

Despite my unease with him, he seemed enthralled with Deb. He was courteous, affectionate, and playful. Yet, something still bothered me. I couldn't put my finger on it, although I thought at times he stared at Raven a beat too long. Listened too intently to her when she spoke. But it was probably the jealous caveman inside me more than reality. He was probably concentrating on her voice since it was soft and modulated. I noticed Deb spoke louder on his behalf, and I tried to do the same.

During dessert, Deb smiled at me. "Raven says you're coming to the zoo with us!"

"Yes," I replied. "That's two weeks from Wednesday, right?"

"Yes." She rubbed Stewart's arm. "Thanks to this guy."

I nodded in agreement, and even Raven spoke up. "It is incredibly generous of you, Stew. Very kind."

For the first time, his smile looked genuine. "Happy to bring some kids a little joy. I wish I could be there to help."

"I think you've done enough," Deb said. "It's so awesome for the kids."

He nodded. "Maybe we can do dinner again once I get back."

I hummed, noncommittal. He made Raven uncomfortable. She covered it well, but I already knew her. She hadn't spoken much, eaten little, and her smiles and laughs were strained. She was stiff beside me. He was decent, although I found him a little pompous and full of himself. For someone Deb had described to Raven as quiet, he certainly talked. I put it down to nerves—having dinner with his new lady's friend. That could be nerve-racking. He could be very comfortable in a business setting and not as much in a personal situation. Lots of people were like that. He might relax more as we got to know him. But until I spoke to Raven in private, I wasn't agreeing to another dinner out with Stewart.

"We'll have to touch base again."

He inclined his head. "Sure." He slid a card my way. "Feel free to get in touch." I picked it up, noticing it was the same one Raven had a picture of. I slipped it into my pocket. "Thanks."

I turned to Raven. "I hate to break up the party, but mind if we get going? I have a meeting early tomorrow."

"We can drop her off. Her place is on the way to Deb's," Stewart offered. At my frown, he shrugged. "Deb told me where she lived. I thought the girls might want a little more visiting time."

"I'll take my date home, thanks."

By home, I meant my place. We'd gone back to my apartment late Saturday night. There had been no Andy sightings all day or evening at her place—or since then.

He waved me off, not at all put out. "Right. Of course."

We said our goodnights, and we were silent until I pulled away from the restaurant. My car had been delivered to me earlier, the new windshield in place, and it felt good to have it back. I felt Raven finally relax beside me.

"You don't like him," I stated.

"No, and I don't know why. He's a bit uptight and pretentious, but he obviously likes Deb. He was all over her tonight. Held her hand, kissed her. He listened when she spoke. He seems kind and certainly generous, but he makes me nervous."

"I got the feeling he was trying to impress us. Or you, at least, given you are her friend. He was trying too hard."

"Maybe that's it. There were times he looked almost irritated. Then he would clear his expression."

She was observant. I had noticed a few odd looks on his face but thought I'd imagined them.

"Maybe he had gas," I teased.

She laughed. "Well, there you go."

I took her hand. "We don't have to do another dinner."

"Deb will be so disappointed." She sighed. "I am kinda glad he will be away for the zoo trip."

"Yeah," I agreed. "I can't picture him helping out with kids, to be honest."

"Me either, but Deb said he told her he would have. He says he likes kids."

"Well, time will tell. Deb seems a good judge of character, and she certainly seems to like him."

She sighed and rested her head against the leather, looking at me. "You're right. I'll give him the benefit of the doubt."

"I'll be there if we do dinner again. I can always fake a sudden stomach ailment or something."

She giggled. "I'll tap my ear as a signal."

I laughed at her teasing. "Noticed all the tapping did you?"

"It must be difficult not being able to hear in one ear." She huffed. "Maybe you're right. He might have been nervous."

"I guess we'll find out." Then I snapped my fingers. "Damn, I used all the cream this morning." I changed lanes and pulled into the grocery store. "God forbid I send you to work without coffee in your system." I shook my head and looked sorrowful. "Poor little children. They'd be traumatized." I was joking, but not really. Raven needed two cups of coffee to be human in the morning.

She laughed, knowing it was true. Once she got to school, she had another cup or two. She loved the stuff as much as I did, perhaps even more.

"Maybe we could get a snack," she mused.

"You didn't eat much dinner."

"It's a nice place, but the food wasn't to my taste. Far too many ingredients I couldn't pronounce."

It had been as eclectic as the reviews stated. A

little pretentious, much like the man who chose the restaurant and exclaimed the food perfection. I hooked my arm around her waist, and we headed inside. "Okay, let's get some cream and a snack."

Raven perused the deli counter, pursing her lips at the pile of chicken wings. I nudged her. "Go on, then. Get them." As she spoke with the clerk, I heard my name being called, and I looked over, a smile breaking out on my face. I hurried toward the woman, laughing as she flung herself into my arms, hugging me tight.

"Hey, stranger," she huffed out as I set her on her feet. "Come to my place, eat me out of house and home, fall asleep, then not call me for days? Weeks, even? Seriously," Sofia admonished me.

I laughed. "You were away and, since coming back, working double shifts." I cuffed her under the chin. "Troublemaker."

"I heard there's another reason," she teased, looking over my shoulder. "And there she is, looking a little upset, I think."

I turned, seeing Raven staring, looking confused. She was distraught, her tells working overtime. Her teeth were buried in her bottom lip. Her toes tapped an uneven rhythm in her sandals. She smoothed her hair away from her face, approaching slowly as I waved her over.

"Oh boy, you need to make an introduction and fast," Sofia muttered.

I glanced between her and Raven, then I stepped away from Sofia, astonished.

Was Raven jealous? Thinking of what Sofia had said and how I had hugged her, I realized she was. I tried not to laugh.

She came close enough I could pull her to my side. She was tense. But before I could speak, she squared her shoulders. "Hi. I'm Raven. And you are…?" She let the question trail off, lifting one eyebrow. Her countenance was serious, and her tone held no friendliness.

Sofia chuckled. "Damien's cousin, Sofia."

Raven jerked a little, all the tension leaving her body. "Oh, of course! Sofia, it's so nice to meet you," she enthused, her sudden change of mood making me hold in my amusement. Raven held out her hand. "I've heard so much about you."

"And I you," Sofia said, her own amusement evident. "Not from this lug, though. He seems to have forgotten I exist."

"That's my fault," Raven insisted. "Entirely. And Egan. I know he's been extra busy because of me. He is such a great guy. So handsome and charming. Talented. He cheats at cards, though."

For a second, Sofia was taken aback, then she smiled. "I agree to all those things. Especially the cheating at cards. Backgammon too." She narrowed her eyes. "Sounds like he has a fan in you. It seems mutual."

Raven waved her hand. "Oh, I think he's great. He likes me because I tell him stuff straight. He is crazy for you, though. Totally gaga. I mean—"

I cut her off, pressing a finger to her mouth. "I think Sofia knows, baby."

She pursed her lips against my finger. "Oh. Right," she mumbled. But she kept talking. "You should give him a chance."

For a moment, Sofia stared, then she began to laugh. "I like her, Damien. You should keep her."

"I plan to."

"We should do lunch one day," Raven said. "Just us girls."

"Sounds like a plan. I'll pop upstairs, and we'll figure out a day."

"Awesome." Raven leaned forward and hugged Sofia, whispering something to her. Then she turned and went back to get her wings.

Sofia looked at me. "She is going to keep you on your toes, cousin."

"She already does."

She studied me with narrowed eyes. "You're in as deep as Egan said. Deeper, I'd say."

I didn't deny it. "As deeply as Egan wants to be with you."

She began to shake her head, and I gripped her arm. "Let the past go, Sofia. Raven is right. The man is crazy about you. Totally gaga."

"Oh my God, the two of you sound alike."

"It's the truth. He would lay down his life for you."

"You know I don't want that."

"It's still true. Don't think of the bad what-ifs. Think of the joy. Remember how great love is."

She frowned, then hugged me. "All I can remember is the pain it causes."

"Try harder," I urged.

She nodded slowly, reached up and kissed my cheek then walked away.

Egan had a long road ahead of him. I hoped he was up for the monumental task.

Raven came over, holding her box of wings.

I glanced down at her with a smile. "Ready to go home, my little jealous ball of fire?"

She rolled her eyes. "I saw a strange woman hugging you, talking about you having dinner and sleeping over. I didn't know that was Sofia."

I tucked her to my side, pressing a kiss to her head. "I liked you all jealous and possessive. Putting Sofia in her place with your '*And you are?*'" I chuckled. "You were fierce."

"I'll show you fierce when we get home."

"I look forward to it."

She looked up at me, her eyes twinkling. "After the wings."

I laughed. "Of course."

CHAPTER NINETEEN

Damien

Two weeks later, Raven shook her head, trying to convince me it was time for her to go back to her apartment. "Damien, Andy's stopped. You yourself said so."

"I just meant I was cautiously optimistic. Not that I was convinced."

Frustrated, she ticked each item off on her hand. "Not one sighting. Not a single hidden message, hang up, even a hoodie-wearing glimpse while we're outside with the kids. The bugs you examined were no longer activated. Face it. Andy's given up and moved on. Your men have better things to do."

I shifted, lifting the mug of coffee she'd handed me after dinner and taking a long sip. Raven was right on all accounts. It was as if Andy had vanished. I had spoken to Jeff from The Real Connection, who praised the tight security he had allowed us to install on his system and informed me all breaches had been stopped dead with our software. He also told me he'd done a thorough search in his system and tightened more protocols.

"I found no trace of any outsiders anywhere. I also spoke to other site managers, and they have locked themselves down tighter. As a personal favor, they searched their systems and found no trace of his presence either."

"We can't find him," I admitted.

"Perhaps he has moved on. I am sorry your friend experienced what she did, but I think this Andy, whoever he is, got the message loud and clear."

"I had wanted to stop him from doing it to someone else."

"If I hear anything, I will be in touch."

"Thank you."

Unfortunately, he hadn't returned to the off-site building, or if he had, he hadn't accessed the computer there. And even if Andy had given up, moved on, or whatever you wanted to call it, I still wanted to know who he was. Make sure he stayed away. Ensure he didn't do this to another woman. I had to keep overturning rocks until he crawled out from the one he was hiding under.

"I could ease up a bit on the men," I agreed. I'd cut it down to one man watching her, but I wasn't ready for her to be off the radar yet.

"And I'm sure you want your space back. I must be cramping your style. Sharing your bathroom vanity, taking over your kitchen, and all," she said lightly, looking over my shoulder, her gaze focused elsewhere.

I leaned forward, taking her chin in my hand, forcing her to meet my gaze. "No," I said shortly. "You're not."

She blinked, and I saw the worry in her eyes. I held her firmly. "I don't want you to go back to your apartment, Raven."

"You don't?"

"No. I want you to stay here with me." I drew in a deep breath. "Permanently."

Her breath caught.

"I realize the normal thing would be that you go back to your place. That we date. Text. Call. I pick you up. Take you home after the date. Or bring you here. Stay over on the weekend. But that's not what I want."

"No?" she whispered.

I brushed my fingers over her jaw as I shook my head. "No."

Silence hung between us. She stared at me, uncertain but hopeful.

"Ask me what I want, Raven."

"What do you want, Damien?"

"I want you beside me at night. I want to wake up with you wrapped around me like a little kitten, happy and content. I want to push aside your lotion bottles on the vanity so I can find the toothpaste, listen to you humming as you cook in the kitchen. I want to go grocery shopping with you, argue over who ate the last of the popcorn and what movie we're going to watch."

Her eyes glistened.

"I want to make love to you every day. Listen to you laugh. Watch over you and know you're safe." I ran my thumbs under her eyes, catching the tears that were spilling over. "I want to live my life with you *now*, Raven. That's how we're going to end up, so why not begin right away? Why wait for our happiness?"

"I make you happy?"

With a groan, I pulled her into my lap. "Yes, you do. Very much so. Don't go back to your place, Raven. Stay with me. Let me love you. Love me back. Please."

When she didn't reply, I tapped her nose. "Tell me what you're thinking in that beautiful head of yours."

"That I want this. More than anything."

"I'm not your ex, Raven. I'm never going to hurt you that way."

"I know."

"Tell me."

"What if, after all this worry ends, and we start living just a normal life where you don't care that I'm out alone or late coming home from school, you realize it was a mistake to move so fast?"

I had to laugh. Leaning down, I kissed her, holding her face in my hands. "First off, I will never not care if you're late, and I will worry myself sick every time you're out without me. As for a normal life, I think we're anything *but* normal. But I want that, baby. With you. I love you. You consume me, and it's not because of the situation or the worry. I adore everything about you, and I want you in my life. Full stop."

"Really?"

"I will always be overprotective. Worried. It's part of who I am. My training and my past only heightened it. I worry about Sofia, my mom, my men, but the way I worry about you tells me how imperative it is to me that you're in my life." I rested my forehead on hers. "Stay, Raven."

She slid her arms around my neck. "Yes."

I pulled her tight to my chest, our mouths melding. She tasted of the sweetness of the cookies she'd eaten, the hint of coffee, and her. Raven.

I deepened the kiss, feeling the euphoria of the moment fill me. She was going to stay. I got to keep her. Love her. Protect her. She belonged to me.

Mine.

She shifted, and I lifted her so she straddled me. Our mouths never separated, the need to feel her lips on mine paramount. I groaned as she slid her hand under my shirt, drifting her fingers over my torso and running her hands up to my pecs. She whimpered as I ground against her, my cock hard and pressing. I slid my hand up her legs, taking her pretty skirt higher, teasing the soft skin of her thighs. I traced the edges of her lacy underwear, pleased when she widened her legs.

I broke from her mouth. "You want my fingers, Raven? You want me to touch you?"

"Always," she gasped. "Please, Damien."

I buried my head into her neck, kissing and licking along the elegant column, dragging my mouth across her collarbone as I dipped under the lace and found her slick and ready.

"Oh, my girl wants me," I crooned, parting her folds and caressing her already hard little clit. She gasped, gripping the back of my neck. I strummed her, smiling as she began to undulate her hips, wanting more of my touch. I pressed my thumb to her nub and slipped two fingers inside, thrusting slowly.

"Yes," she pleaded. "Oh fuck, Damien. *Just like that.* Touch me. Rub me. Oh God, *fuck* me."

I loved it when she got vocal. Talked a little dirty. Told me what she wanted. I moved my fingers faster, watching the pleasure ripple across her face, her back arching as she began to shake and whimper my name. I bent and sucked a nipple through the thin material of her blouse, giving in to my desire and tearing it open, the small buttons hitting the floor and rolling away. I pushed down her bra, her full breasts spilling over, and I sucked her nipples until they were red and stiff from my mouth. I fisted her long hair in my hand and pulled on it, the whole time working her with my other hand. She moaned and whimpered, whispered my name, and pleaded in a breathy voice that drove me insane with desire.

"Like that, Raven? You want more?"

"Yes," she half sobbed. "Your cock. I want your cock."

I waited until she was writhing, begging. I lifted my hips, and between us, we yanked down my sweats, my engorged cock springing free, already weeping for her. I raised her, sliding in slowly, watching as she took me in, her need and desire evident. Fused together, I placed a hand on her, my fingers spread wide on the bare skin of her back. "Ride me, baby. Take what you want from me."

She gripped my shoulders. Began to move. I held her hips, watching, groaning at the sight of my cock disappearing into her over and again. Sucked her nipples, biting gently at the soft skin. Pulled her close and kissed her. Clasped her hips harder and began moving her faster. She cried out, locking down around me. That set off my orgasm, and I thrust into her wildly, gripping her hard as I roared out in intense pleasure. My balls tightened, my orgasm burning through me. I felt everything tenfold. Our slick skin sliding together. Her hot breath in my mouth. Her pussy milking me, the flutters of her muscles gripping me like a lover's embrace inside her. Everything was sharp, clear, and intense. And then… there was peace.

I leaned back, gasping for breath, holding her

close. The air around us cooled our overheated skin. My mind drifted, my body sated. Her head was tucked into my neck, her beautiful hair tickling my skin.

"Okay, Raven?" I managed to ask.

She lifted her head, her sleepy gaze meeting mine. "Oh yeah, I'm good."

I kissed her softly. "That's *our* normal, baby. And that's how we're going to be together."

She snuggled closer. "Okay, then."

"Okay."

We pulled up to the school, Raven looking excited. I peered up at the overcast sky, the sun struggling to break through the clouds. "I hope the rain holds off."

"It's supposed to, until around four. We'll be back at the school well before then."

We got out of the car, and I stood with the other parents and volunteers, watching Raven and Deb organize their little charges. They explained patiently that every group had a leader and a follower. There were four groups of five children, and ten adults. Each of us would be assigned to a group with one adult at the head and one at the end of the rope the children would hold on to. We would stay together as much as possible. They had mapped the route in the zoo, Deb coming to my apartment, where they spent hours planning every detail. I had smiled, watching and listening to them, thinking they were as excited as the kids. I brought in pizza, made sure they had wine, and even asked about Stew. Deb smiled, obviously still infatuated.

"He's great. Away a lot the last couple of weeks at another new office they are setting up out west," she explained. "But he says he'll be around more after next week. We can do dinner!"

I nodded and didn't commit. We couldn't avoid it forever, but a little longer for sure. Then Raven either had to tell Deb her true feelings or decide to put up with him on occasion. If they were serious, Raven was going to have to get used to him or never see her friend. I knew she would hate that idea.

A short while later, we loaded up the school bus, the children excited, the parents amused as they watched the kids waving to cars, fidgeting in their seats with anticipation, and talking about the animals they would get to see. I leaned close to Raven, who was seated in front of me.

"Last time I was on a school bus, I was sixteen."

"Was it a school trip?"

"We were headed to a basketball tournament."

She turned her head slightly. "Did you misbehave?"

"Never," I insisted. "But the captain got in trouble. He dressed his girlfriend as a player and snuck her onto the bus. Made out with her in the back seat. Got caught."

After a quick glance around that no one was looking, I pressed closer, brushing my mouth to her neck. "We can reenact it later if you want. I'd love to make out with you in the back of the bus. Or maybe behind a bush at the zoo while all the little buggers are busy."

She shivered, then used her best teacher voice. "Behave, Mr. DeSalvo. I don't want to have to put you in time-out."

With a low chuckle, I dropped another fast kiss to her skin. "I'd make out there with you too."

Then I sat back. She shook her head and looked out the window, saying something to the little girl she sat next to. But I saw the soft color on her cheeks and the way she was smiling.

Mission accomplished.

We broke for lunch about 11:30. The morning had been busy, but fun. Everything was going well. The kids were well-behaved, and the biggest problem we had faced was all the bathroom breaks that were needed. Someone constantly needed to stop and never all at once. But Raven and Deb were patient, as were all the parents, and I just went with the flow. I was watchful, especially when it was Raven taking a child into one of the restrooms. But everything seemed fine. I saw nothing suspicious in the park.

Families and couples strolling, lots of kids, tourists, and locals alike, taking pictures, enjoying the day. Guided groups, staff members walking around. Maintenance crews keeping the park clean of litter. Nothing was out of place. Still, I remained vigilant, staying close to Raven, watching her, a niggle of anxiety pulling at me. I had a few men and women around the park, and they were watching too. Mike and Tracey were volunteers. Raven had trackers on her, and we could all see where she was. I had eyes on her every moment I could.

I had learned in my business that when things seemed good on the surface, it often led to chaos. I wanted to be prepared.

I sat next to Raven at lunch, enjoying the simple sandwiches, cut-up veggies, and cookies that were provided. The kids all ate well, and I made sure Raven got a chance to eat, although she was far more concerned that Jenny wasn't being picked on by Tommy or that John wasn't eating Lori's sandwich. I played referee with a couple of them while she ate her lunch, winking at her across the table and making her blush again. I loved doing that.

We continued on our tour, the clouds moving in, the kids a bit more restless and tired. I understood why they chose the morning for the large part of the day, and we only had an hour or so left in the excursion. I had a feeling the bus would be pretty quiet on the way back to the school. Maybe I could make out with Raven in the back. The thought made me grin.

"Ms. Raven—I have to go!" Cindy's voice piped up. "Now!" she added, panicked.

Raven swooped her up in her arms and headed for the restroom up ahead. I took the end of her rope, and we all paused to look at the ducks swimming across from the building. A few moments passed, and I grew restless. I hated it when she was out of my sight for very long, even though I knew each trip was five or six minutes. I glanced at my watch after seven minutes had passed, about to call to Deb to hold both ropes, when I saw the door open. Except it wasn't Raven who came out. Only Cindy—and she was crying. She hurried our way, and I rushed toward her. "What is it? Where is Ms. Raven?"

She wiped her face. "I don't know. I heard her talking to someone, but she wasn't there when I came out. I tried to wash my hands, but I got water everywhere," she whimpered.

"Mike!" I yelled. "Take over!"

I burst through the door, surveying the empty room. I hit my alarm, knowing it would signal everyone I had in the park. They knew if I activated it, Raven was in trouble. I barked into my headpiece. "Missing. I repeat, Raven is missing. All eyes open wide."

I headed to the back, shocked to see another door at the end of the stalls. It hadn't been marked on the map of all the entrances and exits. I rushed through it, back into the park. It was semi-hidden in the bushes. I ran through them, my gaze taking in the scene. Families, kids, couples. A maintenance man emptying a garbage can, adding to the bin he was pushing.

No one running, nothing suspicious—which made everything suspicious. I hurried back into the restroom, calling Egan. "I need every camera. Get everything. Call the park security and get them on it." I headed back out to the maintenance man, who had moved forward. "Did you see anyone come out of that restroom?"

The older man looked up, startled. "What?"

I pointed to the restroom. "Over there—did you see anything?"

He wiped his rheumy eyes. "No. This was on the ground, though." He reached into the bin and held up Raven's purse. "I was gonna take it to the office."

Cursing, I grabbed it and headed back to the restroom. I looked around, seeing what I hadn't in my rush through the room. Some specks of blood on the edge of the sink. The imprint of a set of men's shoes in the dust on the floor. The wastebin knocked over as if there'd been a struggle. Mike came in. "How did this happen?"

"Back door," I growled. "It wasn't on the list because it wasn't supposed to be in use. Someone broke the lock." I passed a hand over my face. "He's been here the whole day, watching. Waiting." I looked at Mike. "He got her."

I had to lock down my feelings of panic. The emotion I felt for Raven. She didn't need Damien her lover right now. She needed Damien the man of Hidden Justice to find her. Save her.

A short while later, we were ensconced in the security room at the zoo. The children were gone, a story that Ms. Raven was ill pacifying them. Mike and Tracey ensured they were all on the bus and headed home. Safe.

We sat in front of the multiple screens, scouring them. My people had torn the park apart, searching for her. We found nothing. No trace of her or Andy. Somehow, he had simply blended in. I hadn't given Andy enough credit for his persistence or his intellect. Because there was no doubt, this was Andy.

Raven's tracker wasn't working. It had been blocked somehow. As we scanned camera after camera, Egan called me over. "I got something."

I watched Raven walk into the restroom. Another camera caught the maintenance man as he stepped out of the bushes by the back door, pushing his bin. I watched in horror as moments later, I spoke to him, then he disappeared.

"She was right there," I murmured. "Right

fucking there under some bags." My breathing picked up. "That was Andy?"

"In disguise," Egan murmured. "I'm trying to track him with all the cameras."

The maintenance man moved through the park slowly, never rushing. He passed some of my people, not even reacting. He veered off the road and disappeared off-camera.

"Find him," I growled, already dispatching men to the location.

"He had this all planned. He followed us all day, waiting for the right moment. He hid in plain sight. I fucking talked to him." I grabbed my hair. "He gave me her purse, and she was right there. Right fucking there!" I roared.

He had access to the buildings. He knew his way around. He'd planned every step of this. He hadn't gone away the way Raven had hoped. He'd stepped back and planned this out. He knew he would find a moment he could grab her.

But how? How did he know we'd be here? How was he doing this?

"How did he turn off her tracker?"

Egan shifted. "I think the blood we saw was her head hitting the sink. I think when that happened, the tracker was broken. It was in her earring, right?"

"One of them, yes."

The thought of how hard she would have hit her head, that she was hurt, held hostage by Andy, made me ill. Once again, I had to force down the terror and focus on finding her.

We were given more room, and I sat beside Egan, helping track Andy down. I fixated on the task, refusing to give in to my panic. Raven needed me now, and I would not let her down.

Ten minutes later, we had traced his steps. We caught the tail end of the cart as he went off the main path, and we found him walking into an old, unused shed. Seconds later, he emerged, his disguise gone, his usual hoodie in place. He carried a heavy bag over his shoulder and jogged around the building, only to disappear again. Egan began scanning the perimeter cameras and pointed. "There!"

Andy emerged from behind the building and headed to a small, inconspicuous gray car that was parked in the bushes. He tossed the bag into the trunk and slammed the lid, hurrying to the driver's seat. Knowing Raven was inside that bag, I became more furious. Seeing the careless way he handled her made my hands clench. I would be repaying every bump, bruise, and injury he caused her, tenfold. The car lurched forward, disappearing off-camera.

"How long ago?" I asked.

"Twenty minutes."

"Did you get a plate?"

"No. I can hack into traffic cameras. But I need to get to the office."

"Send all this footage there."

"Done."

"We need to go there *right now*." My people wouldn't find her here. We were too late.

He pressed a comforting hand to my shoulder. "We will find her. End him," he added. "He will pay for touching what is yours."

"Yes." My gaze drifted to the screen.

"Hang on, Raven. I'm coming," I whispered.

I could only pray she knew that and would be strong until I got to her. I needed her to be.

I was terrified to think of what would happen if I was too late.

CHAPTER TWENTY

Raven

I woke, pain the first conscious feeling. Terror was my second. Caution, the third. My head ached, my body was sore, and my cheek felt as if it was on fire. I slowly opened my eyes, only seeing blackness. The ground beneath me was cold, damp, solid. I tried to flex my feet and hands, surprised to find them working. Something cold and heavy was on my neck, and I lifted my hands, shocked to feel a thick metal collar around my throat. I traced the edges, feeling the weight of the chain it was attached to. Tamping down my fear, I carefully sat up, dizzy and disoriented, my stomach lurching as I moved. There was a wall behind me, and I leaned against it, wetting my dry lips and swallowing. Struggling to remember what happened. Desperately trying not to scream. I knew it would bring someone running, and I was certain I didn't want that.

Taking Cindy to the bathroom was my last coherent thought. Rinsing my hands off in the sink, hearing a noise, and glancing up, shocked to see an older man behind me. "I think you have the wrong restroom," I said. "The men's room—"

He smiled, an evil, twisted smile, and raised his arm. A wooden mallet was the last thing I saw before pain exploded in my head. The feel of the cold, hard porcelain sink hitting my face was all I remembered before the dark claimed me.

I hadn't recognized the older man. I shook my head as a shiver ran through me.

Who was he?

I had my answer a few moments later. The scraping of a heavy door echoed in the room, and dim light spilled in. Lifting my head, I blinked, trying to focus. Through the pain and the tears in my eyes, it was difficult. Until he spoke, and ice ran through my veins.

"Well, well. What have we here?"

Andy.

I stifled a sob, too frightened to speak. To make a sound.

"Tsk. Cat got your tongue?" he asked snidely, advancing.

I curled up as tightly as I could, unsure what he was going to do next.

He hunched down, his face close to mine. "You treated me like a dog, Raven. Threw me a few scraps and ran, leaving me hungry." He lifted the chain, pulling on it. "I thought I'd give you a taste of your own medicine."

I couldn't stop the whimper that escaped my throat.

"Not so tough when your bodyguard isn't around, are you?" He laughed, the high-pitched sound making me grimace.

"Please, Andy, don't do this," I begged, my voice hoarse. "Let me go."

"After all the trouble I went through to get you?" he asked. "No."

"Damien will find me. He will punish you. If you let me go, I'll make sure he doesn't touch you."

He laughed again, shaking his head. "Still lying. I'll cure you of that."

"He'll find you. He's going to be so angry," I said, trying to sound threatening, but instead, my voice was weak. Pitiful.

"Not going to happen, *Ms. Raven*," he mocked. "You can't find what doesn't exist."

I frowned. "I don't understand."

"Exactly," he spat. "None of you did." He tugged on the chain, sending me to the ground, the chill seeping into my skin.

"You are going to stay here and rot until you learn to love me. By the time I'm finished with you, I will own you. Every single inch of you. Forget about everything and everybody else, Raven. Your inept bodyguard will never find you. No one will. He'll forget and move on. You'll be mine once you accept the darkness." He strode to the door. "And me."

The sound of the metal slamming sent shudders through me.

I shut my eyes, letting my tears soak the ground.

"Damien," I whispered. "Please. Please."

Another sob escaped.

"Find me."

DAMIEN

"What the fuck are we missing?" I yelled, standing and pacing the room. It was four a.m., and I had nothing. No clues. No way to trace Raven.

Egan had located the car on the traffic cams. We got the license plate, only to find it had been reported stolen and was found not far off the exit we traced it to. I had Leo go and dust it for prints, which he was running now. There were so many, it was going to take time. I didn't expect anything, but I was desperate.

"How can someone not leave a trail?" I ranted. "No digital, no paper, nothing. I fucking need a crumb—something to go on!"

Egan sat back. "No trail? Easy. By not being the person you said you were."

I sat down heavily. "I know Andy Smith is an alias. But the man exists—I saw him. But who the fuck is he?"

Egan grasped my shoulder, shaking it. "We'll find him. But you need to sleep. You will not do her any good if you cannot think from exhaustion."

"I'll sleep when she is home."

"I think you should sleep now." A voice came from the doorway.

I looked up, startled. "Julian?" I asked, confused. "Marcus?"

They walked in, looking serious.

I stood. "What the hell? How did you get here so fast?"

Marcus shook my hand. "We were already on the way for another reason. We detoured when Egan called."

Julian stepped forward, hugging me hard. "You helped me find my wife. You took down the bastard holding her hostage. I'm here to help you find Raven. We both are."

Marcus nodded. "But Egan is right. You need to rest."

"I can't. Not when I know she's out there, scared, hurt, and God knows what else."

Julian began to speak, but I held up my hand. "You didn't rest until we got Tally back."

He nodded. "Then let's get at it."

Hours later, I rubbed my eyes in frustration. "Whoever this asshole is, he is good. He's fucking invisible."

"Have you spoken to this Stewart guy who arranged the trip? Asked him who all he told about it?" Julian mused. "Maybe Andy overheard somehow?"

"No. He flies back today. I assume Deb will have contacted him and told him what happened, but I don't know for sure." I rummaged around my desk. "I have his card here. I'll leave him a message to call."

I called the number, leaving a message. "I'll call the office and leave a number on his voice mail there as well." I frowned as I studied the card. "Huh. Only his cell number—I hadn't noticed that before." I snorted. "Not that I looked. Stewart and I will never be buddy-buddy." I typed in the web address on the card, bringing up the page. It took me directly to his profile, which had a picture and his bio plus his contact info.

"Jesus, this is badly done. They need a website overhaul," I muttered, hitting the home page button and getting nowhere.

Julian took the card. "I'll do it. I need to make a call as well. You concentrate on those fingerprints." I had taken some to cut down on the time we needed. We were running every print Leo got through the

Hidden Justice portals. It was slow work, but it had to be done. Julian left the room, closing the door behind him for privacy. I was sure he was calling Tally to check on her and the kids.

The room was quiet except for the clicking of keys, the odd grunt or noise, or the printer spitting out something we needed. The scent of coffee was heavy in the air, the aroma of the sandwiches they had brought in lingering. At their insistence, I ate the turkey club they ordered for me, the food tasting like ashes in my mouth. But I knew they were right and I needed the energy. Leo was downstairs running the building, doing what he could from his computer. Egan was trying every camera he could think to access to find an angle that would give us a hint of the kind of car Raven had been transferred to and where it went.

I tossed aside another set of prints that came up with nothing. I had six others running. Egan glanced at his phone and left the room.

I checked on Raven's still unworking tracker, then studied the footage we had again, looking for a clue. Any clue. My computer beeped as a hit came in, and I pulled up the information.

"I may have something."

I scanned the screen, suddenly on my feet as adrenaline flowed into my body. "Fingerprints came back with the name John Andrew Allan," I read out loud. "Files are sealed."

Marcus looked over my shoulder. "Not to us."

I slammed my hand on the table. "No known address. Motherfucker—this is him. I know it is. The mug shot looks like Andy. Younger, but it's him."

Julian walked in with Egan. "I have something too, Damien."

"What?"

"Stewart Anderson doesn't exist. He mirrored a website from a company in the States and dropped himself in there. He created a whole fake profile."

"But I met him."

"I think we found your crumb." He paused. "I think you met Andy's alias."

I gaped at him. "How is that possible?" I asked. "They look nothing alike."

"Or so you thought." He handed me the sketch Egan had done of Andy, then the picture he'd obviously printed off the fake website.

"Nothing alike," I said again.

He handed me another piece of paper. "Look without the glasses, the colored contacts, or the wig."

I stared down at the picture. "Holy fuck."

"Take away the prosthetic add-ons, the scruff, and the padded shoulders..." He trailed off.

"It's him." I stood, rage setting in. "You mean to tell me I had dinner with that fucker—that he sat across the table, acting like someone else, planning all this? That he set this all up?"

"I think so. I think he does this a lot. Andy,

Stewart, the maintenance man. He pretends to be someone else."

"But how is he living?"

"Under yet another fake name and life. Now we have to find him." Julian rested his hand on my shoulder. "And when Stewart calls you, and he will, because we all know how these psychos work, you have to pretend to still be in the dark. Almost beg him for help. He has to think he's ahead of us. Still controlling the game. Let him get careless."

"Why can't we go find him and beat him until he tells us?" I snapped.

"Because he's already underground. I called the real financial company, and they have never heard of him, which came as no surprise. He will respond to your message as Stewart and pretend to be shocked. Horrified. Drop some red herrings about who he told so we can chase our own tail. We're going to trace the call and see if we can find where he is. Then we find Raven."

"I can't believe I didn't see it." I yanked on my hair. "How the fuck did I miss this?"

"He is an expert manipulator. Add an accomplished hacker with a flair for acting? It's a scary trifecta," Marcus mused.

Julian nodded. "You missed it because you're not a field agent, Damien. You weren't trained for this. Your focus was on Raven. On protecting her." He shook my shoulder. "There's a reason doctors don't operate on their spouses. You can't separate those feelings. You can't be an objective doctor and a loving husband at the same time. It's the same here. It was for me and for Marcus."

He ran a hand through his hair. "This man is a genius at disguise. To be honest, I don't know if any of us would have caught on. He's too good at the game."

"I should have. He was right fucking there, and I missed it."

"Stop," Julian insisted. "Stop blaming yourself, and concentrate on finding him."

I hung my head. He was right.

"I wonder where else he has infiltrated your life? Or Raven's?" Marcus muttered.

Egan made a noise and sat at the computer, his fingers flying over the keys. He was muttering in Romanian, the noises harsh and furious.

"What?" I asked.

"His sealed file is downloading. But there is a connection here. One we didn't see before." He turned his computer so it faced us. "I kept going back to the exit he took. I've been on it myself. So have you. It's close to the off-site facility The Real Connection uses."

"But we spent days checking and rechecking the staff of both places. They all came up clean."

"We didn't dig deep enough." He hit a few more

keys. "We took someone at face value. Older, married, wanting to help."

A picture of Jeff Drew that Egan had snapped when he wasn't looking flashed on the screen.

"Think about it," Egan stated. "The sweating, his nerves. How he didn't want us close. A heavy body suit, prosthetics, and a skullcap. A different pair of contacts. Another set of glasses."

"Hiding in plain sight," Marcus mumbled.

It hit me. "His cologne. I smelled it on Andy that night I cornered him. It was fainter because we were outside, but that's why it was familiar."

"Yes."

Suddenly, other pieces fell into place.

"He gave us free access because there never were any profiles to find. He back-doored into his own system to find Raven. Made what looked like a regular profile and moved in on her. He would be the only one with access to that sort of control. He wiped his own trail."

"You said she spoke with a few men. Met a couple for coffee?"

"Yes. She said they were too aggressive. Wanted more than she was looking for. Came on too strong. She liked Andy's gentler disposition. At least until his true nature showed."

"I bet they were all Jeff. If we could get into her profile, I think we'd find he'd blocked any access other than his own. His aggression became too much for him to hide."

"Are we talking split personalities?"

"No. We're talking a stalker. Someone I think has done this before. He's obsessed the way Zander was over Missy. He has access, obviously money, and the ability," Marcus stated.

"And now he has her."

"Not for long."

"Jesus, is Deb in danger?"

Egan spoke. "We'll get eyes on her, but I would say not. Unless he knows his cover is blown."

"We can't let that happen. My God, she is going to freak out when she finds out who the man she was falling for really is."

Marcus stood. "Better now than later." He rolled up his sleeves. "We're going to do what we do best. Find him and get Raven back. Fast."

"And I'm taking him out."

No one argued.

I wouldn't have listened if they had.

CHAPTER TWENTY-ONE

Damien

Now that we had our crumb, our information on John Allan grew quickly.

Egan and I dug in deep. Julian made use of all his contacts. Marcus assimilated all the information. Hours later, we had our profile.

"Okay," Marcus began. "Here we go. John Allan —aka Stewart, Jeffrey, and Andy—that we know of. IQ puts him at the genius level. Wealthy family, only child. Mom died when he was young. Father never remarried. School notes indicated he got bored easily. Needed distracting all the time. That was a constant all his life. Decent kid until he hit his teens. Always into computers, games, and—" he lifted his head, meeting my gaze "—drama club."

"Obviously kept that up."

"Yep. So, he started with petty theft, bullying at school, bothering the girls. He was accused of lurking, being a peeping tom, stealing from the lockers of the girls he liked. He got attached easily, and they never returned his affection. He was written up several times. Kicked out of three schools. At sixteen, charges were filed for forcible confinement, uttering threats, among other things. The charges were dropped, the family of the girl who instigated the charges left town, and of course, the records were sealed since he was a juvenile. Egan found a large payout in the old bank records he dug up."

"So, his father paid off the family, and they moved." I surmised.

"The father paid off a lot of things." Marcus cleared his throat. "Didn't do him any favors."

"Never does," Julian inserted.

"John escalated. Hacking. Drugs. Dropped out of school. At nineteen, his father died of a heart attack. Kid became a billionaire overnight. He dropped out of sight for a while, then he disappeared. Completely off the grid. The money was gone, and so was he." He paused and took a sip of water. "I noted one drama teacher's notes from class stated that John had *'the ability to lose himself so deeply into character, it was almost as if he became that person.'* I think our boy likes to be other people as much as possible."

"So, he didn't disappear," I said. "He became someone else."

"Yes."

I rubbed my face. "How often has he done this?"

Egan grunted. "Probably more than we want to know. I'm looking at similar cases in other cities, but I need time to check them all out. I would say his obsessive tendencies reached epic proportions when he found Raven."

"The only persona that seems constant is Jeff Drew. He pays taxes. Owns property. A decent bank account. Employees. Even has a driver's license, although I'm certain all of them are fake and planted. He has his wealth hidden, somewhere offshore, no doubt. He certainly has the brains and knowledge to make that happen. I think if we dug deep enough, we'd find he was 'born' around the time John disappeared." Marcus sighed. "But I think he only uses that as a cover. I'm sure he is out in the world under many other faces."

"Why was he so careless with Stew's persona?"

"You said Raven and Deb made plans the day before. He wouldn't have much time, so he copied and pasted. Probably assumed no one would look that hard. He would have added other layers the longer the persona stayed around. He wanted to be in that coffee shop and 'bump' into Deb." Marcus rubbed his chin. "Made a quick profile. Printed a few cards. Done. I think he was starting to get careless. First mistake. Second, not wiping down the car. Both have gone in our favor."

"I thought him a bit odd. Raven disliked him.

Said he gave her the creeps. I should have listened to that."

"You can't blame yourself. She spent time with Andy—you didn't. On some level, her psyche knew it was him, and she was reacting. But she didn't recognize him. That was the point. He was flaunting how close he could get to her without her knowing."

I shuddered, wondering how close he was now. I couldn't even think of that or I would go mental.

Julian drained his coffee mug. "He's having the time of his life right now. Think about it. He's acting different parts daily. Fooling people. Using his intelligence to stalk someone, while making more money doing it. It's astounding how much money the dating site makes. I think it's all a game to him. And he's done it before. When he gets bored with it, he simply disappears and adopts new personas. He has the money to reinvent himself. The brains to know how to circumvent the system. No doubt he has legit-looking documents for every character. When he needs more, he gets them. Life is just a huge stage to him, and he enjoys the power of playing the game."

"So, Raven is what in this game?" I asked.

Marcus joined in. "An obsession. I think somehow related to his past. Maybe she reminds him of someone he was infatuated with when he was younger. His mother. I have no idea."

Egan interrupted our discussion. "Listen up. The Real Connection is owned by a numbered company.

Which is owned by another one and so on. Easy for him to dismantle and move. But I have traced two properties to one of the companies. The building where his off-site backups are stored, and a place not far from there. An older house. The building where The Real Connection is located is leased under Jeff Drew's name. There is an apartment there as well. Everything else is hidden."

He moved the screen so we could see his monitor. "I think she's in the house. It's set back from the road, with a gate and a garage that has a private entrance leading into the house. He could have driven right in, shut the door, and moved her undetected. He has security monitors and cameras around the property. That's our best bet."

"We need to override those cameras and system."

He grinned. "Good thing we're experts at that."

"I want some recon too. We need pictures and more information. And it has to happen fast."

He nodded. "We need to make sure he isn't there. He'll be watching—carefully."

Egan pursed his lips. "When we met with Jeff, I noticed he scanned his index and middle fingers to get into the room. I'm willing to bet all his security is controlled the same way." He grinned. "And we have those fingerprints. With some planning and luck, we can override his system and get what we need."

"We need to do this quickly."

Julian met my eyes. "We will. But we have to do it

right. We're only going to get one chance. If he's spooked…" He didn't finish the sentence.

I swallowed down my fear. "I know. He'll disappear, and so will she."

My phone buzzed, and I glanced down. "That's Deb. I wonder if he is with her."

"If so, keep your cool and arrange a meeting for later today. Play the broken, worried man. If you can keep him busy, we can get in and out and then make our plan to get her back. But we have to be sure she is there. If we tip him off, he could move her and vanish."

I shut my eyes and swallowed. Julian was right, but it was going to take everything in me not to beat the shit out of him the instant I saw him. But I had to do it—for Raven.

I answered the phone, making my voice strained and rough. "Hello."

I steeled myself in the car, inhaling deeply. Julian's voice sounded in my ear. "Keep him as long as you can, Damien. Egan's at the house, Marcus is at the off-site building, and I'm at the apartment. If he gets any alerts, clear your throat twice. We'll all be listening."

"Yep."

"Stay calm. This is for Raven. Think of it as an

undercover sting. Remove your personal feelings. I know it's hard. I had to do it for Tally. But Raven needs you to do this."

I straightened my shoulders. "Right."

"Go get him."

I got out of the car and headed to the coffee shop where Deb and Stewart waited. Deb had been upset on the phone, telling me how horrified "Stew" was about the situation and wanting to help. It was typical narcissistic perp behavior. Insinuating themselves into the situation. I told her I wanted to talk to her and Stew if that was possible, and we agreed to meet at the coffee shop. I schooled my features, tamping down my revulsion and hate.

In the coffee shop, Deb was beside Stew, her eyes red and swollen. She offered me a sad smile and a hug before I sat down. I met Stew's eyes, forcing down my real emotions and trying to project worry and confusion.

"Stewart," I murmured.

"Damien," he said, his voice dripping with fake concern. "I don't know what to say. How can I help?"

I spouted my practiced lines. "I'm at my wit's end. I know I'm grasping at straws, but can you think of any time you were discussing the field trip where someone, this man we're looking for, might have overheard you?"

He was a great actor. He paused, seemingly searching his thoughts. He picked up his coffee cup,

MELANIE MORELAND

taking a sip, pursing his lips, furrowing his brow. "Obviously, the donors, the sponsors, people at the firm. I don't recall mentioning it otherwise. I wasn't looking for attention or praise."

It was all I could do not to lean over the table, grab his collar, shake him, and scream in his face, calling him a liar. Instead, I simply nodded.

"Can you tell me about this man? What he looks like?"

"Late twenties, wears a hoodie, shaggy hair. I only saw him once," I said gruffly. "Kinda homely if I recall right," I added, wanting to goad him.

A flash of annoyance crossed his face, and I picked up my coffee to hide my smirk. He wasn't *that* good.

"Doesn't ring a bell."

"Do you have any clues where she is?" Deb asked, her voice rough from crying. "I'm so frightened for her."

I paused, fiddling with my cup.

"In the off-site," Marcus hissed in my ear.

I took another sip, shifting my shoulders, trying to look uncomfortable. Stew had no reaction. No alarms went off.

"Drone over house. Getting info on security," Egan whispered. "Gonna try to send in a heat source detector."

"Mother lode in apartment," Julian murmured. "Taking video."

Stewart regarded me, nothing alerting him. I set down my cup and wiped at my eyes. Then I gave an Oscar-worthy performance. I leaned forward, earnest and upset.

"Nothing, Deb. The man doesn't exist. The police have zilch. Some blurry footage that might be nothing. No clues. I don't even know if it was Andy or a random act."

"But you run a security firm."

I scrubbed my face. "I can protect her if she's here and someone comes at her. My men are brawny and strong. I don't hire them for their brains." I tapped my head. "Some of them are pretty empty up here."

"I heard that," Leo muttered in my ear.

I coughed into my hand to cover my smirk. "We protect celebrities, oversee events. I'm not a cop or some kind of detective. I have nothing to go on."

"Have you thought of the fact that perhaps she went willingly?" Stewart asked, his eyes narrowed. "Perhaps she was tired of your overprotective attitude."

I was getting to him. I noticed his eyeglasses were wrong. As Stew, he'd worn sleek black frames. Jeff wore rounder ones. He was wearing those. Another small error.

"It crossed my mind. But she would have told me and broken it off."

"Are you sure? Some women like to play games."

Deb turned to him. "Raven isn't like that, and I don't like your tone."

He put his arm around her, backtracking. "Sorry, dollface. I was just playing devil's advocate."

I waved my hands. "It's fine. I wondered when we found her purse if she didn't leave it behind so I couldn't trace her phone. But I realized how stupid that sounded."

"Do you have any other trackers on her?"

Another mistake. A finance guy wouldn't know about shit like that.

"Other trackers?" I asked with a frown. "I'm not a PI. My company protects people from overzealous fans or exes with grudges. We're not in the spy business." I huffed out a sorrowful sigh. "I wish I were."

"Right," he said, lifting his cup to his lips. But I saw his smirk.

"Out," Marcus whispered.

"Done," Julian said. "Thank God. I need a shower."

Stew frowned, looking at his phone. I cleared my throat twice, pounding my chest. "Sorry, the coffee went down wrong."

"Sorry. That was me. We should be fine now. I need ten more minutes, Damien. Stall." Egan's voice was low.

"Deb, can you think of anything unusual?" I asked.

Stew relaxed, putting away his phone, and I focused on Deb.

"No. Nothing. Everything seemed fine. Then she was gone."

I nodded. "Vanished."

"You have to find her," she whispered. "I feel terrible recommending that site to her. I had met some nice guys through it. It brought her nothing but trouble."

I patted her hand. "You couldn't have known. The guy who owned it had no idea he had a nutjob infiltrating his system."

"He couldn't help?"

"No, we helped him—well, my guy helped him tighten his security, but he had nothing. This Andy was too smart for us all." I almost choked saying that, but it worked since the last part came out muffled as if I was holding back tears.

Deb covered her mouth, stifling a sob. Stew gave a great performance of comforting her.

"It's in the hands of the police," I lied. "I have nothing to go on."

"Don't give up."

I met Stew's shrewd gaze, lifting one shoulder as if to say "No idea how to respond."

He nodded as if in sympathy. I wanted to wipe that superior look off his face with my fist.

"You're not tapping today, Stew. No ringing

sounds in your car?" I asked, trying to keep the snideness out of my voice.

"Oh, ah, I lost it on my trip. A new one is coming. I'm just putting up with it," he lied.

Another error. He was losing his focus, which was exactly what we needed.

"How annoying that must be. Where were you again? I forgot."

"In the States."

Deb frowned. "I thought it was Calgary."

"Both, actually. Two trips in one," he lied again, his voice terse. "But we're not here to discuss boring finance. I want to help if I can."

"Out," Egan's faint voice rang in my ear.

"If I can think of something, I'll be in touch. Your cell number is the best way to contact you, I assume? Not direct at the office?"

"I'm working from home this week, so if you need me, call. I'll be sure to answer."

"Is that close?"

"Yep. I can walk."

I was done. "Good thing. Driving in this city is a bitch."

"I know," he agreed. "I walk as much as I can."

My phone rang, and I answered.

Leo responded to my terse greeting.

"Get back to the office."

"Problem?"

"Yeah, one of the clients is causing a ruckus. I

need you here," he said loudly. "You don't pay me enough to deal with this shit. And you need to cover a shift tonight. Dumbass Dave is drunk again."

Deb cringed, and Stew turned his head to hide his smirk. He now thought my men were deadbeats and I was a total idiot. A paper pusher.

Perfect.

I'd remind him of that just before I killed him.

I hung up. "I, ah, need to go."

"You'll be in touch?" Deb asked, grabbing my hand.

"When I hear anything." I met her eyes. She was upset and hurting, and I couldn't tell her a thing. I had to keep her in the dark and play Stew, Andy, whatever the fuck his name was, along.

"I'm sorry I couldn't protect her better," I said sincerely.

"Find her."

Stew draped his arm around her as I stood. I bent and kissed her cheek, clapping Stew on the shoulder firmly as I straightened. I felt the padding under his suit jacket. "Thank you," I murmured.

He nodded, looking serious and worried. "Anything," he replied.

Liar.

I shook my head in sorrow and walked out.

I slid into the car, hiding my smirk until I was clear of the coffee shop. The tracker I pressed into the material of his jacket was virtually invisible. Untraceable.

But we'd know where he was.

And where to find Raven.

"I'm coming, baby. Hold on."

CHAPTER TWENTY-TWO

Damien

"Jesus," I muttered, watching the video Julian had made. "I feel sick."

"He's beyond obsessed," Julian agreed. "The apartment was basically empty except two rooms." He paused. "The dressing room and the shrine."

One room was filled with costumes, wigs, props. A makeup table. Shoes, hats, glasses. He'd been at her school, posed as a custodian. A homeless man outside the grocery store she had noticed one night and gave money to. I recognized a hat I had seen a man wearing when we were "fighting" in the park. He'd watched us the whole time.

But the shrine was what frightened me. Pictures of Raven on every wall. Laughing, talking, teaching, walking, crying. Happy, sad, upset. Working at her desk. Teaching her kids. Playing with them outside.

Sitting beside me at dinner, my face blacked out with a marker. Anytime I was with her, my face was a black circle. Any of my staff caught in a picture with her had X's through them. There were a bunch of close-up ones I recognized from the dinner we'd gone to.

"His damn earpiece was a camera. Every time he tapped, it was another picture of her. The twisted bastard," I raged.

He had her schedule laid out. A scarf pinned to the wall she'd mentioned trying to find the other day. Chocolate bar wrappers I assumed he picked from her garbage. A calendar where he'd filled in "their" timeline. Chat #1. First sighting. First date. He referred to his stalking as *glimpses*. Each one was marked, the ink soaking so heavily into the paper it bled to the sheet below it.

And the scary part was the crushed daisies pinned everywhere. One for every time he got upset with her.

There were a lot of daisies.

I had to turn away from the phone.

"I took a lot of pictures," Julian murmured. "For evidence, if we need it."

Marcus spoke. "The off-site building is basically empty except for what you saw. He has massive storage potential not being used, but I assumed the room I was in housed all he wanted there. I would love to get into those computers." He shook his head. "Maybe once this is over. I have a feeling there are a lot of answers in those machines."

"You think he's done this before," I stated.

"Yes. Maybe not to this extent, but once he's taken care of, maybe a lot of other women's fears could be put to rest."

"Good idea."

"I did spot a large fireproof cabinet, but it was padlocked and I didn't want to draw attention to my presence by cutting it. Plus, no bolt cutters," Marcus added. "I think that is where he stores all his documents and files."

Julian nodded. "There was a smaller one in the apartment. I assume the ones he's using right now are locked in there."

I looked at Egan.

"I paused the cameras so they didn't pick up on the drone. I got some footage of the house, the grounds, and the outlay. All the drapes and blinds were shut. I sent in a heat source detector, and something inside was giving off a signal." He paused. "Not a strong one."

"She's cold," I said, tightening my hands into fists.

"Like Missy," Marcus added.

Egan nodded, remembering like me how we had found Marcus's wife that day.

"I was in and out as fast as I could. I got blueprints from hacking into old records, so we know the layout. I can run a program that will override the system so nothing shows when we go in. It will play a loop, so if he looks at the screen, he sees nothing.

There is a spot near the back that has little coverage we could access. You can go in while I monitor the system. I can guide you toward the heat source I locked on earlier, and away from him."

"Can we distract him?" I asked. "Maybe get him with Deb. Get in and out while he's gone?"

"We'd have to tell her. And have her covered while she's with him," Julian pointed out.

"Can she handle that?" Marcus asked. "She was already upset. If she knows the truth, can she remain calm and not tip him off?"

I sighed. "I don't know. Raven always said Deb wore her heart on her sleeve. She might find it difficult."

"Then we do it without a distraction."

"I could call him. Ask to meet him then not show up," I said. "As soon as he leaves the house, we move in. By the time he gets back, she'll be safe."

"That might work."

"Then let's make a plan."

RAVEN

Brilliant light filled the room I was trapped in, and I kept my head down, opening my eyes slowly to adjust to the brightness.

Since I'd been trapped in this god-awful room, it

had been the same. Total black or blinding light. Deadly silence or blaring, horrific music. Andy walking in, staring at me, walking out. A bottle of water put just beyond my reach so that I struggled and bruised my skin to get it, only to find it empty.

I had no idea how much time had passed. Minutes. Hours. Days, maybe. There was no way to track the minutes. Hours. I was thirsty. Hungry. My body ached. My neck was rubbed raw from the slightly too-tight metal wrapped around it. I was cold.

And angry.

Angry he got to me. Furious he thought he could treat me this way. Mad that he thought me so weak he believed darkness could break me. I refused to allow that to happen, and I wasn't going to beg him for anything. He watched me constantly. He didn't know I had seen the camera in the corner. The indicator light was covered, but a tiny pinprick of light shone through. I realized when I moved, it turned green, and he would be watching. Red was off. If I moved as slowly as possible, I could fool it. I stared in that direction in the dark, seething. My hatred for him built.

I blinked and opened my eyes, once again using the light to find any way of escaping. The room was about 10x10, and the only way in or out was the heavy steel door. My chain stopped me just short of reaching the door. And I knew it was locked. Still, I searched.

I heard the noise on the other side of the door and braced myself for Andy's entrance. Sometimes he walked in, stared, muttered, and left. Sometimes he rambled, telling me things about his life. Other times, he taunted me. Or threatened. But he never came close enough for me to strike or him to touch. That at least gave me comfort.

The door opened, and I gaped.

"Stew?" I asked, scrambling to my feet, ignoring the pain in my legs and back from the cold ground. "Oh my God, how did you get here? You have to help me!"

He stared, then smiled widely. When he spoke, I was confused.

"Why would that be, princess?" he asked in Andy's voice.

I blinked in confusion, shaking my head. But when I opened my eyes, it was still Stewart in front of me. "I-I don't understand."

"Of course you don't. And thanks to a quick meeting with him, neither does that dolt of a boyfriend of yours. He's lost. No idea where you went. No idea the man who had taken you was across the table." He tilted his head. "You're better off without him."

He was Andy? Andy was Stew?

My anger peaked. "Better off with the likes of you, you mean? The man who would keep me locked and chained in a room?" I spat. "You call yourself a man. Obviously, you have no idea who you even are if you have to wear a mask."

He shook his head. "Such spirit. Another few weeks in here will change your mind."

My breath caught.

Weeks?

The thought of that made me shudder. My resolve not to beg weakened a little.

"It's cold," I said.

"We're supposed to get rain. It'll get damp too. Colder. Maybe you'll warm up to me then."

"Don't do this," I pleaded. "Let me go home."

He narrowed his eyes, pulling the glasses off his face. "You are home. This is where you will be living. With me."

"Andy or Stewart?" I asked, some of my ire returning.

"Maybe someone else." He flashed an evil grin, making me shiver.

"Don't hurt Deb," I asked. "Please, she's innocent in all this."

"Other than being a fly-by-night slut, yes, she is." He leaned on the doorframe. "I'll use her until she no longer has any purpose. Then I'll dump her." He rolled his eyes. "She is so tiresome, but then again, how does anyone compare to you, Raven?"

"You don't even know me."

"We were meant to be. As soon as I saw your picture, I knew it. You're even named after my favorite poem. 'The Raven.' Edgar Allan Poe. You must know it. It was a sign."

"A sign?"

"That you were meant to be mine."

"You're insane."

He only laughed, the sound slightly crazed.

I tried to hold down my building fear. His laughter, his words were signs that he himself was descending into madness like the man in the poem.

"I'll read it to you later," he offered as if we were simply passing time.

"No thanks. I hate that poem."

He waved me off. "You haven't listened to it properly. I'll teach you to love it."

The same way he wanted to teach me to love him. It was never going to happen.

He straightened and approached me. I scrambled back until I hit the wall. I trembled as he stood in front of me, shudders of revulsion racing down my spine.

"You must be hungry," he said softly. "Thirsty."

I refused to answer.

He lifted a finger, tracing it along my cheek. "How long do you think you can go without food or water, Raven?"

I stared at his feet, trying to escape his touch. It filled me with dread.

"Stubborn little pet." He traced a finger over the collar on my neck. "Such a pretty little pet."

I lifted my head, meeting his eyes. They were cold, empty.

"I'm not your pet, you bastard."

Then I drew back my arm and punched him. As hard as I could, right in the nose. Blood spurted, and he howled in pain. I smiled in satisfaction.

He grabbed the collar, yanking me close, furious. His cloying cologne washed over me, and I tried not to gag. Punching him had drained the last of my energy, and I stumbled. He held me up by the collar, cutting off my breath. I gasped, fumbling, clawing at his hands. He held me until black spots formed in front of my eyes, then he stepped back, dropping me to the ground where I lay, terrified and gasping for air.

"Let's see how you feel tomorrow," he muttered and walked out, slamming the door behind him.

Blackness exploded, and I welcomed the dark.

Andy and Stew were the same person. He had seen Damien earlier.

Did Damien know?

I shut my eyes as tears gathered. He *had* to know. He was coming for me. He wasn't what Stew thought he was. He was acting as well. I was certain of it.

Damien was coming for me. It was a mantra I kept repeating in my head as Andy continued to torment me.

In and out of the room.

Taunting. Blackness. Bright lights. Loud, jarring music. A bottle of water with just enough in it to wet my mouth but not slake my thirst. A crust of bread tossed to the ground that Andy called "my scrap for the day."

He made me stand, my legs shaking as he chained my wrists to the ground and removed the collar. The weight of the heavy chains locked my arms down, no doubt in retaliation for punching him. I blindly kicked out with my leg, my foot connecting hard with his groin. He yelped, backing away, bent over, and I kicked again, but this time, he grabbed my foot, knocking me to the ground. My head hit the ground, exploding in pain.

He cursed and yelled, leaving me on the ground. He stormed away, plunging me back into darkness, the metal door slamming so hard behind him it shook my body. I heard him screaming profanity as he moved away, and despite the ache in my head and the knowledge I would be punished for my attack, I had to smile. I was going to fight back as much as I could.

The jarring music started playing again, the sound ringing in my ears. Of all the things he did, I hated that the most.

I lay on the ground, letting the tears roll down my cheeks. I didn't move, not wanting to activate the camera.

I refused to let Andy see me cry.

To let him know that I was, perhaps, already breaking.

Then it began to rain.

CHAPTER TWENTY-THREE

Damien

We converged on the house in the rain. We had our plan, our backup, and we were ready. I put any and all thoughts and fears for Raven out of my mind and became the Damien of old. A man of Hidden Justice. I knew the target, the goal, and how to accomplish it. I would not fail. Egan would run us from here, and I would concentrate on getting Raven out and putting an end to Andy.

Egan spoke in a low voice as we gathered around him in the back of the van. We were parked a distance away from the rear of the property, which he had pinpointed as the least secure. The van was black and totally self-contained. No lights or sounds were visible from the outside. If Andy was scanning the area at all, we were untraceable.

"The house appears to have some sort of cellar for storage. No windows. Accessed only through the garage. I'm sure that is where she is. When I probed the place earlier, that was where the weak heat source was coming from. I've been tracking Andy since he got there, and when I overlay the two images, that is where he goes. I assume he's checking on her."

I nodded curtly, Marcus and Julian also remaining quiet.

"He's not answering your calls, Damien, so we have to go in with him there."

"Deb says she tried to call him as well, and he isn't picking up," I replied, my eyes stuck to the tiny mark on the screen. The one I knew was Raven.

"We can handle him. We'll go in and separate. Damien—what do you want, to rescue Raven or kill Andy? You might not be able to do both."

"I want both, but Raven comes first. Whoever gets the kill shot, take it."

Julian's hand was heavy on my shoulder. "You took out the man threatening Tally. Let me return the favor."

"Fine."

Egan spoke again, changing screens. "You'll go in here." He indicated the grainy image. "Stay low until you get to the back of the garage. There is a door, and once inside, you should find another door that leads you down the steps. What is down there, I have no idea." He glanced up. "He's not expecting us, and although he has the house monitored at the front, there is little out back. He isn't anticipating anyone showing up."

"He thinks he's invisible. Undetectable."

"We need to wait so I can tap into his security feed and create a loop. I'm hoping with the rain, he'll assume it's a little glitch."

"How long?"

"As soon as I can, Damien. You know we have to do this right."

I tightened my hands on my gun. I knew he was right, but my anxiety was high. I wanted to get to her as soon as possible.

Marcus met my eyes. "Patience, Damien."

Egan kept talking as he typed. "I want to hack into his system and see what he's got going on. Knowing how he likes to stalk her, I'm sure he has a camera trained on her."

I let my head hang, rolling my shoulders. Outside, the rain picked up, the sound of the water hitting the roof loud. Thunder rolled, and Egan grinned. "Perfect."

A few moments later, he grunted. "I'm in."

I watched over his shoulder as his fingers flew and he set up the loop, fed it into the grid, and then moved on to hacking into Andy's system.

His annoyance was evident as his fingers hit the keys in hard thumps. "Bastard is good. I'll give him that," he muttered. "But I'm better." He glanced up. "We're in."

Then he sucked in his breath. "Jesus."

I froze as I looked at the screen. Raven was visible, her body curled up into itself on the ground. The room flashed with lights. She had her ears covered, and the sight of the heavy chains and clamps around her wrists made me curse. Her eyes were shut against the lights. Her entire body trembled. Then the room went dark.

"He's trying to break her. Sight and sound deprivation," Julian muttered. "Then he'll retrain her. That sick bastard."

"He's not going to have a chance. He's a dead man walking, and his time is about to expire. We ready?" I snarled.

"Five minutes. Get her and get back. Sofia is on standby, and we'll treat any injuries as best we can until we get her there."

I checked my gun. "Let's do this."

Something I learned during my time with Hidden Justice was all criminals have a weak point. Often it was their ego. Andy was a master at manipulation. At pretending to be someone else. Hiding in plain sight and enjoying the twisted satisfaction of doing so.

But he also underestimated those around him. And thought because he was so smart, he couldn't be found. He was careless with the fact that he left the back of the house vulnerable. He'd been playing his game so long and so well that he assumed no one would ever put the pieces together and find him.

But we did, and we walked right into his hideaway. The security on the back door was simple to override. Egan blocked it, and Marcus had the lock open in only a few seconds. The double garage was black inside, our night vision goggles letting us see what we needed. One car, a nondescript dark sedan, was parked to one side, closest to the house entrance. There were two doors. One leading in and one leading down. Just as we advanced, the loud music ceased. Marcus held up his arm, signaling for us to stop, and we waited but heard nothing.

Egan breathed in our ears. "Proceed with caution. He's on the move."

Julian pulled out a knife, slashing the tires on the car. "He can't go far now."

"He'll head for her once he knows we're here."

"I'll cut him off," Julian whispered. "Go get her. Be alert, boys. I have a feeling he has some surprises in store."

The cellar was freezing. Damp. It smelled of mold and decay. The metal door ahead of us had a bar across it that we lifted, opening the heavy door with caution. My breath caught in my throat at the sight of Raven lying on the hard, cold ground. The darkness around us burst into light, and I tore off my goggles as it exploded in front of my eyes, leaving me stunned for a moment. I stumbled as I headed to Raven, calling her name. She remained motionless on the ground. Falling to my knees, I dropped my gun and gathered her up, carefully lifting her into my arms. She winced, her eyes firmly shut.

"Raven, baby, it's me. I got you. You're safe," I repeated over and over. I ran my hands over her, horrified at how cold she was. "Baby, open your eyes."

I hauled her farther up and over my knees. I could hear shouting, shots being fired, running feet, and Marcus glanced behind him. "Go help him," I yelled. "Don't let him get away."

I ran my hand over her head, fury mounting even higher at her injuries.

Raven's eyes blinked open, the green hazy and filled with pain.

"I got you, baby. I'm here."

A smile tugged on her lips. "I-I knew—you'd—come," she mumbled, her voice low and raw.

I examined the chains holding her. "Search his pockets for keys," I ordered into my earpiece.

I heard more commotion upstairs, gunshots, then silence.

"I'll have you out in a few minutes, Raven. You're safe now."

"Andy?" she asked.

"Dead, I think."

She shuddered, and I shrugged out of my coat,

draping it around her and carefully tugging her close again.

"I'm taking you home, baby. You're safe now," I said, talking into her ear. "Everything is going to be fine now." She made a small noise in the back of her throat.

I straightened and froze. A red dot was visible in the middle of her forehead. I followed the light. Andy was in the door, a gun in his hands, the laser sight pointed directly at Raven.

"She isn't going anywhere. Neither are you."

I observed him dispassionately, refusing to let him see my fear. "I beg to differ."

"You'll be begging, all right. I took out your friend fast, but you, I'm going to enjoy killing. You made me suffer, so I'll let you suffer." An evil grin spread over his face. "And she can watch."

I narrowed my eyes, studying him. Without a disguise, I could see him fully. He was younger than his other personas. His hair was unkempt, his build slim. He was furious, his eyes crazed. He'd been shot, the blood running down his arm. His hands weren't steady.

"Then aim your gun at me, asshole," I replied.

"Move away from her, or I will kill her."

"No, you won't," I said. "You're obsessed with her. You won't kill her."

His laugh was high-pitched and grating. "I'll be

the one to decide that. I doubt you'll risk it," he said. He cocked the gun. "Now, move."

I looked down. Raven's eyelids were closed but not shut completely. I knew better than to think Julian and Marcus were dead. I simply needed to buy some time.

"Think you're a big shot, aiming that gun at a defenseless woman?" I sneered. "You lazy, worthless piece of shit? Playing games, hiding under masks, and pretending to be different people? You call yourself a man?" I indicated Raven. "This is how you get a woman? Kidnap her? Brainwash her?" I shook my head. "She will never love you. No matter what you do."

The tremor in his hands increased, and I knew he was losing both blood and patience. He swung the gun in my direction, the laser pointed at my heart. "Shut up."

"Go on," I urged. "Do it. You don't have the balls."

It happened all at once. He braced himself to shoot. I shifted just as Raven moved. She rolled and grabbed my gun from the ground beside her, aiming it blindly and pulling the trigger. Shock registered on Andy's face as the bullet struck his knee. His arms flew up, his gun falling. He pirouetted, an ungraceful arc that spun him. Another gunshot sounded, and he fell to the ground, blood spurting from his chest. Raven collapsed onto the ground, my gun falling from her hand. Julian rushed in, Marcus on his heels.

"Keys," I yelled. "I need keys."

Marcus dug in Andy's pockets, then hurried over, knelt beside me, and we lifted Raven's hands, unlocking the metal cuffs. Red welts bloomed on her skin, the bruising already starting. Her neck matched, and her head and face showed signs of trauma. I was ill at the sight of her injuries. She stared blankly at the ceiling, not reacting.

"Egan, get here," I snapped into the mic. "Drive right through the fence."

"On my way."

I met Marcus's gaze as I lifted Raven back into my arms, wanting her off the cold ground.

"How is she going to get over this?" I murmured.

"With time and love," he assured me. "She will."

I shut my eyes as I gathered her close. "I have you, baby. You're safe now."

She didn't respond.

There was a loud crash outside, and Egan appeared. He had blankets in his arms, and he hurried over, helping me wrap Raven in them. She was motionless, but from across the room, I heard Andy gasping for air, a couple of low moans escaping his mouth. I made a decision and carefully handed Raven to Egan. "Get her out of here. Take Julian. He's been hit."

"It's a flesh wound," Julian protested. "Barely a

scratch. Fucker walloped me with a fry pan then took a potshot as I was weaving around. That hurts way worse than my arm. He was a lousy shot."

"Take them, *now*."

Egan stood, lifting Raven.

"We leave in ten. Tell Sofia our ETA."

I stood and approached Andy. He was slowly bleeding out. Marcus joined me, meeting my eyes.

"You okay?" I asked, noticing a darkening bruise on his forehead.

"He tried to bean me too. Idiot. My head is too hard for that. He shot at me but hit the floor. I think I got a sliver in my leg. Julian's right, he's a lousy shot."

"Lousy human being."

I leaned over Andy. His eyes were open, his life slowly draining from him. His breathing was harsh. "Help," he groaned.

"You think I'm the right person to ask for help?" I shook my head and bent low over him. "Here's what is going to happen, Andy, Stewart, Jeff, John, whatever fucking name you want to go by right now. You're gonna die, and I'm going to watch you. And while you're rotting and burning in hell, writhing in agony for all of eternity, remember this. I will be loving Raven. Protecting her. She will be by my side until death parts us. I will touch her every day. Kiss her mouth. Make love to her. Watch our children grow— together. And you will simply be a small blip in her life. I am going to love her so hard she will forget you ever existed. In fact, the entire world will. I'll make sure of it. So, this game you've been playing? You lost."

My bullet ended his miserable existence. My satisfaction at ending the life of the man who tormented the woman I loved helped temper my rage.

Marcus nodded. "So that solves that. What do you want to do now?"

"Get Raven to Sofia, then I'll come back with Egan. I want everything he had. I am going to trace every woman he ever hurt and make sure they know he is dead so they don't have to live in fear. And I'm going to let Egan out of his cage. This house needs to be destroyed. He's been dying to blow something up."

Marcus shook his head. "Stay with Raven. She needs you."

Julian appeared, a bandage around his arm. "Marcus and I will stay and start gathering. By the time Egan gets back, we can help him set it up to blow and leave."

"Your shoulder—"

He cut me off. "Seriously, I'm fine. Once we're done here, Sofia can check me out. The fucker might have given me a little concussion, so I owe him. I look forward to messing this place up." His face darkened. "Then we'll go to the other building and dismantle the shrine. Erase all traces of the men he pretended to be."

"What about his money?" I asked. "His company?"

Julian met my eyes. "Hidden Justice will take care of it all. You are still one of us, Damien. We all are. We protect and help our own. Now go upstairs and get your girl. She needs you. She was getting agitated and saying your name."

I kicked Andy's foot. "Him?"

"Leave him," Marcus growled. "The cold is good for corpses. We'll add it to the pile before Egan lights the torch."

In my ear, I heard a chuckle.

"Excelent," uttered Egan. "Kaboom."

I turned and hurried to Raven. I had a lot to say to the three men who helped me. But that would come after.

Raven took priority.

CHAPTER TWENTY-FOUR

Damien

I held Raven as tight as I could without hurting her, whispering in her ear constantly. Reassuring her, telling her how much I loved her. How brave she was.

"We're going home now, Raven. You're safe."

I didn't know if she heard me, but she nestled closer. She moved her hands, gripping my shirt. I could see the marks on them. Marks he'd put there. I hoped he was already rotting in hell.

I carried her up to Sofia and put her on the hospital bed she had waiting. But as I tried to move away, Raven became distraught, whimpering and clutching my shirt tighter. Her eyes remained shut, and I leaned close. "I'm not leaving, my beautiful girl. I'll be right here. But I need to let Sofia examine you. Please."

"Lights," she whimpered. "It hurts."

Sofia offered me a towel, and I held it over

Raven's eyes. "As soon as she is done, we'll lower the lights, okay?"

"You won't leave?" she breathed out, her voice dry and rough-sounding.

"No. I'll be right here."

Sofia was swift and professional. I watched as she inserted an IV, then checked Raven's injuries, a deep frown on her face. My anger grew bright again seeing the welts and bruises on her wrists and neck. The swelling from where she'd hit her cheek and head. Sofia took some X-rays, working quickly so Raven didn't panic when I had to step away. I spoke to her the whole time, so she heard my voice. Sofia allowed me to give Raven some ice chips to soothe her thirst, and finally, I was able to get some electrolytes in her. Raven sipped the cold liquid greedily. I turned the lights down and took the towel off her eyes.

"Sofia is going to put some drops in, okay?" I asked. "They'll help ease the ache in your eyes."

Raven let Sofia add the drops, and she lay back, still clutching my hand. Sofia spoke to her quietly. "Raven, I want to give you some pain meds. They'll help, okay?"

"Can we give her a sedative?" I asked.

"No. She's hit her head twice. The X-rays show no swelling, but I'm worried about a concussion. We need to keep waking her every two hours."

Egan knocked and came in, carrying a tall container. "I made a protein shake for her. She must be starving, and I know you'll want her to get some nutrition inside. I added chocolate. She likes that."

Sofia smiled at him. "Good thinking."

Raven heard him, and she lifted her shaking hand, searching for the cup. He chuckled and gave it to her, and she sipped the thick beverage with a sigh.

"Baby, I have to talk to Sofia. I'm only a few feet away, and Egan is right here. Okay?"

She frowned but released my hand.

I walked across the room to Sofia. Egan stood beside Raven, talking to her.

"Tell me," I said to Sofia.

She laid a hand on my arm. "Nothing life-threatening. Her bruises and lacerations will heal, Damien. No swelling in her head. I'm shocked she didn't break her cheekbone from how hard she hit her face in the bathroom. I have salve for the marks on her neck and wrists to help heal and ease the pain."

"The bastard chained her like a dog," I hissed.

Sofia nodded in sympathy. "She is going to be in a great deal of discomfort for a while. She's dehydrated, so lots of fluids. She needs to eat, drink, and rest. I want to monitor her closely."

"I won't leave her."

"Good." She hesitated as if unsure what to say.

"What?"

"She's emotionally fragile right now. She's still terrified. She is going to need you to be strong. Keep her calm." She met my eyes. "It might get rough.

Outbursts, crying jags. She may laugh unexpectedly. Or she may be withdrawn, not wanting to be touched. Everyone handles this differently. You have to let her feel what she feels—as hard as that will be to see. I think she should talk to someone."

"I still keep in touch with the woman Marcus used to help us when we went through harder cases. I'll call her."

"And you need to find a way to channel your anger, Damien. Away from Raven. Take it out on the punching bag, talk to a professional. Go to the shooting range and empty a few rounds. You have to look after you as well so you can look after her."

"I just need her to be okay."

"It's going to take some time."

"I know. Matteo and Marcus offered to let us go to the island. Get her away for a while."

"That might be a great idea. Let's make sure she's healthy enough to travel first, though, all right?"

"Yes. Is there anything she can't do right now? I know she'll want a bath," I asked.

"Just stay close. She may be dizzy. She may have flashbacks. Don't leave her on her own, and watch her carefully. Wake her every two hours tonight. I'm home, and I'll check on her in the morning. But if you are concerned, call me."

I met my cousin's warm gaze. "I don't plan on leaving her side at all, Sofia. I'll make sure she's okay."

She smiled. "I knew you would." She paused. "Egan said he's going back out?"

I nodded. "He has to help Marcus and Julian. He won't be long."

"He is going to blow something up?"

"Yes. And when Julian and Marcus get back, check them out, please. Julian took a graze to the shoulder, and they both got hit in the head."

She rolled her eyes. "I'm sure whatever hit those two in the head suffered more damage than their noggins did. But I'll check them out."

"Thanks."

I bent and kissed her cheek then returned to Raven. I watched Egan stop to speak to Sofia and kiss her cheek before leaving. She met my eyes, tossing her hair and busying herself with some task. I tried not to grin. Egan might actually be making some headway.

I traced over Raven's uninjured cheek gently. "You ready to go home, baby?"

"What about that?" She indicated the IV pole.

"It comes with us. I can switch out the bag. Sofia will probably remove it in the morning. She just wants to get your fluids up, and she added some pain meds."

"Okay."

She began to sit up, and I shook my head. "Nope."

"I can walk."

"Yes, you can. Tomorrow. Tonight, you're in my arms."

She didn't protest as I gathered her up, and Sofia followed us upstairs and into the apartment. Raven began to cry when I walked into the bedroom and sat down, holding her. Sofia offered me a small smile, left the supplies I needed, and headed back downstairs.

"I-I didn't think I'd see this room again," Raven wept. "I was so scared."

"I know, Raven. I was too. But you're safe, and he can't hurt you again. He can't hurt anyone."

"He's d-dead?"

"Yes."

"Is it wrong that I'm not sorry?"

"No. I'm not either."

She cried for a few moments, and I rubbed her back in comforting strokes.

"May I have a bath?"

"Yes."

"Will you stay with me?"

I stood, carrying her to the tub. "Always."

There seemed to be no problem with me touching Raven. In fact, she was calmer when I was close. I helped her into the bath, my eyes mapping the bruises that stood out on her body. Shadows of pain that showed on her pale skin. She winced as she sat down, then sighed in relief as the warm water surrounded her. I had capped off the IV so she could relax. I tossed her clothes into the garbage, knowing she would never want to wear them again.

"My earring broke."

I sat down next to the tub. "I know." She reached for my hand, and I entwined our fingers. "I think it caught on the edge of the sink when he grabbed you. We found your hair clip and one shoe in the cart he was pushing. And I had your bag and your cell phone. Five trackers, all useless."

She nodded, leaning her head back, shutting her eyes. I slipped a rolled towel under her neck and sat back. The dark, painful-looking ring around her neck made me angry all over again. I had to concentrate on staying calm. Sofia was right, and Raven didn't need to be witness to my rage. Except all I saw was pain on her body. The bruises and cuts. The marks left by the metal biting into her skin.

"Can you get past this?" she asked, startling me out of my growing turmoil.

"Me?" I questioned. "I'm worried about you, Raven."

"I need some time, but I won't let him take away all the good I found. If I did, then he wins."

I lifted her hand to my mouth and kissed her knuckles. "Neither will I."

She shut her eyes again and was quiet.

"He was right in front of me the whole time," I confessed quietly. "I said I would keep you safe, and I failed."

Her eyes flew open. "He fooled all of us, Damien. You can't blame yourself because you didn't see through his disguises. You weren't looking for costumes and masks. You were looking for a real person."

"He hurt you. I don't know if I can forgive myself for that."

"I forgive you."

I studied her. "Just like that?"

"Just like that. I knew you'd come for me, Damien. That's what kept me going. So, there is nothing to forgive." She reached out and took my hand. "I love you, and you did save me. You found me and brought me home."

"Your faith in me…" I shook my head. "I can't believe it."

"Believe it. I love you, Damien."

I leaned over and kissed her. "I love you, my Ravenna Jade. I'm never letting you go again."

"Good. Please don't torment yourself, Damien. Let it go. Don't let him win. He's gone."

I pressed a kiss to her head with a quiet okay. I marveled at her strength. I would talk to Marcus and Julian again. Maybe a professional. But for now, I would concentrate on Raven.

"I'm hungry," she said suddenly.

"Tell me what you want, and I'll get it."

"Toast and honey. And some tea."

"Okay." I began to rise, but she grabbed my hand. "No," she pleaded. "Stay."

I sat back down. "Okay. When you get out."

"I'd like a shower now."

I assisted her into the shower, and she turned to face me. "Are you coming in?"

Discarding my clothes, I got in and helped her wash her hair and her back. She leaned into me, obviously exhausted. "Feel better now?" I asked quietly.

"I needed to get him off me. That smell was on my skin."

"Did it work?"

"Yes."

I soaped up and rinsed off, ridding myself of any trace of the past few hours as well. Clean and dry, we sat at the table, Raven sipping her tea, her toast untouched. I picked up a piece, tapping it to her lip. "Eat, baby. Please."

"Did I kill him?"

I set down the toast, cupping her face. "No."

"I shot him."

"You shot him in the leg. You injured him, but you didn't kill him."

"Oh."

"Was that bothering you? Thinking you killed him?" I didn't want that on her conscience, and I was glad to clear that up for her.

"I don't know." But she picked up her toast and bit into it, chewing and looking thoughtful.

"I was aiming for his head."

For some reason, her words made me grin. "Well, you missed."

"I guess I'll leave that stuff up to you."

I leaned close and kissed her cheek. "Not that we'll need it again, but yeah, let me do the heavy lifting."

She ate more of her toast.

"How high on his leg?"

"His kneecap."

"Huh. I thought I'd be better at that."

"You often think of shooting people?" I teased.

"Not really. But at times…" She shrugged. "I'm pretty good with darts and stuff. I guess a gun is different."

My lips twitched. "Somewhat." I wasn't sure if I should tell her, then decided to be honest. "Egan flashed through some video Andy took. He told me you punched Andy and kneed him in the nuts."

"He got too close, and I didn't like it."

I ran my fingers down her cheek. "You're incredibly brave, Raven. I am in awe of you."

"Is the video…" She let her voice trail off.

"Gone. It's all gone."

"Okay."

She was quiet for a moment, then spoke. "Would you teach me?"

I knew what she was asking. I hated the thought of her touching a gun. But I realized why she was asking. She needed to take back her power and not be afraid.

"If that's what you want, then yes."

She finished her toast. "Okay, good."

I woke her every two hours all night, not that she slept much. For the first time, darkness frightened her, and she panicked when I snapped off the light. So I kept one on, dim enough not to bother her eyes. She would begin to fall asleep, only to jerk awake, gasping and clutching at me. I would talk to her, whispering reassurances until she fell asleep again, only for the pattern to repeat itself.

Finally, as dawn broke, she fell into an exhausted slumber. I slipped away, wanting her to sleep and too restless to stay beside her.

I wasn't shocked when Marcus and Julian showed up before seven, both exhausted and grim.

I poured them coffee. "All done?"

Marcus grunted as he sipped the hot beverage. "Damn, that's good. Yeah. All done. The house burned fast. We have everything, and it will all be looked after." Before I could protest, he held up his hand. "Not by you, Damien. HJ will take it over. They've already moved in and smoothed the waters.

No questions will be asked about the house, Raven's name will not come up. If there are any other victims, they will be helped. You concentrate on Raven and you."

"And Sofia cleared you?"

Julian chuckled. "Yep. She was waiting." He rolled his shoulder. "All bandaged up and the lecture about no more bullets duly noted." He touched his head. "She also had some rather snarky views on my head versus the fry pan the asshole hit me with. Something about how hard it was."

Marcus chuckled. "Me too. She had a lot to say on that subject."

I grinned. Sofia had no problem expressing her opinions. I told them about the conversation I'd had with Raven about killing Andy. Julian nodded. "Little flashes of humor help. It shows how strong she is. She'll recover and move past this. You will as well, but you need to step back and let HJ finish this."

"I will. But I have one thing I have to do. I need to tell Deb the truth. Or a slimmed-down version. She should know he won't be around anymore and why."

Marcus drained his mug. "Do that, and shut the door. Come back to the island with us, and let the peace and beauty help Raven heal. I know how much it helped Missy. She said it helped her focus and move past all the horrors she went through. We'll have the private plane, so she'll be comfortable. You need the break as well."

"They're right. And I'd like that," Raven said from behind me. I stood and turned. She was in the hall, wearing my T-shirt and a pair of leggings. Her hair was down and messy. She was bruised and worn.

And the most beautiful woman in the world.

She came forward, her steps slow. "We haven't officially met," she said as Marcus and Julian stood to greet her. "Thank you for what you did." She extended her hand, the tremor obvious. I knew strangers would make her wary now. But she was trusting my relationship with these men. She knew they helped rescue her, and she was making the effort.

They shook her hand, offering her a kind smile and gentle words.

Marcus pulled out a chair. "Join us, Raven. Let me tell you about the island. I have some pictures too."

She sat down, reaching for me. I shifted my chair closer, taking her hand. I felt her relax, and I tugged her closer. With a quiet huff of air, she leaned into my side.

"Do you have pictures of your kids?" she asked. "Both of you? I would love to see those."

And right then, they fell in love with her.

Deb pressed a hand to her mouth, horrified. She looked between Raven and me, shocked. I had been as honest as I could be, telling her that Stew had used her to get close to Raven and it was he who had kidnapped her.

"It was all a lie," she murmured. She reached for Raven's hand. "He hurt you."

"I'll recover."

"That bastard!" Deb spat out. "I knew something was off. He was too perfect."

I bit back my smile. I was glad to see her anger.

"I knew it wasn't going to work," she added. "But I didn't expect this."

"None of us did."

She tossed her hair. "I met someone last night. My neighbor's brother moved back into town. He asked me for a drink, and when I told him why I couldn't right then—how upset I was about you, Raven, he was great. He sat and talked to me about life in general. Distracted me."

"Maybe you should take him up on the offer," Raven said.

"Maybe I will." She paused. "Where is Stew now?"

"Where he can't hurt anyone," I lied smoothly. "He won't be back."

"Good."

Egan knocked and came in, stopping when he saw Deb. "You got a moment?" he asked.

I stood. "I'll give you girls some time to talk. Raven, are you okay if I go downstairs with Egan?"

She paused, then nodded. "Yes."

"I won't leave her until you get back," Deb offered.

"Okay."

Downstairs, Egan showed me a file he thought I'd be interested in. I stared at the image on the screen. It was a younger version of Raven—or a very close facsimile. "Who is that?"

"The girl Andy stalked when he was younger. I think he created his site to look for replacements. He saw Raven's picture, and that was that. I found several files on his computer of women he went after."

"Were they hurt?"

"Not to the extent of what just happened. It escalated with Raven."

"You give this to Marcus and Julian?"

"Yes. They're going to make sure a complete investigation is done and anyone who needs it gets help. Financially or mentally. They told me to show you and then you could move on, knowing the why. He was mentally unstable and fixated on a certain type. Unfortunately, he had the wealth and talent to do something about it."

I stood. "Had is the operative word. He's gone. He can't hurt her or anyone else again."

"Nope."

I stuck out my hand. "Thanks for everything, Egan. You've been amazing."

He stood and hugged me. "You are my friend. And soon to be my cousin. Of course."

"Sofia know about the cousin thing yet?"

"No. I like to prepare. She's like building a bomb. One careful piece after another. Each one perfect." He grinned. "And I am excellent at building a bomb. She will be my greatest detonation. Fireworks like never before seen."

I laughed and headed back upstairs. I had a feeling Sofia had no idea what she was up against.

And I hoped Egan got his wish. With him beside her, I wouldn't have to worry about her happiness, safety, or anything. I knew him well enough to know that. I hoped she could see that too.

CHAPTER TWENTY-FIVE

Damien

The look of sheer delight on Raven's face as we approached the island let me know I'd made the right decision in bringing her here. We'd traveled with Julian and Marcus, the private plane making her comfortable as they suggested. She still shied away from bright lights, loud noises, and strangers. Even going for a walk caused her anxiety. She clung to my side, pressed as close to my body as she could when people would walk our way. She'd been unable to return to work at the camp, and Deb had told her the replacement they hired wasn't as much fun to work with, although she understood why Raven wasn't coming back.

She needed time, space, and love to recover, and I planned on giving her all of them. Leo and Egan were running Elite in my absence, Egan thrilled to be donning a suit and looking businesslike and professional. He informed me Sofia liked that look, so he was going with it. He carried a briefcase and made sure that she saw him as often as possible in his business attire.

"I wear her down. Brick by brick," he told me. "The wall is going."

Sofia, of course, had no comment on the subject, although I noticed her softening toward him.

"It's so beautiful," Raven murmured, bringing me back to the present.

I held her close, her back pressed to my chest. I had my arm wrapped around her tight, and I gripped the rail of the boat to keep us upright. I lowered my head and pressed a kiss to her cheek. "Almost as beautiful as you."

She laughed softly, squeezing my arm. I glanced down, pleased to see the welts and bruises beginning to fade. I hoped the sun, peace, and beauty of this place helped the memories fade as well.

We arrived and were greeted enthusiastically by the crew. Missy, Tally, and Evie were all smiles and welcoming hugs. Matteo shook my hand and waited until Raven extended hers before approaching her. He was still larger-than-life, his presence intense, his countenance serious. But his voice was gentle and careful while interacting with Raven. I appreciated his holding back, knowing he would make Raven nervous.

But once she saw the children, it all changed.

Moments later, she was sitting in the sand, one child on her lap, the others all vying for her attention, regardless of their age. She was in her element, talking, exclaiming, asking questions. The kids all gazed at her in wonder. She was amazing with them.

Matteo chuckled beside me. "She is lovely, Damien. A natural with children."

"She adores them."

"You adore her."

I glanced his way. "I would lay down my life for her."

He clapped his hand on my shoulder. "I know. It's good to see." He heaved a sigh. "What happened was horrible. But it's over. You have her in your life now. She can rest and recover here with us. Then you can decide where the future takes you." He shook my shoulder in rough affection. "No rush, no deadlines. Just the sun, the sand, and good friends. This place is magical with its healing powers. I saw it with Evie and me. Missy and Marcus. Julian and Tally. It'll do the same for you and Raven." He paused then chuckled. "Although you might have trouble getting alone time with her if the kids have anything to say about it."

I had to laugh. "Whatever makes her happy."

"I think we found one thing already. Look at her smile."

Raven glanced up, meeting my eyes. Hers were clear and bright. Happier and calmer than I had seen them since we pulled her out of that room. Perhaps even before that. I had never known her before the threat of Andy was in her life. Now it was gone, and we could concentrate on each other. I winked at her, and she smiled at me, content, at ease, and in her element. I looked forward to seeing that smile more now.

"Now, let's take your bags to the guesthouse. You can settle in, and the girls have a huge welcome dinner planned for later."

I grabbed our bags. We had packed light, planning on buying what we needed when here. Raven stood to follow, the children falling into step with her, not yet ready to let her go.

I didn't hold back my grin. Matteo was right. I was going to have to fight for time with her for the next while.

But that fight I would happily lose. It was worth the happiness on her face.

RAVEN

The night air was balmy, the sky filled with stars. The water swirling around my feet was warm, the feel of it on my skin soothing. Across the water was the mainland, the subdued twinkle of the lights barely visible. Around me, the air was peaceful, the only sounds were the wind and water and the muted murmurs of the families that lived here. On occasion, the high-pitched giggle of a child would ring out as their parents readied them for bed. Or a name being called affectionately by a spouse.

I had never witnessed so much love. The serious, intense men who were involved in vigilante justice and could kill someone without blinking were not the men who inhabited this island. They became doting parents and loving, devoted husbands the moment they stepped on the sand. And they had all embraced Damien and me. I had met Gianna, Vince, Geo, and Lila. Alex and Roza were away on one of their many trips, but I looked forward to meeting them before I left. They were all kind and welcoming, although Gianna, Matteo's sister, was more reticent. She stayed close to her husband, and Damien explained she'd suffered a huge trauma in her past that made her wary of new people. I hoped she would warm up to me, seeing how much we had in common. She loved to spend time with the children, the same as me. Their innocence and joy were a balm to my soul, and I suspected she felt the same way. The rest of the women were gracious, open, and warm, including me in everything. The men were protective and openly affectionate with everyone. The love of their wives was so plain and effusive, it was astounding.

I loved the sun, the peace, and the absence of the darkness that had been in my life before I met Damien.

I sighed as I sat on the sand. We'd been here a week. Only a week and yet it felt as if I was home. I liked the pace here. Each family had their own space, their privacy, yet daily, they gathered. You never had to be alone if you didn't want to. This beach was the common area, and there were games and play sets, chairs, and tables. The men had built a large gazebo, covered and welcoming, with places to sit and read. Relax in the shade. Enjoy some peace or be surrounded by everyone. In the short time we had been here, I had already come to love them all, and I was going to miss them when we left.

I stared at the water, feeling sad. Damien hadn't said a word about leaving, but I knew he would have to go back soon. We would have to go back soon. I would have to prepare for another year of school, set up my classroom, and get organized. Damien would be back at Elite, and we would find our life together—this time without threats or darkness hanging over us.

I brushed at the sand on my feet, wondering if we would have a life together. Since arriving on the island, Damien had been wonderful. Caring, sweet, protective, and patient. He held my hand, kissed my cheek or forehead, stayed close. At night, he was beside me, holding me, helping keep the nightmares at bay.

But he hadn't touched me sexually. Hadn't kissed my mouth or made love to me. I feared something had changed, and I wasn't sure how to get past it.

Missy had noticed me watching Damien earlier and must have seen something in my expression because she leaned over and patted my arm, her eyes sympathetic and filled with understanding.

"Give him time, Raven. He is trying to come to terms with things too. Marcus and I struggled a little as well, but we got through it." *Evie and Tally had nodded in agreement, offering me their silent support.*

I appreciated it, but I was still unsure how to bridge the gap I felt growing between Damien and me.

I was so lost in my thoughts, I startled when Damien sat on the sand behind me, his powerful legs caging me in and his strong arms wrapping around my waist.

"Raven," he murmured into my ear. "What are you doing out here alone in the dark?"

"Nothing," I replied. "Enjoying the peace."

"I thought you'd gone for a bath while I talked to Leo. I couldn't find you in the house. I was worried."

I stroked along his forearm, his muscles contracting under my touch. "Sorry to concern you."

"Are you all right?"

"I'm fine."

He was quiet for a moment, then he tightened his arm, drawing me close to his chest. His hard, chiseled chest I missed so much. "My married friends inform me if their woman says she's fine, she is anything but. Talk to me, Raven. Tell me what's on your mind."

I looked at the dark water, watching the waves break on the sand, the gentle, pulling rhythm soothing. "Did what happened with Andy—him kidnapping me—change how you see me, Damien?"

He didn't respond right away. Then his answer broke my heart. "Yes."

Tears welled in my eyes at the pain the simple word caused me. Then he spoke again.

"I always thought you were brave and amazing before. That you fought to stay that way and came out of that room even stronger made me realize just how incredible you are. I am in awe of you, Raven. And more in love with you than I ever was."

His declaration shocked me. I turned in his arms, resting my head back on his shoulder and meeting his gaze. I touched the side of my face that was still healing. "I thought maybe my scars might change your mind."

He covered my hand. "These will fade, Raven. We all have scars. They show we survived something. A mark on your face doesn't change anything for me."

"But you haven't touched me. Kissed me. You haven't made love to me since then."

He lifted my hand to his mouth and nuzzled it. "I didn't want to rush you, baby. I wanted you to heal. I worry about hurting you. Is that what's upsetting you? You think I don't want you anymore?"

"Yes."

"Nothing could be further from the truth. I want you as much now as before. More."

"I thought maybe you only saw me as a victim now."

"You aren't a victim. You're a survivor. Fierce. Strong. And you're mine. You always will be."

"Then make me yours again, Damien. I want—"

I never finished my sentence. He crashed his mouth to mine, his tongue sliding in and taking control. He banded his arms around me tight, holding me close. He deepened the kiss, moaning into my mouth. It became carnal, wet, intoxicating. My head swirled, my body lighting up for him. With him. Everything else faded away. Except him. Us. The need growing between us. He stood, lifting me with him, his mouth never leaving mine. I clung to his neck, not wanting our mouths to separate. He carried me into our room, setting me on my feet, plucking at the bows on my shoulders that held up my dress. I yanked down his shorts, feeling his cock, hard and hot between us. He tore his muscle shirt down the middle, our lips still locked together. He lifted me again, and I wrapped my legs around him, groaning at the sensation of him nudging at my entrance. He lowered us to the mattress, his body pressing into mine, and he slid into me, slowly stretching me, filling me until we were flush.

He dragged his mouth to my ear. "Now I'm home," he whispered. "Inside you."

"Damien," I pleaded. "Please. I need you."

He began to move, long, leisurely thrusts of his hips. Taking his time. Not wanting to hurt me. I gripped his neck. "More. I'm not made of glass. Show me how much you want me."

He covered my mouth with his again and began to move. Faster. Harder. Lifting my ass and sliding in deeper. He kissed my mouth, neck, ears, and chest. Sucked at my nipples until they were wet and glistening. Swiveled his hips and hit me exactly where I needed. Mumbled words of praise and love. Groaned and hissed in pleasure as I licked and bit at his chest and neck, clutched his shoulders, pulled on his hair. I arched my back, taking him as deep as I could, crying out in the pleasure of it.

My orgasm grew like the waves outside. Slow, continuous building. Then it crested, the ecstasy so great I cried out his name, gripping him hard. He buried his face in my neck, his long groan of gratification low and satisfied as he climaxed. He stilled and rolled, sliding from me. He pulled me to his chest, breathing hard. We were quiet for a moment, recovering.

"Does that put your fears to rest, Ms. Raven?" he asked.

"It was a good start."

He chuckled, tucking me closer. "I'm sorry I made you feel as if I didn't want you, Raven. I always want you. I was trying to give you time."

"I don't need time, Damien. I need you. I always need you."

He pressed a kiss to my head.

"I want to leave the past behind us and move forward. Together. I don't want what he did to define us. I want *us* to define us."

He sat up, and we faced each other. "We do define us, Raven. Our love defines us. However it started, what we have is us. It's all I want."

"I love you so much," I whispered.

He cupped my face. "I love you, Raven. More than I can adequately express. And I want a life with you."

"Me too."

"Then let's enjoy this place and each other. Decide on the future when we're ready."

"Do we have to leave soon?"

He smiled. "No. Leo and Egan have it well in hand. I can take a few meetings via Zoom if needed. We can stay as long as you want." He paused. "We never have to go back if you don't want to. Matteo offered us a place here if you want that."

"Really?"

"I'll show you the spot tomorrow. Or if you want this place as a haven, we can build a smaller house and use it when we need it. We don't have to decide right now."

"I'd like to see the spot."

He leaned forward and kissed me. "Then I'll take you tomorrow."

I draped my arms over his shoulders, pressing my mouth to his. "In the meantime…"

He pulled me onto his lap. "I think we need to catch up on lost time. I need you to really know how much I love you."

"Yes, Damien. Show me."

DAMIEN

Raven was transfixed by the spot I took her to see. Slightly set away from the rest of the houses, it had a breathtaking view, and the trees behind it offered shade and privacy.

"It's so beautiful."

"It's yours if you want it," Matteo said, strolling toward us. "I had been planning to add another couple houses in the next few years. We can do it now or wait until you're ready."

"A couple?" I asked.

He smiled, leaning on one of the large boulders. "I figured you and Egan would be along at some point. I picked out a spot for each of you. You can live there or use them as guesthouses when you visit."

"Does Egan know this?" I asked.

He crossed his arms. "He does. I had Marcus tell

him while he was there. I thought if Sofia knew there was a retirement plan in place, she might be more, ah, accepting of his suit."

I laughed. "Sofia would love it here, but she'd miss being a doctor."

"She doesn't have to. They are always looking for doctors at the clinic on the mainland. She could work there. She would make a huge difference in the lives of people here. It might give her satisfaction she can't get in a big-city hospital."

I nodded thoughtfully. "She would like that."

"I'll let Egan tell her when the time is right. But, like you, if you want this place, it's yours for the asking. Whenever they or you are ready." He stood. "I'll let you wander. I have architect plans at the house afterward if you're interested."

"Thank you, Matteo."

He tilted his chin in acknowledgment. "Something I've learned, Damien, is that life is short, and when you find happiness, grab it. You've been the Watcher for a long time. Maybe let someone else take that burden and enjoy the gift you've been given. You deserve it." He glanced at Raven. "I think you've been given something very precious. Grab it and hold it close."

I wasn't sure who was more shocked when Raven suddenly launched herself at Matteo. She flung her arms around his waist, hugging him hard. She hadn't displayed open affection like that to anyone except the children since we arrived. We had reconnected last night, but of all the men, Matteo was the one she was most skittish with. Seeing her hug him was surprising.

He looked at me before slowly wrapping his arms around her. He rocked her like a child, murmuring something to her. She looked up, nodding, then rose on her toes and kissed his cheek. He smiled at her with genuine affection, then tapped her nose. "You are welcome," he said. "Damien is family, and now so are you. Whatever you decide, that will not change."

He strolled away, and Raven approached me. I tugged her close. "What was that all about?" I asked.

"He is offering me a life without fear. A place to build new memories with you. I realized how big a heart he has under that gruff exterior."

"He does. Family is important to him." I sat down on the boulder Matteo had vacated and cupped her sweet face. "Is this what you want, Raven? To live here?"

"I'm torn. My first instinct is yes. But does that mean Andy won? If I leave Toronto, am I giving up on my dreams because of him? I wanted to teach."

I studied her. "Maybe your location would change, but you can still teach. There's a school on the mainland where the kids go every day. Matteo says they are always looking for teachers."

"Oh."

"We can go home, let Matteo build, and make our

decision once we pick up our life again. You may want to stay, or you may want to move."

"What about you?"

I tugged her close. "Wherever you want to live, Raven, is where I want to be."

"But your company. The system you watch over. The people you protect—"

I silenced her with a long kiss. "The only person I want to protect is you, Raven. I've been the Watcher long enough. I have great people to take over. Leo will run the company. He can hire his own staff. The only thing keeping me there is you. And if you want to be here, then so do I."

She threw her arms around my neck, burrowing her face into my shoulder. "I love you," she whispered. "I love you so much."

"I love you too. So, will we tell Matteo to build, and we'll figure it out?"

She pulled back, the tears glistening in her eyes, happy ones.

Her smile said it all.

EPILOGUE

Damien

EPILOGUE – TWO YEARS LATER

I broke through the waves, the water refreshing on my skin. It had been a hot day on the boat, and I was grateful for the cool. I swam back to the shore, not surprised to find Raven waiting, towel in one hand, a cold drink in the other. I walked toward her, smiling.

Her skin was sun-kissed, a golden glow that set off her dark hair and emphasized her beautiful eyes. These days, they were relaxed and at peace all the time.

The choice to move here came easily. Once we were back in Toronto, Raven became fearful. Even though she knew Andy was dead, it haunted her. Even with counseling, she admitted she couldn't let go of the memories. I wasn't surprised. Everything that was part of us was associated with the events of the past. The pub where we met. The coffee shop. My apartment. The school. Even driving past the zoo made her uneasy. Deb, Tracey, Leo. All were reminders.

I called Matteo, and a year after leaving the island, we were back. Raven finished her school year, and I closed up my life. We returned to the island, and Raven flourished. She loved teaching on the mainland, and I enjoyed the outdoor life and helped out some days with the charter business Alex and Vince ran. Alex was off on another trip with Roza, so today, I filled in.

But it had been a long day, and I smiled as I approached my wife, grateful it was done and behind me. I bent and kissed her full mouth, and then, unable to resist, nuzzled her bare shoulder. She shivered, making me smile.

"You're all wet," she murmured, pushing the towel into my arms, edging away.

I caught her waist. "Give me five, baby, and you will be too."

She laughed, pushing me away. "We're having dinner with the crew tonight. Save it."

I pouted but took the glass she offered and downed the fresh, cold beverage. Raven loved to mix the various fruits on the island and from the market, to make her own juice. This was one of my favorites —passion fruit, pineapple, and mango.

"You look very pretty," I commented. "I like that dress." I waggled my eyebrows. "Especially those little bows on your shoulders."

She rolled her eyes. "Do you only have one thing on your mind today?"

"Yes."

"Well, forget about it until later."

"What time is dinner?"

"Thirty minutes."

I could work with that.

Teasing, I shook my head, covering her in a spray of seawater. She jumped back, but it was too late.

"Damien," she scolded in her best teacher voice. "Now my dress is wet!"

"Oops." I dropped the glass and grabbed her, throwing her over my shoulder. "Might as well finish the job."

She gasped in outrage, smacking my back. "Don't you dare!"

I strode back into the water, dunking us both. She came up sputtering and spitting in her anger. Then she launched herself at me, and I caught her in my arms. We kissed endlessly, the dinner forgotten, nothing else mattering but us. We'd be late, if we ever showed up.

We were newlyweds after all.

I'd married my Raven at sunset on the beach in

front of our house last month. We were surrounded by our friends whom we considered family. Egan and Sofia were there. My mother and stepfather flew in, marveling at the beauty of the island, but luckily not interested in living somewhere so remote. Raven's brother watched via Zoom with his family.

It was a perfect evening, filled with love. We ate under the stars and danced in the moonlight. There was much laughter, lots of hugs, far too much champagne, and at the end of the night, just my wife and me. As I had already stated—perfect.

Raven floated in the water, her dress discarded, her legs wrapped around my waist, anchoring herself to me. Moving here was the right decision. The memories were far away, banished by the sun and water.

Her long hair was spread out around her, and she was beautiful. I traced a finger down her torso, swirling it over her skin. She giggled and pushed my hand out of the way. She stood in the water, shaking her head. "We don't have time for round two."

"They'll understand."

She shook her head. "Marcus is making his linguine, Damien. With the lemon cream sauce and chicken. We can't miss that."

I began to laugh. "Already? You're tired of me already? Pasta wins over sex with me?"

She moved closer, cupping my face. "The baby wants it."

"Well, if the——" I stopped. "*What?* What baby?"

She moved my hand to her stomach. "Your baby."

"Raven, you're pregnant? We're having a baby?"

"Yes."

"How long? How far? Is everything okay?" I asked, joy filling my entire soul.

"It's early, but everything is fine. I saw the doctor who works with Geo yesterday, and he says everything is good."

"Did I miss something? Why didn't you tell me?"

"I wanted to be sure. And you didn't miss anything but a blood test. You can come for the ultrasound."

I picked her up and held her close. I kissed her until we were breathless, and she wrapped her legs around me again. "What's another fifteen minutes?" she whispered against my mouth. Then her stomach grumbled.

I swung her into my arms. "Nope. The baby is hungry, and there is pasta waiting."

She laughed. "How the tables have turned."

I strode toward the house. "Food first, then sex." I paused. "We can have sex, right? It won't hurt the baby?"

"We can have lots of sex. I understand soon I'll want nothing but sex. And food."

"Then I'm stocking the fridge and staying home," I replied.

I set her on her feet and dropped to the floor. I

kissed her stomach, spreading my hands wide around the place where our child would grow. He or she would be safe and protected for the next eight months within Raven's body. After they were born, I would protect my child and my wife with my life.

The Watcher once again, only different.

This time, it would be done for love—as a father and a husband.

There was no better job than that.

Thank you so much for reading THE WATCHER. If you are so inclined, reviews are always welcome by me at your retailer.

I enjoyed writing this couple's story and hope to have the final installment of this series to you soon.

If you love a growly hero, Richard and Katy VanRyan's story begins with my series The Contract. You meet an arrogant hero in Richard, which makes his story much sweeter when he falls.

Enjoy meeting other readers? Lots of fun, with upcoming book talk and giveaways! Check out Melanie Moreland's Minions on Facebook.

Join my newsletter for up-to-date news, sales, book

announcements and excerpts (no spam). Click here to sign up Melanie Moreland's newsletter
or visit https://bit.ly/MMorelandNewsletter

Visit my website www.melaniemoreland.com

Enjoy reading! Melanie

SNEAK PEEK

of the final installment of Hidden Justice

CHAPTER 1

The hallway was dim, the walls crumbling. Dusty from years of unuse. The mold and decay were all around me. I traced the miles of cable, checking and rechecking every inch. Ensuring the charges were in the correct place, the amount of dynamite exactly as needed to bring down the building in a perfect synchronization of an inward sequence.

As always, I felt the thrill of anticipation. The high knowing all the work, the planning, and the intricate details would soon pay off. Shortly, where a tall building once stood, only a pile of rubble would remain.

Hours passed as I did the final inspection. Everything was perfect. I had overseen every detail, calculated and recalculated the explosives.

The building would fall faultlessly.

Outside, I headed to the control area. I was alone, which seemed odd, but I continued. I did one final sweep of the building, finding zero heat sources. I hoped no small animals wandered in at the last moment seeking shelter, but I knew it happened at times. The haven they sought became their final resting place, but better them than a homeless person or a curious onlooker. That had never happened, thank God.

I checked all the cameras, pleased to see them working. The implosion would be captured as the building went down, both inside and outside. I would use it to study, seeing if I could have changed something, if something needed fixing next time, or God forbid, it didn't explode the way it should have today. But I was confident. Ready.

I looked around as dawn broke. The building would collapse as the sun rose. One life ending as another day began. Some sort of poetic justice there.

I flicked open all the controls. Checked the area. Began the countdown over the loudspeakers that was followed by the warnings. Had the thumbs-up and okays from all the people connected to the project. We were all clear. Far from the building on the edge of the site, some people gathered to watch the building come down. They were distant enough to be safe but have a great view as the building collapsed. For some, it was a hobby watching buildings being demolished—their fascination endless. Security kept them from getting too close. I frowned as I looked around, wondering why no one else was on-site with me. Usually, a few people watched from behind the controls, but today, it seemed I was alone. Once I had the final all clear, I pressed the button, the one-minute timer beginning to count down to one.

Something niggled at me, growing in my mind. I felt a sudden swell of anxiety, then one of pure fear blossom in my chest. I stumbled back from the controls, gasping for air, unsure what was happening. A small light came on, indicating a heat source in the building. Ignoring the crippling agony in my chest, I checked the cameras, shocked to see a person in the building. I zoomed in, terror dripping from my throat as I focused on the face of the woman sitting on a chair in the middle of an empty building.

Sofia. *My Sofia.*

How had she gotten there? What was going on?

I pressed the kill switch, horrified when nothing happened. "Get out!" I shouted, pressing it again. "Sofia, my love, get out!"

She stared at the camera, shaking her head. I saw she was tied to the chair, helpless.

She was trapped high in the building, and I couldn't get to her.

I began to scream her name, desperately hitting the control keys, trying sequence after sequence to stop the explosives from detonating. She looked at me, her lips moving.

"I love you," she said.

Then the explosions started, and the screen went black. I fell backward, the pain of the moment overwhelming and intense. It felt as if I had been blown apart in that building with her.

Add The Specialist to your TBR

ACKNOWLEDGMENTS

As usual, a few thanks.

Lisa, many thanks. Many laughs. Many, many red strokes. Good thing I don't learn—it's job security. LOL.

Beth, thank you for your support and insights. You always make my words better.

Melissa, Trina, and Deb, thank you for your encouragement, laughter, and support.

Sisters Get Lit.erary Services, thank you for your eagle eyes and assistance. So appreciated!

Kim, you do an amazing job for me. One day explain it okay? But involve wine. It's always better with wine. My brain gets smarter.

Karen, this is you. This is me. THISISUS. I love you. Embrace it. Thank you for everything. I can't list it all because that is an entire book in itself.

Nina (Valentine PR). Thank you for your calm, your humor, and your guidance. I appreciate all you do.

To all the bloggers, readers, and my promo team. Thank you for everything you do. Shouting your love of books—of my work, posting, sharing—your recommendations keep my TBR list full, and the support you have shown me is deeply appreciated.

My reader group, Melanie's Minions—love you all.

MLM—for all you do I cannot say thank you enough. I wish I could hug you all. Maybe one day.

ABOUT THE AUTHOR

NYT/WSJ/USAT international bestselling author Melanie Moreland, lives a happy and content life in a quiet area of Ontario with her beloved husband of thirty-plus years and their rescue cat, Amber. Nothing means more to her than her friends and family, and she cherishes every moment spent with them.

While seriously addicted to coffee, and highly challenged with all things computer-related and technical, she relishes baking, cooking, and trying new recipes for people to sample. She loves to throw dinner parties, and enjoys traveling, here and abroad, but finds coming home is always the best part of any trip.

Melanie loves stories, especially paired with a good wine, and enjoys skydiving (free falling over a fleck of dust) extreme snowboarding (falling down stairs) and piloting her own helicopter (tripping over her own feet.) She's learned happily ever afters, even bumpy ones, are all in how you tell the story.

Melanie is represented by Flavia Viotti at

Bookcase Literary Agency. For any questions regarding subsidiary or translation rights please contact her at flavia@bookcaseagency.com

 facebook.com/authormoreland

 twitter.com/morelandmelanie

 instagram.com/morelandmelanie

 bookbub.com/authors//melanie-moreland

ALSO AVAILABLE FROM MORELAND BOOKS

Titles published under M. Moreland

Insta-Spark Collection

It Started with a Kiss

Christmas Sugar

An Instant Connection

An Unexpected Gift

Harvest of Love

An Unexpected Chance

Following Maggie (Coming Home series)

Titles published under Melanie Moreland

The Contract Series

The Contract (Contract #1)

The Baby Clause (Contract #2)

The Amendment (Contract #3)

The Addendum (Contract #4)

Vested Interest Series

BAM - The Beginning (Prequel)

Bentley (Vested Interest #1)

Aiden (Vested Interest #2)

Maddox (Vested Interest #3)

Reid (Vested Interest #4)

Van (Vested Interest #5)

Halton (Vested Interest #6)

Sandy (Vested Interest #7)

Vested Interest/ABC Crossover

A Merry Vested Wedding

ABC Corp Series

My Saving Grace (Vested Interest: ABC Corp #1)

Finding Ronan's Heart (Vested Interest: ABC Corp #2)

Loved By Liam (Vested Interest: ABC Corp #3)

Age of Ava (Vested Interest: ABC Corp #4)

Sunshine & Sammy (Vested Interest: ABC Corp #5)

Men of Hidden Justice

The Boss

Second-In-Command

The Commander

The Watcher

Reynolds Restorations

Revved to the Maxx

Breaking The Speed Limit

Shifting Gears

Under The Radar

Full Throttle

Mission Cove

The Summer of Us

Standalones

Into the Storm

Beneath the Scars

Over the Fence

The Image of You

Changing Roles

Happily Ever After Collection

Heart Strings

Made in the USA
Monee, IL
14 January 2023

25045400R00197